I0629436

The Pied Piper

A Maureen Gould Legal Thriller

Keenan Powell

Three Hooligans Press

Copyright © 2024 by Keenan Powell

All rights reserved.

No portion of this book may be reproduced in any form without written permission from the publisher or author, except as permitted by U.S. copyright law.

Praise for the Maureen Gould Legal Thrillers

Praise for *Implied Consent*, winner of the Ippy Gold Medal

Powell has written a book that dares to be legal thriller, family drama, and polemic. Remarkably, she succeeds at all three. – Booklife Reviews, Editor's Pick

Keenan Powell has penned her most memorable heroine to date. Powerful and authentic. *Implied Consent* is a must read! — Bruce Robert Coffin, award-winning author of the Detective Byron Mysteries

Sharp-witted, big-hearted and authentic, *Implied Consent* is a knock-out of a novel from a writer who knows both the letter of the law and the messiness of real life. Treat yourself - you won't regret it. — Catriona McPherson multi-award-winning author of *In Place of Fear*

Praise for *The Millionaire*

Book two in the Maureen Gould legal thriller series will keep you up into the wee smalls! The author, a lawyer herself, invests private attorney Gould, her prosecutor husband Jake, and daughter Quinn (an attorney wannabe) with such authenticity that I feel they are family. I even adore their kitty Germaine Greer. The court scenes explode as Gould defends Tony Paredes, accused of murdering his former coach Oscar, who raped him at school. Oscar's wife contends Tony is guilty. Senior Prosecutor Vivian Thandie, who has never lost a case, agrees. Gould fights for justice, all the while contending with her own scars as an abuse victim. I was so gripped as the taut story unspooled that I skipped meals and virtually ignored my husband (sorry, babe). If you love legal thrillers that are smart, jet-paced, and ring with such truth that you can't put them down, THE MILLIONAIRE is for you. Highly recommended! — Char Jones, Reviewer

Powell's second Maureen Gould thriller (after *Implied Consent*) packs a wallop. Trial lawyer Gould now represents Tony Paredes, a young man accused of murdering his abusive childhood chess coach, Oscar Wenderholm. Despite a successful prior trial against his coach, Tony and Maureen faced an overturned verdict due to a technicality; now under arrest on suspicion of Oscar's murder, Tony is imprisoned and brutally beaten, giving Maureen added incentive to save him. Meanwhile, Maureen's own difficult childhood rears its ugly head, making the case exponentially more taxing. -Booklife Review

To Mary Patricia Malloy Gannon, my grandmother, who baked

Contents

Prologue

When the security buzzer hummed its ugly little tone, I was seated at the head of the table closest to the conference room door, symbolically controlling who entered and left. I had been flipping through my scripted questions and occasionally making a scribbled note, deliberately ignoring the other attorney.

Everyone seated around the conference table turned to look through the glass wall into the reception room, hoping the witness had finally arrived. He was already twenty-five minutes late. At the far end of the table, the court reporter put down the phone she had been playing with, then tapped her keyboard, waking up her sleeping laptop.

I picked up my coffee cup, noticed that it was nearly empty, and wondered if I should make a bathroom run before we started the deposition.

Paul Lewis, the witness's young attorney – expensive haircut, Italian suit – had selected a chair as far away from me as possible, and was angled away from the table, ankle on knee, occupying as much space as he could. He had been tapping a pen on his legal pad when the buzzer sounded. He glanced at his watch and wrote a note before he twisted around to see if his client had arrived.

Seated beside me was my client, Esme Castillo, who also happened to be the niece of my paralegal/office mom, Yolanda Martinez. Dressed in a conservative navy-blue suit, her only jewelry was an Our Lady of Guadalupe medal. Her thick black hair was pulled back into a low ponytail. Uncharacteristically subdued, her hands were clutched so tightly, her knuckles were white. Her head was bowed. Praying, perhaps.

Behind her, the windows overlooked the historical Jackson Square neighborhood. Overhead, seagulls wheeled in a dazzling blue sky, washed clean by the previous night's drizzle. Beneath them lay the San Francisco Bay, hidden from view by brick buildings on tree-lined streets, some of which survived the 1906 earthquake.

When the buzzer sounded, Esme's head jerked up.

Farther down the table was Quinn, my daughter, who worked part-time with me while she went to law school. She appeared very grown up, in a gray blazer that accentuated her gray eyes, the color of which she had inherited from her father. While we waited, she scrolled through her laptop. Before anyone arrived that morning, I told her to look occupied and give minimal attention to the witness and his lawyer. Quinn was the image of me, tall, athletic, with unruly red hair, so the effect would be to have two Maureens refusing to give them power. When the buzzer sounded, she glanced at the door, then looked over at me, watching to see what I would do.

We were waiting for Alfred Tanzini, the man who swindled Esme out of her business and then sued to prevent her from opening a competing enterprise. My goal was to win back her company, which meant far more to her than simply a job. It was her heritage, her identity.

I would show Tanzini no mercy. He didn't deserve it.

Yolanda sat behind her desk on the other side of the glass wall that separated the reception from the conference room. She studied her monitor, the screen of which I couldn't see. The buzzer sounded again, longer this time. She gave me a frown and a quick shrug, then pushed herself out of her chair and crossed the few feet to the entry door, which remained locked during business hours due to a recent violent trespasser.

Yolanda threw the deadbolt, then cracked the door just enough to greet the visitor. The voice in the hallway was too garbled to understand. She stepped back and swung the door wide open, permitting two people to enter.

Neither of them was Tanzini.

They were detectives, easily enough to identify by the shields hanging from their necks. One was an African American woman. She was almost as tall as me, with her hair in a short natural, dressed in a black pantsuit with a cotton shirt and flat comfortable shoes. Behind her was an Asian man, who appeared slightly younger. He stood over six feet tall, with a thick shock of stylishly cut black hair, in jeans, a button-down shirt open at the collar, and a lightweight zipped jacket.

I rose from the table and walked out to greet them, intending to preempt their questions and wrap up their visit quickly. "Good morning, detectives. I'm Maureen Gould. This is my office. Is there something I can help you with?"

"Detective Dobson," the woman said. "And this is Detective Chong. We're here about Alfred Tanzini."

Cops showing up to a deposition was not a good sign. As far as they were concerned, the rest of the world could pause its business. If they wanted to talk to the witness, the deposition may never happen. It would take weeks to reschedule and could push the trial date off into the distant future. Meanwhile, Esme wouldn't be able to earn money.

I knew from my years as an assistant DA, there was no saying "no" to the police. I hoped they'd only need a few minutes and then we could start the deposition late.

"He should be here any minute, detectives, if you would care to wait." I gestured towards the couch.

A gasp came from the conference room. Dobson and Chong both glanced in that direction. Yolanda, who was standing behind the visitors, looked past me and subtly shook her head at whoever had made the sound.

Dobson zeroed in on me with a look she had clearly perfected for stopping people in their tracks. "I understand you represent Esmeralda Castillo."

"I do."

"Is she here?"

I turned to find Esme standing in the conference room doorway, one hand against the doorframe for support, the other covering her mouth. Her straight black eyebrows gathered in worry. Her dark complexion had paled.

Normally, Esme was the kind of person people would describe as a "spitfire," small, slight, intense, perpetually in motion. The kind of woman who could work her way through culinary school as a janitor, then work fulltime in a restaurant, while baking cookies at night in her grandmother's kitchen, and then make early morning deliveries to coffee shops on her way into work. She was the kind of woman who could build a thriving business, Esme's Casa de Galletas.

The fragile, frightened woman bracing herself against the doorjamb was not the Esme Castillo I knew.

Tanzini's attorney shouldered past Esme. As he stalked across the carpet, he reached inside his blazer, then extended his hand with a business card held between his first two fingers. "Paul Lewis, attorney for Alfred Tanzini. What's this about?"

Dobson gave Lewis that drop-dead stare. He stopped short. I liked her.

"We'll need to speak with you shortly, Mr. Lewis," she said. "If you would make yourself comfortable, we'll be right with you." She nodded in the direction of the conference room.

Lewis glanced at his watch. "Can't it wait? You can call my office to make an appointment. Later in the week, perhaps."

The silent Detective Chong accepted Lewis's card, ran his thumb across the linen paper, eyebrows raised in an artificial show of admiration, then stashed the card in his pocket. I knew from my husband Jake, a former police officer and now an assistant district attorney, that most cops disliked most lawyers. It wasn't just an urban myth popularized in crime fiction. Lewis didn't pick up on the snub. He puffed up, apparently thinking the detective appreciated his good taste in stationery.

"You're all waiting for Alfred Tanzini, is that correct?" Detective Dobson asked.

"We are," I answered. "He should be here any minute."

Dobson shook her head. "I'm afraid Mr. Tanzini won't be coming. His body was found this morning."

Chapter One

Two months earlier

I worked in my mother's former bedroom in the family's Beaux Arts style mansion, staring at grant applications piled on the plastic folding table I used for a desk.

The mansion was located in the heart of San Francisco's hilly Pacific Heights neighborhood. Originally, Victorians were built, but after the 1906 earthquake damaged many of the quickly built wooden structures, mansions constructed from stone – like mine – were erected to house San Francisco's elite—those who had earned fortunes in the gold mines, selling mining equipment, entertaining miners, and rebuilding the post-quake City by the Bay.

The room was bare with the exception of a few folding chairs stacked against a wall, two beat-up file cabinets, and my old law office photocopier.

Gone was the antique four-poster bed my mother was born in and where I had played hide and seek with the maid. The end tables, the chairs, the dresser, and the vanity where I had rummaged through my mother's jewelry were gone, too. The fireplace mantle was empty, no longer displaying the silver candlesticks I dented playing with as a child. Even the curtains were sold to a woman who specialized in marketing vintage fabric.

I'd inherited the mansion. It wasn't until my mother's funeral that I was told it belonged to me, and had belonged to me, since my great-grandmother, Elizabeth Shaughnessy, died. When I was ten years old, Lizzie left the mansion to me with a life estate to my mother.

In lay terms, that meant my mother was allowed to live there for the rest of her life, after which it was mine to do with as I pleased. Lizzie also left funds for the house's upkeep, which my mother turned over to my father for prudent management. Who could be more trustworthy than a successful business attorney who drove a Jaguar and spent his days in his Embarcadero law firm?

Just about anyone, as it turned out.

After informing me that the house was mine, Frank, my father, cheerfully delivered the news that the money was gone and I owed him compensation for maintaining the mansion. Furthermore, he had no intention of leaving the premises until he was paid off so, he said, we were housemates. Perhaps, he suggested, my mother's death would open the door to a renewed level of intimacy in our relationship.

Not bloody likely.

I evicted him from the mansion and began preparations to open the Foundation in Lizzie's honor. She had been my only champion in a house where there was otherwise not much love. The Foundation's goal was to provide educational opportunities, job services, and free daycare to displaced women, and to assist them in finding safe housing as they transitioned into new lives. I felt she would have approved.

Lizzie had been widowed at a young age, pregnant with her first and only child, and living in the mansion. Lucky for her, she was rich. She didn't need a helping hand. Not all women are so lucky.

I sold every stick of furniture I'd inherited, including the family's antiques, the art, and even Lizzie's cherished Diego Rivera landscape to refurbish the structure that had been badly neglected while my father was in charge. Major repairs were carried out on the roof, the heating, the plumbing, and the electrical systems to satisfy the city permitting department.

It was a miserable day. Overcast, gray, with the threat of rain that never materialized. Without drapes and furniture, the house felt drafty and cold. Being in the mansion made my muscles twitch and the scars on my arms burn. Memories of my childhood lingered.

I hoped they would be replaced with new memories as a haven for displaced women and children.

Now refurbished, the occupancy permit had just been issued by the City of San Francisco. I had an empty house, a big dream, and no way to finance it. The Foundation was getting by on volunteer staff and donations so far. One grant application was pending. We needed money to purchase computer equipment for training, hire a director, and fund the housing services.

That was why after a week of sitting at my law office desk, I was spending a Saturday afternoon sitting at a folding table instead of running, or at least walking, up and down San Francisco's mosaic stairways as I had pledged to my daughter, Quinn, I would do.

I had been groping for ways to connect with her. She recently came back into my life, a virtual stranger who looked exactly like me except for her father's eye color.

After she moved in with my husband, Jake, and me, we set up a rotating cooking schedule. On Jake's nights, we usually ate Italian food. On Quinn's nights, something vegetarian. On my nights, take-out – unless I felt domestic, in which case I made my famous pancakes. She took an interest in the law, which pleased me as both Jake and I are both lawyers. She was accepted to law school and began working in my office part-time.

But she was still a stranger to me. So, when she suggested a shared activity, I usually jumped at the chance. She was trying to get me to exercise more, without much luck. Something was always getting in the way.

To be fair, Quinn wasn't running the stairs that day either. She was in the mansion's third-floor ballroom entertaining children while their mothers learned about nutrition from Esme Castillo in the kitchen.

As I contemplated the byzantine nature of grant applications and googled "grant writing for dummies" on my laptop, Yolanda appeared at my door. This being her day off, instead of wearing one of the natty suits she preferred for the office, she was in leggings and an oversized purple sweatshirt that her kids had decorated with puffy paint flowers and given to her for Christmas.

"There's a man at the door asking for Esme," she said. "He's not a friend of hers. I know all of them, but I don't know who this guy is. I told him that she wasn't available, but he won't leave. Should I call the police?"

"Let me talk to him first." Grateful for a break, I followed Yolanda down the wide stairs, running my hand along the smooth, century-old carved banister as I did every time I descended. Lizzie Shaughnessy had picked it out herself. She said the banister was an emblem of our family aspirations. It told guests exactly who we were and where we were going. We might have come from potato farmers, but we were as grand as anyone, she said, and they all needed to know it.

In truth, the family wasn't always so grand. Black Jack Shaughnessy had won the beginnings of his fortune in a poker game. He owned a saloon in the Barbary Coast red light district. But he was in the process of moving into more conventional investments when he left for World War I and never came back.

At the foyer desk, I pushed the intercom button, identified myself, and then said, "Please state your business."

On the portico was a white man in his thirties, wearing a softball cap, a hoody, and jeans. Behind him, high gray clouds scudded across the sky. "I'm here to make a delivery."

"We aren't expecting one," I said.

He looked at the papers in his hand. "Is there an Esmeralda Castillo on the premises?"

I took my hand off the intercom button and turned my back just in case he could read lips. I said to Yolanda, "He's a process server."

"How can you tell?"

"Nondescript, relentless, with papers."

"How does he know she's here?" Yolanda asked.

"He could have been following her for days, and she wouldn't have noticed. I suggest she accept service so we can figure out what's going on. If he doesn't find her here, he'll catch her somewhere else. You keep an eye on him. I'll get her."

"Fine," she said sharply. She wasn't fine about it at all.

In the kitchen, Esme stood before a rolling whiteboard, marker in hand, as a half dozen women sat around the kitchen table, taking notes. On the counter were bowls of fruit, breakfast cereals, sugar, food scales, and measuring cups. She wore her usual leggings and a sleeveless T-shirt with colorful bracelets that went halfway from her wrists to her elbows, and big silver hoop earrings with her hair tied back.

"Got a minute?" I asked.

She raised a marker in protest. Obviously, she was in the middle of something, and I was interrupting.

"It's important," I said.

"Okay, ladies. While I'm gone, I want you to weigh out a cup of cereal and a cup of fruit, record the weight, and calculate how much sugar is in each."

I led Esme into the hallway where I told her a process server was at the door looking for her.

"Who would sue you?" I asked.

She shook her head. "No one that I know of."

"If you don't accept service here, he'll track you down somewhere else and get you then. Better to get it over with," I said. "Then we can deal with it."

"Fine." She used the same tone Yolanda had.

She followed me to the foyer where we found Yolanda standing in front of the desk, arms crossed, staring at the man outside on the stoop. I unlocked the door and opened it with Esme beside me.

"Are you Esmeralda Castillo?" he asked her.

"I am."

"You are hereby served," he said, shoving the papers at her so quickly, her instinct was to grab them.

At that moment, a dark blur appeared from the shadow of the monkey puzzle tree. It was a man. I had only enough time to clock that he was in his forties, had a stony face and wore a buzz cut. He pushed the process server, flinging him against the portico wall. Without thinking, I thrust my open palm at him, with a move I had learned in self-defense class but forgotten I knew. I locked my stance just before my hand landed squarely on his chest. He flew backwards, propelled by his own momentum. As I overcame my surprise that my body had reacted before I could think, he staggered backwards a few steps and regained his balance as he wiped spit from his face with his sleeve.

I stepped out of the house, pulling the door closed behind me.

"You bitch!" the man shouted. "I want to see my wife! She's in there. I know she is."

I moved a few inches to one side, hoping to draw the man closer to the surveillance camera. He took a step towards me and then realized what I had done. He spotted the camera.

"This isn't over, Counselor. Not by a long shot." He bit out the words, then jogged down the walkway to the street and jumped into a waiting red Mustang with a white racing stripe before it sped away.

The process server had pressed himself against the wall, keeping out of the way. He was younger than I had first thought, probably not long out of high school. He looked shaken.

"Are you okay?" I asked.

"Who was that guy?"

"No idea. Do you need to sit down?"

He balanced himself on both feet and literally gave himself a shake, like a Golden Retriever shedding water. "No, ma'am. I'm good." He turned to leave.

The angry man's threat hung in the air. *"This isn't over."* He had called me "Counselor" as if he knew me from court. But I hadn't recognized him. I had been in the DA's office for years before I opened my own practice. It would be impossible for me to remember every person I'd met in the hundreds of cases I'd handled.

"Wait!" I called to the fleeing process server. "If I need to talk to you about what happened, where can I find you?"

"It's on the papers I handed to the lady." He started jogging. After he crossed the street, he jumped on a parked motorcycle, shoved on a helmet, and pulled into traffic.

Yolanda let me back into the mansion where I found Esme flipping through the papers. "I don't get it. Am I reading this right? I'm suing myself?"

She handed them to me. The case caption read, "Esme Inc, plaintiff, versus Esmeralda Castillo, defendant." The document on top said, "Temporary Restraining Order."

Esme had just been thrown out of her own business.

Chapter Two

ESME, YOLANDA, QUINN, AND I gathered in my mother's drafty bedroom. The nutrition students had taken their kids home. I double-checked to make sure the front and back doors were locked. The stack of grant applications now lay on the floor next to my table, and Esme's paperwork was spread out before me.

Quinn sat on the hardwood floor in a crossed-leg yoga pose with her feet on top of her thighs. I don't know if I was ever that limber, but I certainly wasn't now. The unruly auburn hair she inherited from me was held back by a scrunchie. She focused on the laptop stationed in front of her. She was my online research whiz kid. She could find information faster than I could tell her what I wanted.

Esme sat nervously in one of the folding chairs with Yolanda sitting closely beside her.

"Esme," I peered at her. "The last I heard your bakery was doing great." Everything I knew I'd heard from Yolanda's Monday morning reports. "But according to this, not so much. What happened?"

Yolanda frowned at her niece. "Have you been keeping secrets from me?"

"I didn't want to worry you, Tia."

Yolanda wrapped an arm around Esme. "I could tell. You haven't been the same lately. You seem preoccupied."

"It all went wrong." A tear slid down Esme's cheek, quickly followed by another, then another.

Yolanda pulled a tissue out of her sweatshirt's kangaroo pocket and passed it to her niece.

We waited a few minutes while Esme sobbed. Through the open windows, the sound of children laughing and shouting in the playground across the street drifted up on a breeze.

Yolanda stepped out of the room and returned a few minutes later with a glass of water. She once told me that crying makes kids thirsty and if you wanted them to stop, you gave them something to drink. She handed the glass to Esme, who sipped obediently, and instantly calmed down.

Yolanda amazed me with her wisdom and maternal skills. I hadn't raised Quinn so I didn't know the first thing about mothering. What little I knew, I had learned from Yolanda.

"What happened?" Yolanda asked as she rubbed Esme's back. "You can tell us. Maureen will fix it for you."

I gave Yolanda a look that was meant to convey, "I wish you had talked to me first before you committed me." After all, I was the lawyer. Yolanda was my employee. She could at least pretend I was the boss.

I had reason for concern about this case. Esme's lawsuit was business law. My only experience with this area was a class I took in law school years ago, which I had difficulty remaining awake for. Right after graduation, I joined the District Attorney's Office so I could put away the bad guys. Now, I was in private practice, rescuing the good guys. My heart was in helping people, not in pushing paper.

The stare Yolanda spiked at me said, "My niece needs us."

When you've known someone as long as I've known Yolanda and worked with someone as closely as I've worked with her, a lifted eyebrow or a twist of a hand speaks clearly. A pointed stare was as good as shouting.

There's an unwritten rule in the legal business that office employees get free legal representation. It's one of their perks for putting up with lawyers.

"Start from the beginning," I said.

Esme wiped her eyes with the tissue and peeled tear-saturated hair from her face. "Things were awesome at first. I had more accounts than I could handle. That's when I quit my job and rented the kitchen. I hired Consuela and a couple of her friends to help me bake. And Jojo started doing deliveries for us."

"Where did you find these people?"

"Consuela is my cousin," Yolanda informed me. "And Jojo is my nephew." I knew Yolanda came from a large family, most of which was still in the Bay Area, but I hadn't learned all their names yet.

"We were doing great," Esme continued. "Selling out every day. But the business was in the red. I hadn't figured on the cost of insurance and employer taxes and all that stuff. The more we sold, the bigger my debt was. I had to pay the bakers and Jojo first and then take care of the kitchen rent. Plus, there was the cost of the ingredients. I only use the best,

Tia, you know that. Then I got a cease-and-desist order from the state because I didn't have workers' compensation insurance."

"Esme!" Yolanda scolded.

"I didn't know all this business stuff when I first started, but I found out. I took care of it." She held up her hand, like a witness swearing to be truthful. "Honest, I did. Anyway, that's when Al showed up. He said he'd heard about my business, and he wanted to invest in it. He said he was an entrepreneur and that he made his money by helping other businesses succeed. He told me that I was just experiencing growing pains and it was normal and he could help me over this hump. He believed in me, he said. So, I agreed."

I interjected. "This paperwork says a corporation was formed in the name of Esme Inc, and you contributed your assets to the company in exchange for which you received forty percent of the shares. This Alfred Tanzini put up money for which he received another forty percent. And there's a third shareholder, named Rita Osteen, who also contributed funds and received twenty percent."

"That's right. Rita is an investor friend of Al's. I only met her when we signed the papers. She seemed nice enough. At first."

I looked over at Quinn. "Find anything on Tanzini?"

"Without a date of birth or a middle name, I can't figure out which one he is. The Tanzini who practiced law years ago? The Tanzini who lived over a butcher shop? There's so many of them. Do we even know if that's his real name?"

It hadn't occurred to me that Tanzini could be an alias. Nothing in the incorporation process forced someone to prove who they were. There were papers that had to be notarized, but notaries only asked to see identification. Anyone could get a fake driver's license.

"According to this," I said, patting the paperwork, "you recently started a competing business."

"I wasn't competing," Esme said. "They had all my old accounts. I was just doing online sales and pop-ups downtown in front of the Ferry Building. That wasn't their market."

"You walked away from Esme Inc?" Yolanda asked.

"Walked?" Esme scoffed. "No way. More like I was thrown out."

The sounds of tires, engines, and horns honking rose, drowning out the children in the playground. Pacific Heights was a popular tourist weekend drive-by even in January. Midday traffic backed up on the street below. I got up and closed the windows so I could focus on Esme.

"Can you explain to me what happened?" I asked.

"Before I started the pop-up, I worked every day for the bakery. I was vice president and marketing director, so I was busy hustling accounts. I wasn't baking anymore. I didn't know that they started using cheaper ingredients. Then one morning, I walked into the kitchen and saw this junk Consuela was baking with. Cheap margarine. Cheap vanilla. Crap flour. And that's when Consuela told me they reduced her pay to minimum wage. And that they had laid off Jojo that morning because they said they could save money by hiring a delivery company. Later, at the shareholder meeting, they told me they'd let Lydia go, too, because they said they needed a corporate accountant, and she wasn't qualified."

"Lydia is one of my sisters," Yolanda interjected.

Esme said, "Right. So, that night, I went to the shareholder meeting and complained. That's when the other two told me I was fired and unelected from the board and they'd cash out my shares, but the company was still in the red because they were paying off my debts. So, I still have forty percent, but it's forty percent of less than nothing."

"What?" Yolanda cried out. "Why didn't I hear about this before?"

"I didn't want to worry you, Tia. I swore Lydia and Jojo to secrecy. I figured I'd sort it all out and everything would be okay."

I interrupted. "I'm afraid it isn't going to be okay. The company obtained an injunction against you from selling baked goods."

"Can they do that?" Esme asked.

"They can. You signed a noncompetition agreement. And the assets that you sold to Esme Inc include your recipes, your brand, your goodwill, your name, the business name, and your likeness. None of that is yours anymore."

"What's a brand?" Quinn asked. She was young, but she had an eager mind and learned quickly.

"It's your unique business identity, like Keebler's or Famous Amos. When Esme sold her goodwill, she sold her ongoing business accounts."

"Her likeness?" Yolanda asked. "You mean her face?"

"Any image of Esme, yes."

"And my recipes?" Esme asked. "But those are my grandmother's recipes. They're traditional. I just tweaked them a bit. How can I sell something that I don't even own?"

I pawed around the desktop looking for a highlighter. Yolanda knew I was about to mark up the only copy of the document we had, which meant later she would have to get a clean copy from court. She pulled it out of my hands, pried out the staple with her fingernails, and fed it to the rickety old photocopier. Meanwhile, I rooted in my purse where I found three highlighters and six pens rolling around.

Yolanda hammered the copied pages with a stapler, then handed them to me. I highlighted the assets listed under Esme's contribution, then passed the document to her.

Meanwhile, Quinn tapped away on her laptop. While Esme reviewed the package, I asked Quinn, "Did you find anything?"

"The case was filed yesterday and assigned to Judge Rediger."

"Sharon Rediger?" I hoped it was her husband, Walter. He was a doll. Her – not so much.

Quinn shrugged. "It says, 'S. Rediger'."

Yolanda registered the concern in my voice. "Is that a problem?"

Sharon Rediger hated me. She accused me of prosecutorial misconduct in a case when I was an assistant district attorney and sanctioned me. I appealed, and the sanction was reversed, which in turn embarrassed her. Every case with her after that was a nightmare. I had to fight with her to get every piece of evidence admitted.

"I might not be the best lawyer for Esme," I said. "This judge doesn't like me."

"Can't you move to disqualify her?" Quinn asked.

"I could, but she's the one who will rule on it. She'll deny the motion stating that I failed to show she was biased. I could appeal. But generally, 'the judge hates me' isn't good enough to get a reversal. So, then we end up stuck with a pissed-off judge."

"Wouldn't that force her to be fair?"

"That would force her to look fair. She'll just be more careful."

Esme stared at the papers in her hands.

"Look, Esme, it'd be better for you if you consulted with Ian Napier."

Ian was my father's former law partner. When my father was disbarred, Ian continued their practice. He was a good man, if perhaps gullible. He had nothing to do with my father's illegal activities.

"Napier will want to get paid," Yolanda protested, again invoking her right as a law office employee to free legal representation.

Esme handed the documents back to me. "I thought I was just incorporating my business, not selling it to someone else. I didn't know that I was giving up my name and my face and my recipes. That's like I sold me, like I sold out my grandmother, my heritage. What, do I stop being Mexican now?"

I needed to focus on the most urgent issues. I stashed her heritage comments in the back of my mind to think about later. There were specific questions I needed answered now.

"Esme, did you read the corporation agreement?"

"Of course I did."

"Did you have an attorney review it before you signed?"

"No, why would I? I trusted Al. He said it was just standard contract legalese, that I wasn't to worry."

"Esme!" Yolanda shook her head in exasperation.

"I'm sorry. I guess I screwed up." Esme's wild-eyed gaze met mine. "So, like, does that mean it's over? I can't go into business for myself ever again?"

Chapter Three

PAUL LEWIS SAT BEHIND his sleek Scandi modern desk in the seventh-floor office on Market Street, across the street from the Ferry Building with its distinctive clock tower, a San Francisco landmark that survived the 1906 earthquake. Still in use, ferries chugged across the bay bringing office workers in the morning and returning them to their East Bay homes in the evening. The building itself was full of high-end open-air specialty shops.

With his back to the windows, Lewis' view of the large office was gray-on-gray uncluttered low horizontal lines that dissolved into the fog on inclement days. A cabinet that had once held paper files but was now empty since the world converted to digital. A long table, once used for organizing said files, also now obsolete. A couple of low, gray-upholstered visitors' chairs across from his desk, symmetrically placed so they framed the ever-closed black door, better to keep the witches out, my dear.

A Bluetooth in his ear rang the number he'd called. Ankle on knee, he contemplated a snag in his silk stocking.

It all felt foreign to him, like he had awoken in an alternate universe. One day he was skiing with his friends in Utah. Then, suddenly, he was trapped in this tower, hundreds of feet above Market Street, disconnected from the bustling world below, and kowtowing to a client who treated him like a lackey.

How did he get here?

His father's likeness materialized in his mind's eye.

When Rita Osteen's voice sounded in his ear, he pushed the image away.

Without a hello, she asked, "What's the status?"

"Judge Rediger signed the injunction this morning. It was served on Esme a few minutes ago."

"So, she's out."

"Not entirely."

"What's that supposed to mean?"

"She's still a shareholder with forty percent of the stock. Together you and Al have the majority, but she's entitled to profits."

"What if I bought her shares?"

"Then you would be the majority shareholder. Essentially, it would be your company to run, but Al would still get a percentage of the profits."

"I see."

An electronic crackle let Paul know that Rita was still on the line. She tended to take long pauses. She expected him to wait, as if she owned his soul. Which, of course, she did.

Paul pushed away from the desk and wandered to the window. The overcast sky had drained the view of color. Cars wove around buses. Horns blared. Pedestrians strode heads down along the sidewalk. Life on Market Street went on without anyone knowing he existed.

He ran his finger along the cool metal enclosing the glass. The building was old, but the windows had been replaced with those that couldn't be opened. Not that anyone had jumped to their deaths from one of these offices. That's what the Golden Gate Bridge was for.

In the distance, the flags of the Ferry Building hung limply. It was the place where Paul had found Esme Castillo, working. He had walked down to pick up a sandwich for lunch. She was selling cookies in a pop-up booth,

Esme was so busy that she didn't see him. If she looked, she should've recognized him. They'd met when she came to his office to sign the Esme Inc paperwork.

He had liked her. Pretty, young, ambitious, creative. He had wanted to warn her about Rita, but he didn't. Because Rita Osteen owned his soul.

It was bad enough that Rita and Al shoved Esme out of the company she had created. It didn't seem fair to push her out of the industry altogether. But Esme signed a non-competition clause. She had agreed to never sell baked goods again outside of Esme Inc. Never. For the rest of her life.

If Rita Osteen found out that Paul knew Esme opened a new business, she would – and could – destroy him. So that afternoon, when he returned to the office, he'd called Rita and told her.

Rita spoke, disrupting his reverie. "Make her an offer. Ten thousand for her shares."

"What about Al?"

"I'll worry about Al. You just be a good boy and make sure your friend at the county doesn't sign the contract."

Paul considered calling Andy to reinforce the mandate.

As soon as Esme Inc was formed, it sent a proposal to the county of San Francisco to lease a café space on Concourse C at the airport. Andy was in charge of the department that processed the contracts. Rita commanded Paul to pay Andy a large sum of money to ignore Esme Inc's proposal. When Rita was ready, Andy would receive another large sum of money to sign the contract. She didn't explain her reasons for delaying the contract. Paul didn't ask.

But it was obvious now. Rita was waiting for Al to default on his loan, so she could take his shares before the business became profitable.

"Send Ms. Castillo the offer. Ten thousand dollars," Rita said.

Ten grand for Esme's hopes and dreams. That might be fair if Esme could start over.

"And the non-competition clause. Are you willing to set that aside?"

The line went dead.

Chapter Four

AL TANZINI PUSHED AWAY the plate that was covered with the bloody remains from a slab of prime rib and a baked potato and slapped himself on the belly with both hands. Then he wiped the carnage from his switchblade and dropped it into his slacks pocket. "And that, my friends, is why they call me 'The Great Tanzini'."

His punchline didn't get him the laugh he'd expected. Although the lights had been dimmed in his apartment dining room so the glittering night view of San Francisco could be appreciated, he could see well enough to know that the others weren't enjoying themselves as much as he was. Despite the good food and expensive booze, they'd all been somber the entire evening. But this was a night to celebrate. Party he would.

He'd bet Rita that he could get the airport permit pushed through. She didn't believe him.

But hot damn! He got it done.

Without the permit, Dahlberg Kemp International, the huge food manufacturing and distribution corporation, wouldn't buy Esme Inc's franchise rights. Until the franchise deal went through, there wasn't enough money for Al to pay back Rita and secure his rights to his shares.

If he didn't repay her six months from the date they incorporated Esme Inc, he'd forfeit. He would be out on the street, starting over. Fancy condo gone. He couldn't even live in his car. The rental company would take it back. All he would have were the clothes on his back.

Al shook his wrist to make his gold chain bracelet jangle. The sound of the metal clicking reminded him of the coins men once played with in their suit pockets. Al Tanzini was born to have pockets full of coins. It was his destiny.

Rita sat primly to his right, legs crossed, wearing a beige suit that probably cost more than the old gold Ford Torino he drove the night he left New Jersey, heading as far west as he could, as quick as he could. Her hair, rolled up behind her head, had been dyed the color of champagne to cover the gray. Her makeup was subdued except for the violent red lipstick that made her thin mouth look like a wound.

"Get it?" he asked, "The Great Tanzini!"

She smiled politely at his joke, then settled back with a deep sigh. She could be such a wet blanket sometimes, but there was passion in her, too, as he well knew. And she had the bucks and enough smarts to see that Al could be a business tycoon, if only he had the breaks. Hitch yourself to my star, baby, and I'll fly you to the moon, he had said to her once. It was the only time he heard her laugh.

A belch bubbled up. Al covered his mouth with his fist just in time. If he was alone, he would have loosened his belt. His gut was straining with food, but he wasn't quite drunk enough yet. He could find room for more booze. "Where's that brandy?"

"We haven't finished the prosecco yet," Rita said. She motioned for that weasel Henry to fill Al's flute, but Al covered the glass with one beefy hand. "No more of that sissy stuff for me. I need a man's drink. What about you, Henry? How about some brandy?"

Weaselly Henry Watkins was Al's man at the County Department of Transportation. Henry answered the phone one day when Al called to follow up on the permit. For some reason, Anderson was never available to take Al's call. No matter, Henry gave Al what he needed.

Henry Watkins had hardly spoken through dinner. He was a funny little man, pale, round head, balding with white-blonde hair, and black horn-rimmed glasses. He probably hadn't seen the inside of a gym since high school where the sight and smell of all those naked boys would have frightened him. But this bean counter from the San Francisco County Transportation Department was the link to Al's future empire. For the time being, Al needed him.

"Not for me, sir." Henry pulled out the inhaler he had puffed on all through the evening and took another hit. "Not with my asthma medication."

Rita said, "Let's wind this up. Do you have the paperwork?"

Henry reached into an old-fashioned briefcase he had set by his chair and pulled out a sheaf of papers. He held the document aloft, not knowing whether to give it to Al or to Rita.

"Give it here," Al said. "Got a pen?"

Henry pawed through his briefcase, found a gold pen, and handed it over. Al signed the papers with a flourish, then passed them to Rita.

Al stood, slipping Henry's pen into his breast pocket. When he shook Henry's hand, Al's gold bracelet jingled. He liked the feel of the cold heavy chain slapping against his wrist. He liked, too, how impressed people were when they noticed it. It was real gold. The pawn shop guy told him so.

With their hands locked in a manly shake, Al slapped Henry on the upper arm.

Henry grimaced.

"It's a pleasure doing business with you," Al said.

Rita rose from her chair, hinting to Henry it was time to leave.

Now that Al was on his feet, his clothes weren't cutting into him so much, but he wanted to get out of them. Maybe Rita would lend him a hand. He gave her an inquiring look. But she was still playing the ice queen – for Henry's benefit, no doubt. She'd warm up as soon as they could get rid of that little pipsqueak.

And squeak he did. "Um, Mr. Tanzini, that's my pen." Henry pointed at Al's breast pocket. "I wouldn't say anything, but it was a gift from my mother."

Rita snorted. She slipped the pen out of Al's pocket and gave it to Henry.

"Thank you, Mrs. Osteen, Mr. Tanzini, for the dinner." But he didn't leave. He just stood there, next to his chair. On the seat was that briefcase, now gaping open, like a hungry mouth. Henry wanted to get paid.

After all, a deal is a deal.

"Rita, can you?" Al said. Al never carried cash. Other people did that for him.

Rita snapped open her slender purse. She pulled out an envelope and handed it to Henry. "I think you'll find it's all there."

"Oh, I trust you, Mrs. Osteen. No worries there. Thank you. Thank you very much."

"Remember, mum's the word," Al said. "You got that? There's nothing wrong with friends helping friends out with a little cash, but some people might take it the wrong way."

"Absolutely, Mr. Tanzini," Henry said. "Mum's the word."

Chapter Five

WHILE I SET OUT dinner, Quinn opened canned cat food and Germaine Greer, "my" Siamese cat who hated me, swirled around her ankles, purring loudly. It was my night to cook, which meant Quinn and I picked up Chinese on our way home.

A vegan carrot cake was stashed in the fridge. We were having an early birthday celebration for Quinn. Her real birthday was on Sunday, a school night. There was little I knew about mothering but sugaring up your kid on a school night was a bad idea. Even if she was turning twenty-five years old.

Jake, my husband, was still at the office when we arrived. An assistant DA who specialized in white-collar crime, he had been working nights and weekends for the past few weeks on an investigation he wouldn't talk about. That was okay with me since I was obsessed with breathing life into the Shaughnessy Foundation, and white-collar crime put me to sleep.

Quinn was still new to the family. She had been given up for adoption at birth. I was only fourteen years old at the time and had no choice in the matter. I wasn't happy about it.

I had planned to name her after my great-grandmother, Lizzie. Daydreams of playing on the floor with my baby in the mansion's third-story ballroom-turned-nursery were tinted with yellow. My imagination had provided yellow gauze curtains fluttering in the breeze as we crawled across the floor and giggled. On the third floor, it would be just my baby and me. The rest of the family roamed the lower floors, ghostlike, in my imagination.

Raising a baby wouldn't have been a financial burden. My family was rich. My mother was an heiress, having inherited the Shaughnessy silver mining fortune. We literally lived in a mansion in one of the most prestigious San Francisco neighborhoods.

The problem – for the family – was the shame of a teenaged single mother. Even worse was the scandal of who fathered that baby. So, before I began to show, I was sent away to a so-called "girls boarding school" back east, really a home for unwed mothers, and my baby was taken from me.

Dreams of being reunited with my baby had become so painful over the years that I suppressed those thoughts. To shut them out, I filled my mind and heart with passion for my clients and their cases. It was the only way I could function.

The baby was raised by good, kind people. Unfortunately, both adoptive parents had passed away before she finished college, which inspired her search for her biological family. She connected with my mother online.

Unbeknownst to me, my mother signed up on a DNA website hoping to find Quinn. She then arranged for Quinn to come to San Francisco for a Mother's Day reunion but died before it took place, without confiding her plans to me. When Quinn showed up at my office with no warning, I fainted.

When I came to, on the floor with Yolanda fawning over me, Maureen, the cutthroat litigator, was struggling for dominance with Maureen, the want-to-be mom. My life since then has been attempting to negotiate a truce between the two Maureens on a daily basis. That's why I was setting the table with recycled plastics placemats, cloth napkins, and chunky earthenware.

My dream had come true. Quinn lived with Jake and me in my open concept urban chic condo in a South Beach converted warehouse, just south of the Bay Bridge and a little more than a mile from my office, complete with polished concrete floors, brick walls, and pipes hanging from the tall ceiling that apparently had no purpose other than to collect dust.

Before she came to live with us, Jake and I would have camped out on the couch in front of the TV and passed the takeout boxes back and forth. But now I was living out my visions of maternal goddess, just like on old TV sitcoms.

I crossed the great room to the sliding glass windows that led out to our little patio. Being January, the sun had set early. I pulled the drapes shut to block out the dark.

While Germaine Greer lapped at her meal, Quinn brought out two pilsner glasses filled with Tsingtao beer and settled beside me at the dinner table. She and I each took a carton of food, helped ourselves, then exchanged them and filled our plates.

Quinn had been quiet all day. I'd only had a few months with her, so I didn't know if her silence was a bad sign. Had I offended her during the day? Was she rethinking our living arrangements? I didn't want to lose her again.

"Is there something bothering you?" I asked.

Quinn's chopsticks hovered over her rice. Then she laid them to rest on her plate and sat back in her chair before she answered. "I envy Esme. She's lucky."

Esme had just been thrown out of her business and robbed of everything she had struggled for. When she and Yolanda left the mansion, she was in a rage. I was afraid for Esme's state of mind, but Yolanda promised she'd take her niece home where Yolanda's four children, each a life force unto themselves, would wear her out.

"Esme lucky? How so?"

"She knows where she came from and where she belongs. She has a heritage, a culture. She grew up in a big family with her grandmother who she adored, and lots of aunties and cousins. Did you know about their Sunday dinners? Sometimes twenty or more people show up. It's like a big party all the time. But it's not just her family. It's their traditions, their shared experiences, their history, how they pull together to build futures. That must be comforting to her when things go wrong."

"Must be," I murmured.

I couldn't offer Quinn a family like Esme's. We weren't the kind of people who pulled together when there was a crisis. We were the kind of family that shut our problems away in a girl's boarding school. Besides, there was only one of us left – me – since my mother died.

I would have been happier pretending Quinn had been the product of unfertilized conception, like a Komodo dragon. But she had not. Francis E. Gould was alive and in prison, convicted of money laundering for a pedophile ring a few months ago. Out of sight and out of mind. That was just fine with me. Frank was my father. He was Quinn's father, too.

Quinn registered the expression on my face. "It's not your fault," she said.

"It's not something I can fix."

Fixing is what I did, who I was. I put my clients back on the road to a productive life. But I couldn't do that for my own daughter.

"I'm not talking about *him*," she said. "Tell me about your ancestors before your parents, the Goulds and the Shaughnessys. Where did they come from? How did you end up in San Francisco?"

Quinn's eyes lit up with expectation. It was her family, too. If she wanted to know, she was as entitled to our heritage as I was.

"Lizzie always said her family were poor Irish potato farmers. Her husband, Black Jack, won the silver mine in a card game. I don't know much more than that."

"Black Jack? Was that his name?"

"No, I suppose it was John. But that's what they called him because he had a great big black handlebar mustache. From the way she talked, he must have been bigger than life."

"What happened to him?"

"In 1914, he joined the Army and went off to fight in World War I. His ship sank on the way to France. The body was never found, so she had him declared dead. She was pregnant with their son, John, at the time."

"Sad," Quinn said.

"She made the best of it. As they say, she led a rich and fulfilled life."

"What about the Goulds?"

"Irish, too. My mother married my father because they were Catholic. Lizzie hated him, but her parents were delighted because his family were lawyers and judges. Very respectable. Beyond that, I don't know."

Family heritage had never been important to me. Maybe it was because I hated my father and resented my mother. I didn't care about what led up to them becoming who they were.

Germaine Greer raced to the front door in a beige blur. A few seconds later, I heard the door open, a briefcase drop, and the manly purr of, "There's my girl," answered by a delighted feline purr. She was definitely not my cat.

"Is that Chinese food I smell?" Jake called from the hallway. "Did you save any for me?"

"Mongolian beef." I pointed to an unopened carton on the table. Quinn and I had been eating tofu stir-fry, rice, and fried veggie rolls in deference to her diet.

My tall, dark-haired, handsome, broad-shouldered husband came into view in the kitchen behind the breakfast counter, wearing his favorite SFPD sweatshirt with a patch of cat hair on his shoulder. It was the weekend, so he didn't need to wear a suit at the office.

Germaine Greer slinked across the granite counter. She and Jake both knew I hated her walking on the food prep surfaces, but he indulged her, and she enjoyed irritating me. They could claim victory on this issue. Long ago, I had decided to pick my battles.

Quinn sock-shuffled into the kitchen and pulled a third Pilsner glass out of the cupboard and a bottle of beer out of the fridge. When she was turned away from him, he gave me a quick, sly smile, and patted his front jeans pocket.

Jake was just like a little kid. He couldn't keep a secret about gifts. Inevitably, every birthday and Christmas, he'd give me my presents early and then dash out at the last minute, so I'd have something to open on the big day.

He hadn't really been late coming home from work. He had to drive across town to the jeweler, where I had left Lizzie Shaughnessy's pearl necklace for restringing. One of the pearls was to be set on a pendant with a gold chain. It was our birthday gift to Quinn.

"How was your day?" Jake asked. He practically giggled, excitement bursting at his seams.

Quinn was back in her chair. She frowned quickly at the strange note in Jake's voice, then said, "We had a gate crasher at the mansion."

Jake focused on me. "What does Quinn mean, a gatecrasher?"

"Not a big deal," I said, hurrying to change the subject. Once Jake heard about the event at the mansion, Quinn's birthday would fly out of his mind. "How about you?" I stared pointedly at his pocket.

He played up the reveal. Scratched his head. Looked around the ceiling, like he expected a fairy to fly by. Quinn gave me a "what's up with him?" smile.

Finally, he patted his jeans. "Oh, look here! There's something in my pocket!"

Quinn rolled her eyes. I choked down a snort of laughter. Jake was delighted with himself.

He pulled out a small, square black jewelry box and set it in front of Quinn. "Happy birthday!"

Quinn frowned in confusion. Except for small hoops in her pierced ears, she didn't wear jewelry.

"Open it," Jake said.

"The suspense is killing him," I said. "You'd better open it."

She picked up the box and slowly lifted the lid. When she saw the pearl, her face went blank. I'd screwed up. It wasn't what she wanted. Maybe she had been hoping for a car? Jake and I had talked about buying her a car of her own, but it felt manipulative, like we were throwing money at someone to win them over. I wanted to give her something personal, something that could only be given from me to her. Hence, one of the pearls.

My throat tightened with fear.

Jake broke the silence. "It's one of Lizzie Shaughnessy's pearls. From your mom's necklace. We'd hoped you'd like it."

Quinn sniffed. Her eyes brightened with tears. "You guys!"

She rose and gave Jake a hug. Then she came around the table and wrapped her arms around me and squeezed. It was awkward, but it was heartfelt.

"Did we do good?" Jake asked.

Quinn nodded her head vigorously. She tried to pry the cardboard insert out to free the necklace, but her hands were shaking. She handed me the box. "Can you?"

I took the box and carefully removed the necklace. She held her hair over her head as I draped the chain around her neck and snapped the latch into place. She kissed me on the cheek.

As she lightly caressed the single pearl, she said, "I love it. Thank you."

I looked over her shoulder at Jake. He mouthed to me, "I told you so."

Then he clapped his hands and straddled his chair. "I'm starved."

Quinn went into the kitchen and returned with a placemat, napkin, and plate, which she set in front of Jake. "Some guy tried to force himself into the mansion, but Mom stopped him with a kung fu move."

Jake's entire body tensed. "Are you okay, Red?"

"My wrist is a little sore, but I'll live."

"Are you sure? Did you get it looked at?" Jake asked.

"If it's not better tomorrow, I will." I pointed at his cartons. "Dinner's getting cold."

He ignored the food. "Who was this guy? What did he want?"

"No idea as to his identity, but he said his wife was inside and he wanted to see her."

"Mom didn't know him," Quinn volunteered. "But he knew her. He called her 'counselor'."

"Someone from court?" Jake suggested. Occasionally a belligerent defendant or a family member would make threats. Most of the time, nothing came of it.

"Maybe," I said. "It wouldn't have been since I opened the practice or I would have known him, but I couldn't possibly remember everyone I've met in all the years I was at the DA's."

"Did you file a report?" Ever the attorney and former cop, Jake wanted the evidence documented.

"For attempted trespassing?"

"Assault. You were put in apprehension of imminent bodily harm. That's a crime."

I laughed out loud. "The cops aren't interested unless there's blood or a body. You know that."

"You should get it on record, Red."

"We have the surveillance, and we all wrote out statements for our records. If it happens again, it's documented."

"Show me that video."

"There's nothing you can do," I said. "Relax. Eat your dinner."

"I want to know what this guy looks like, in case I see him hanging around."

Quinn's backpack was still on the breakfast counter where she'd left it when we came in. She unzipped it, pulled out her laptop, and after a bit of tapping, found her way into the Foundation's security system. We set it up to be accessible online in case there was an alarm at night, so we could see what was going on from the safety of the condo.

Jake looked over her shoulder while she accessed the footage. It began with me talking to the process server in the portico.

Quinn said, "Here he comes."

"Freeze it," Jake commanded. He turned to me. "This guy?"

On the monitor was a flickering still of the man whom I had sent flying off my doorstep. He was coming back at me when he noticed the surveillance camera and looked directly into it.

"That's him," I said.

"That's Dixon Vaughn."

"Sounds familiar."

"It should. You got him fired. He was a uniformed officer with SFPD. Don't you remember?"

There was only one case I was involved in where an officer lost his job. "I didn't get him fired. He did that to himself. And I almost lost my license because of what he did."

"Sorry, Red," Jake said. "You're right. You didn't get him fired. But you reported him, and he got fired. In his head, it's the same thing."

"What?" Quinn asked. "What did you do?"

"Remember I told you how Judge Rediger hates me? When I was in the DA's office, I was prosecuting a rape case. Really awful facts." I didn't want to put the picture of the victim's injuries into my daughter's head. Images like that never go away. "Anyway, this Vaughn guy – who I'd never met – had taken a statement from a witness who said she had seen the victim leaving the bar with another guy, not the defendant. Vaughn claimed he wrote a report, but I never saw it.

"We believed the victim had met the defendant in a bar for a first date and then for unknown reasons, she accepted a ride from him. Someone found her in the park the next day. She had been drugged, so she couldn't remember what happened to her. We got the man's identity from her dating app."

"So, you prosecuted the wrong man?" Quinn asked.

"The cops put together the case. My boss approved the indictment. I did my job. Then, the defense attorney's investigator found the waitress who saw the victim leave the bar with her attacker. When the waitress was shown a photo of the defendant, she was adamant he wasn't the guy, and she said that she had given Officer Vaughn the attacker's name. She'd recognized the attacker because bars circulate photographs of suspicious men, and he was in one of those photos."

"But what about DNA? Didn't they do a rape kit?" Quinn asked.

"The perpetrator didn't leave behind any bodily fluids." The assault was carried out with foreign objects. My response sounded clinical. That's how I distanced myself from the horror that was inflicted on this poor woman. I was grateful that she couldn't remember it.

Quinn paled as she processed my answer.

"Turns out the rapist was a roommate of the defendant," Jake said, in effort to redirect the conversation. "He had used the defendant's laptop, his IP address, and his dating app account to hook up with women."

I picked up the story. "So, the defense filed a motion to dismiss the case for prosecutorial misconduct. They claimed I suppressed evidence that would have vindicated the defendant. I asked the department to find out if Officer Vaughn had taken a statement. The report was found. It had never been turned over to me. But Judge Rediger didn't believe me, and she sanctioned me. I was fined ten thousand dollars and removed from the case. I appealed, and the sanction was reversed. If I had known about the statement, I would have turned it over. The defense was entitled to it because it proved the defendant's innocence. And I would have recommended to the DA that we dismiss the case."

Jake continued the story. "Vaughn lost his job over it. He blames Red because she was the one that made the department find his report. The department was in the middle of switching from paper records to digital and he claimed he gave it to a secretary to input into the system. The man's no loss to the force. He was lazy and crooked. Turns out the rapist was a friend of Vaughn's."

"Creep," said Quinn.

"Dangerous creep. Red, you need to stay on your toes. Print off that picture for the office so Yolanda knows what he looks like."

"Yolanda was there. She saw the whole thing."

Jake tried not to look surprised. I told him the night before she was going to the Foundation with me for the day. He wasn't listening. I would take offense if it weren't for all the times I was preoccupied and had blocked out what he said. It's expected when you're married to a trial lawyer.

Quinn hit the play button on her laptop. Dixon Vaughn sprung to life, shouting "This isn't over yet, Counselor!"

Jake focused on me. "I don't like this, Red. I don't like this at all. If there's one thing I know about this guy, Dixon Vaughn, he's relentless. He appealed his termination as far as he could take it. Made everyone in the department miserable. Hearings, depositions. He even filed a lawsuit – which got thrown out. He was obsessed. And now he's obsessed with you."

"I'm not letting that man intimidate me," I said. "He's nothing but a bully. You know what? It's time to brush up on self-defense. It'd be great to offer a self-defense class to our Foundation clients. But we'll do a test class first. Yolanda would be up for it. Maybe Esme, too. Quinn, I'd like you to come, too."

"I don't want to hurt anyone."

"Of course you don't," I said, hoping to channel Yolanda's persuasion techniques. "But you don't want anyone to hurt you. That's the key. And I worry about you wandering around San Francisco by yourself."

"OK, fine. I'll do it," Quinn said, invoking the juvenile expression of passive-aggressiveness.

I turned to Jake with a warm smile. "Do you know anyone who could teach us?"

Chapter Six

GERRY WALDRON WAS JAKE'S best friend. They had been cops together. Gerry retired when he was injured in the line of duty and still walked with a slight limp. He was bigger than Jake, over six feet tall, stocky, and wore a shaggy beard. A teddy bear.

When someone burglarized my office a while ago, around the same time that my private investigator was murdered, Jake had asked him to stay with me until things blew over because I refused to quit working.

At the time, I had a case going to trial soon. I had to go to the office. So, Gerry sat on the reception room couch every day all day long. And when I left the office or the condominium, he tagged along. He even went with Quinn and me to our Mother's Day brunch. That was when Yolanda had taken a liking to Gerry. They were a couple now.

Gerry was also a sixth-degree black belt in kung fu.

Our first lesson was at the mansion. Gerry and I pushed the living room furniture against the walls. The newly installed carpet that had replaced aging Oriental rugs would make for a soft landing when we fell.

Gerry wore a karate gi with a black belt. He told us to wear loose, comfortable clothing. Quinn and I wore sweatpants and sweatshirts. Yolanda and Esme wore yoga pants and baggy T-shirts.

Yolanda paired off with Esme. I was Quinn's partner.

Gerry clapped his hands. "Okay, ladies, are we ready? The first thing we are going to learn is how to break a wrist grab. Maureen, you've had some training, so if you would step up here, let's do a little demonstration."

Gerry took hold of my wrist. I stepped closer to him and leveraged my arm through his fingers. Then I faked a hammer blow to his nose. He took a step backwards with his hands covering his face.

I'd forgotten I knew that move.

"Good job!" Gerry said. "Now pair up and practice. I'll talk you through it."

I returned to Quinn's side.

She said, "But I don't want to hurt anyone."

"Here's the thing, Quinn," Gerry said. "When a man attacks you, he has already decided to do you harm. He's planned out his moves. He's ramped up his courage. And he's waited for the exact moment that you are the most vulnerable. So, he already has the advantage."

"I'm always aware of my surroundings," Quinn said. "No one's going to sneak up on me."

"That's great," Gerry said. "But there's a guy who has it out for your mom. He's unpredictable. Vengeful. He has a track record of abusing women. With a guy like that out there, you need to keep your options open. Since you're here, and your mother and your friends are here, and I came over here this afternoon to show you some techniques at Jake's request, would you like to participate?"

Quinn crossed her arms and dug her chin into her chest, letting her red hair hide her face. I had never seen her behave so petulantly. I wondered how much of my perception of her was based upon my fantasy and to what extent I really understood the person she was. In some ways, we were very much alike. How we looked. Our devotion to justice. Our commitment to family.

Yet, there were times when she was a total stranger to me. When she chastised me over my ancestors' exploitation of Chinese laborers and then sulked in her room. And now.

Gerry continued. "Listen here, ladies. If a man touches you without your permission, he intends to hurt you. Period. Again, it's your choice how to react. With training, you will have choices. Without training, you're helpless. What will it be? Decide now, or I'm wasting my time with you. Choice or victim?"

Gerry stood in front of Yolanda and Esme. "What will it be? Choice or victim?"

"Choice!" Yolanda said.

"That's my girl." Gerry moved down the line. "Esme?"

Normally, I called men out on their use of "girl," but since Gerry was here to help us, I decided to let it slide today.

"Choice!" Esme echoed her aunt. Esme bounced on her toes, like a prize fighter itching to get into the ring.

"Good girl," Gerry said.

Gerry moved in front of me. "Choice or victim?"

"Choice."

"I knew that about you," he said. Then he stepped in front of Quinn.

"What will it be?"

I held my breath. I had rescued Quinn from a dangerous situation once. Before she knew how evil Frank was, she thought of him as only her long-lost grandfather. That was my fault – I hadn't told her the truth. One night, when I was looking for a witness in the East Bay, he invited her to dinner, promising he'd tell her about her father. Instead, he took her to the mansion. He got drunk while she looked on, paralyzed with uncertainty. Her yearning for a family fought with her rising panic as she sensed something was wrong. If I hadn't arrived when I did, I don't know what he might have done to her.

Everyone in the room watched Quinn. Her face reddened with embarrassment. When she spoke, it was without conviction. "Choice. I guess."

"Excellent!" Gerry picked up a short bamboo baton he had stashed to one side of the room and tossed it to me. "Now we're going to learn how to defend ourselves from a knife attack."

Chapter Seven

HENRY WATKINS HUDDLED AT his desk, hidden from view by a flimsy gray partition, dizzy from that last puff on his asthma inhaler. He faced his monitor, fingertips resting on the keyboard, but he couldn't work. He couldn't think. His face stared back at him – a ghost image washed out by the bright overhead lighting. The ghost blinked. It had a surprised expression on its face when their eyes met. Focused on the hushed conversation taking place a few yards away in the bullpen, he and the ghost tried to make out the words. So far, he had caught, "subpoena," "grand jury," and "corruption."

When he peeked over the barrier, he saw the two men speaking. Anderson and Sinclair were both supervisors in the department. Anderson was Henry's immediate superior, even though he was ten years younger than Henry. Sinclair oversaw a different group. They were best buddies, by the looks of it. They wore the same black slacks, the same starched button-down shirts, the same blue silk tie. Same height, both dark-haired, styled in the same way. Young, hip, with college degrees in public administration, they were what the chief called "fresh blood" and "go-getters."

Henry Watkins wasn't a go-getter in anyone's eyes. He was dependable, accurate, and efficient. He was the tortoise. But that wasn't good enough for the chief. Before Henry came to the Department of Transportation, he worked in the county's Finance Department, where he reviewed procurement contracts. He was the man who made sure forms were filled out correctly and sums added up. It was a dead-end job. He topped out in the salary range and still couldn't afford to buy a car, much less park it in San Francisco. With the rate of inflation, by the time he retired, he wouldn't be able to pay rent on his apartment. He'd have to leave and move in with his sister, the shrew, who had inherited their parents' decrepit 950-square-foot bungalow in hotter-than-hades Vallejo.

So he took a lateral transfer, hoping there would be opportunities in the Department of Transportation to move up the ladder. When his last supervisor retired, he put in for the job. With four years in the department by that time, Henry thought he had a pretty good shot at it. Every kind of contract had passed through his hands. His knowledge of the regulations was so thorough, he could recite them. He was mature, responsible, and had a two-year degree in accounting.

But the chief hired Anderson instead. Runner-lean. Expensive haircut. Fresh out of college, ink barely dry on his degree. After Anderson came to work, it became apparent that he didn't know a thing about requests for proposals, bids, or single-source procurements, and wasn't interested in learning. He relied on Henry to keep the group running smoothly while he hung around with Sinclair, sometimes in Anderson's windowed office overlooking the bullpen, sometimes in Sinclair's office next door, as they apparently plotted their career advancements. Today they weren't in either office, but instead standing in an aisle. The only complete sentence Henry heard from either of them was, "I think my office is bugged."

Henry's lungs felt like they were collapsing. He plunged the inhaler into his mouth again and sucked deeply. Within moments, he was light-headed, and his lungs relaxed.

He wasn't the only worker bee straining his ears. Every other cubicle was occupied, but there wasn't a call in progress, no papers grinding out of the communal printer, not even tapping on the dozen keyboards in the office. The only sound was the whirling computer fans mixed with the hum from the ventilation system, together producing a drone of conspicuously loud white noise when you're trying to eavesdrop.

Henry's monitor pinged an incoming email. It was from Nancy, in the next cubicle. "Is there any coffee left?" He didn't respond – it wasn't really a question. It was code. Nancy wanted to meet in the break room, apparently with hot gossip to share. A few moments later, he heard her stir, then saw the top of her frizzy blue hair as she bobbed past his partition.

Per their usual routine, he waited a few minutes, then picked up his chipped ceramic coffee cup with "I Heart San Francisco" emblazoned across it, and headed out, watching his feet as he walked so he didn't make eye contact with anyone. You didn't know whom you could trust. As he approached Anderson and Sinclair, they glanced up from their klatch. One sneered, the other rolled his eyes. Then they each walked off briskly in different directions. Sinclair had a folded newspaper lodged under one arm.

When Henry entered the break room, Nancy was sitting at the table, in an oversized cardigan wrapped around her baggy calf-length dress with big, bright flowers. Her mottled plump legs bulged over her sneakers and socks.

She once told him the dresses she'd sewn for herself, all from the same pattern, hid a multitude of sins. He supposed she was embarrassed by her size.

When they first met, he suspected she had a crush on him. After a while, he let her know he wasn't interested. It wasn't her, he told her, she was nice enough – Henry wasn't interested in companionship in any form. He cherished the privacy of his little one-bedroom apartment where he entertained himself reading about historical civilizations and doing crossword puzzles and not talking to another human being. Working in an office was the price he paid for his solitude. His dream was to retire and live out his years as a recluse.

Nancy peered into a grease-stained pink cardboard box someone had left on the table, plucked out a chocolate-iced donut with colored sprinkles and took a bite, then pushed the box in Henry's direction. The reek of fried sugar and bread made him feel sick. He held up a hand, declining her offer. He wasn't there to consume empty calories. He was there for information. Nancy, however, was not going to part with it until Henry sat down.

He filled his mug and took a seat. "What's going on?"

"Haven't you heard? A bunch of people in Building Inspection were indicted for taking bribes. It's in the paper."

Henry scanned the room. There was normally a discarded newspaper lying around somewhere. But not today. Sinclair must have taken it. When he was whispering with Anderson, a newspaper was tucked under his arm.

"There's always a corruption scandal," Henry said. "What does this have to do with us?"

"Shush." Nancy crooked her finger for Henry to come closer. He leaned across the table. Her breath was a mixture of doughnuts, acrid coffee, and something medicinal.

"Not just that," she whispered, "the chief was taken to the DA's office first thing this morning. They sent a couple of detectives to get him."

Henry's mouth went dry. This was bad. Very, very bad.

The contract Henry had given to Alfred Tanzini was not entirely genuine. It was prepared on the correct form. The blank spaces had been filled in as they should have been. There was a signature on the bottom, that of Andrew Anderson.

But Anderson hadn't signed it.

Henry had attached Anderson's electronic signature. He needed the money Tanzini offered him to fast-track the contract. Anderson would sign it eventually, and then Henry could substitute the genuine document for the bogus one.

The problem was Esme Inc's application had been sitting in Anderson's in-box for weeks. Anderson was ignoring it. Henry didn't know why.

He thought about that envelope full of money Tanzini had given him. Right now, it was hidden in a book on a shelf in his apartment. It was the beginning of his nest egg, the funds he needed to make sure he could stay in his apartment when he retired. With the "bonuses" he'd hoped to earn "expediting" contracts, he hoped to set aside sufficient savings to be comfortably ensconced in his cherished apartment for the rest of his life, surrounded with his books on ancient wars, miles away from the shrew sister and her falling-down shack.

If the department was investigated and Anderson's files were reviewed, the contract Henry had sent him for Esme Inc would be revealed. A smart detective would discover that Al Tanzini had a signed contract, but there was no record of it in the department files.

Henry would be screwed.

The cops would find out about the money Tanzini had paid him. They would call it a bribe. He would go to jail.

Henry needed Anderson to approve that contract today. If anyone found both versions, the bogus and the genuine, they would just think it had inadvertently been signed twice.

Henry took his leave of Nancy, forgetting his coffee cup in the breakroom, and headed to Anderson's office. He stopped at the open door, knocking on the frame three times for attention.

Anderson was on his feet, swirling his blazer like a matador as he slipped one arm into a sleeve. "What do you need, Henry? I'm in a hurry."

"Sir, have you had the opportunity to review the Esme Inc contract?"

"What contract?"

Anderson's mind was a sieve. Henry had told him several times. What was Anderson doing in this department anyway besides taking a paycheck and making connections for a better job?

"The café slot on Concourse C."

Anderson shook his head, then dropped his cell phone into his pocket.

"The Mexican bakery, sir. Remember? Well, there's great news. The vendor is ready to start the build-out. All we need is your signature, and we're good to go." Henry realized he had just used the words spoken at his meeting with Tanzini. Could that be used in evidence against him? How would anyone know?

"I mean, sir. The vendor is very anxious to proceed."

Anderson moved towards the door and paused. Henry blocked his exit.

"Sir, I'm afraid if we don't sign soon, they will lose interest. You know how these businesspeople are. If they aren't making money, they think they're losing it. They may commit to another project."

"Not now, Henry. I have an appointment with my lawyer. If you don't mind –." Anderson jerked his head, indicating Henry should move out of his way.

Henry obliged. As Anderson strode towards the elevator, Henry called out, "When may we expect your return?"

Anderson didn't answer. He banged the call button with his fist, then jumped into the car as soon as the doors opened. Sinclair jogged to catch up to Anderson, bumping into Henry and nearly knocking him over. Anderson held the door for Sinclair. Then the doors slid shut.

Neither Anderson nor Sinclair returned to the office that afternoon.

The contract wasn't going to be signed. Henry needed another plan.

Chapter Eight

PAUL LEWIS ADJUSTED THE Bluetooth in his ear.

On the other end of the call, Andy Anderson hissed, "What the hell am I supposed to do?"

Paul drew in a breath. How should he respond? As a friend or a lawyer?

Andy kept talking. "You don't seem to get how bad this is. The bozo I work for got dragged away this morning by the cops."

Paul opted for friend. "It's –,"

"It means the department is being investigated for corruption. Don't you read the news? The DAs are crawling all over every city and county agency. It's only a matter of time. Do you think someone snitched him out?"

"Your boss, the bozo?"

"Yes, the bozo!"

Paul strolled to the windows. The street below was shades of gray, distorted by rain streaking down the glass.

Andy's voice was a low growl now. "It's only a matter of time."

"You said that. Look –,"

"Look, nothing! You got me into this. You better get me out."

Paul had a dilemma. As a friend of Andy's, and one with legal training, he should advise him to seek a criminal defense attorney. But if Andy did that, and told the truth, any competent defense attorney would tell him to cooperate immediately. The first guy to take a deal got the best deal. And cooperation would mean telling the authorities what Paul had done.

"Did you just call to yell at me, or did you want some advice?"

"Advice."

"Don't answer your phone."

Paul tapped the Bluetooth power button. Instantly, his ear was filled with the hollow sound of nothingness.

If Andy was investigated, the police would find countless calls and messages between Andy and Paul on Paul's private cell phone. Why shouldn't they talk? They were old friends. Went to college together. Hung with the same crowd. That would be the story Paul would tell.

And it was true. But there was more.

After Mrs. Osteen had brought Al Tanzini into his office to work on the Esme Inc paperwork, Tanzini showed up one day without her. He was worried about the Dahlberg Kemp International franchise deal. Tanzini needed to prove to DKI the business was thriving and a good investment. That was why they'd applied for the airport contract. But the process was dragging on, and Tanzini said he was afraid DKI would pull out.

Paul knew the truth. Tanzini needed the DKI money to repay Rita's loan and secure his shares in Esme Inc. If he kept his shares, he would be a millionaire many times over. But if Tanzini forfeited his interest in Esme Inc, he would be worse than broke. He wouldn't even have enough money to hire a bankruptcy attorney.

What Al didn't know was Rita had slowed down the permit so Al would default, and she would end up the majority shareholder.

As it happened, Paul's friend, Andy, had just gotten hired at the County Department of Transportation. Upon Rita's instruction, Paul talked to Andy. Money was paid. The contract went into limbo.

When Al asked how to speed up the process, Paul said that there was nothing he could do.

Impatient, and without telling anyone, Tanzini took matters into his own hands. He had gotten hold of some clerk who then delivered the contract with Anderson's signature on it.

Rita was furious. She called Paul and read him out. Paul called Anderson. He had never signed the contract.

Now there was a bogus contract floating around while Anderson had an unexplainable amount of money, and the authorities were rooting around in the department database.

Paul pulled the Bluetooth from his ear and tossed it on the desk. He leaned his forehead against the cold, wet window and squeezed his eyes shut.

This is not what he expected when he graduated from Stanford. His father had promised him a glowing future with the family law firm. He was set up for a political career if he wanted it. Better yet, Paul could cozy up to his rich friends, get himself appointed to their Boards of Directors, and he'd have the inside track on investment opportunities. Money would stick to him like static cling.

By the time Paul found out what was expected of him at the law firm, it was too late to get out. Rita, and his father, had him exactly where they wanted him. He was their henchman. He did the dirty work. He cleaned up their problems.

Rita Osteen was a legacy client, from the old days when Father handled her late husband's business interests. The truth was all of Paul's clients were legacies. He had not brought in any new business. Even though Paul socialized in the correct strata, sailed in the bay, wine tasted in Napa Valley, and skied in Utah, moneyed people of his age patronized the same law firms their parents had. These days, most businesses were national interests anyway. Even if they had a base in San Francisco, their attorneys were either in Los Angeles or New York City. And the up-and-coming entrepreneurs could not afford his hourly rate.

So, Paul was stuck with his father's old golfing buddies and their widows.

The first time he was called upon to do their dirty work was when Old Man Osteen died. Rita was out of town at a medical health spa getting a facelift. The Old Man sent Paul an email saying he wanted to write a new will. Attached to the email was a photograph of the old man's handwritten notes with his signature and the date. He wanted Paul to write it up to make it look legal and to bring it to his bedside for signing.

The new will cut Rita out and left the entire estate to his children. The old man came to believe that Rita married him for his money and had manipulated him. Now that he was on his deathbed, she was getting a new face to start a new life once he was gone.

Paul did as he was told by Old Man Osteen. When he visited Old Man in the mansion, he talked to him long enough to make sure that he was legally competent. Then Old Man signed the will. The nurse and Paul witnessed it.

By the time Paul returned to his office the next day, the Hag, his father's secretary for decades and now his, gave him the message that Old Man Osteen had died during the previous night.

Rita returned from the spa that afternoon. Somehow, she found out Paul had visited the old man and that a document was signed. She showed up in Paul's office with Father, who had flown up from Baja.

He, dressed like he was on the golf course, escorted Mrs. Osteen into Paul's office, catching Paul playing solitaire online. She, dressed in another silk skirted suit and stiletto heels, held the crook of his elbow, and smirked.

Paul shut down the computer and stood to greet them.

Father, tanned from golf, flicked a finger in the air, gesturing for Paul to step out from behind the desk. With an economy of movement, his father slid into Paul's chair. He held a hand out to Rita, inviting her to take a seat. Paul was left standing awkwardly to one side.

Father rocked back in the chair and swiveled to face Paul. "It has come to our attention that Mr. Osteen executed a document last night, just before he died."

Someone had told. That didn't take long. The maid? The nurse? There was no point in denying what they knew to be true.

"He did."

"Let's see it."

Technically, the will should have been turned over to the old man's daughter, Marigold, who was appointed personal representative. But Rita would learn she had been cut out sooner or later. There should be no harm in letting Rita know now.

Paul leaned across the desk, pulled open the pencil drawer, and retrieved a set of keys. He went into the file room and unlocked the secured file cabinet where wills were stored. He brought the document back into his office and handed it to his father.

His father flipped through the legalese, then took a moment to study the provisions. He gave a long, slow blink of disgust, then pushed the papers across the desk to Rita.

"What?" she asked.

Father nodded at the will. "You need to read it."

Rita took longer to study the document. A lay person wouldn't know where the good stuff was buried. After she reached the last page, she read it again. When she was finished, she dropped the will onto the desktop.

"He cut me out?"

Paul took a step back. Let the old man explain it to her.

"Completely," Father said.

Rita's face turned a deep shade of red, making her light buttery-colored foundation splotchy. With her garish red lipstick and heavily mascaraed eyelashes, she looked like a drunk clown.

Paul choked down a laugh.

"You could challenge the will," he said, hoping to placate her.

She gawped at him. Her left eye throbbed.

If this meeting didn't end soon, he would fall on the floor laughing. Father would not be happy.

Paul spoke more quickly. "You have widow's rights. You're entitled to half the estate, regardless of Mr. Osteen's will."

"Half," she repeated.

Paul felt a sudden urgency to pee. He shuffled his feet to relieve pressure on his bladder. His father spiked a look at him.

"That's the law. There's nothing I can do about it," Paul said.

"And if this piece of paper didn't exist, the last will he made, the one he signed when we were married, leaving me everything, would be enforced."

"Yes, but it does exist."

Rita Osteen reached across the desk for Father with a familiarity that always sickened Paul. They held hands. He didn't know what they meant to each other. All he knew was that they had been friends since before he was born. It was Father who introduced Old Man Osteen to Rita not long after she arrived in San Francisco.

He had no evidence to prove it, but it felt like Father and Rita had set up the old man to get his money.

What Father did next horrified him. He took the will and walked to the file room. Paul heard the shredder grind to life, then mince paper into unrecognizable slivers. When Father returned to his office, he sat behind the desk again and accessed the firm's database on Paul's computer. As Paul looked over his shoulder, his father deleted the will.

The old man's children found out about the new will anyway. Nurse Evans had told them. They filed a lawsuit. The nurse testified that she had witnessed a will. At the trial, Paul produced a trust document that had been purportedly signed on the same day the now-destroyed will was executed. Rita signed both the signatures of her late husband, and the nurse and Paul witnessed it. The forged trust document appointed Rita the trustee and empowered her alone to sell all the properties held in trust, which was the entire estate.

Why had Paul protected his father? He didn't know. He was the obedient son. Always had been. Like all his friends, who enjoyed a luxurious lifestyle because of their parents' income, he readily fell into the future that had been laid out for him. It never occurred to him to rebel.

Now, he wished he would've said no. He wished he had the guts to quit his job. But he was trapped by the money and privilege.

Paul punched the window he was leaning against. A cracking sound, louder than he'd expected, made him jump back. The glass vibrated, but it hadn't broken. Not even a fine line. His hand hurt, though. Skin peeled back from his knuckles, like rumpled bedsheets, revealing pink and white tissue. Blood began to seep from somewhere beneath the raw meat.

"What do you think you're doing?" It was the Hag's sharp voice. She stood in the doorway, her wrinkled face twisted with anger.

Another legacy from his father, the Hag had been the firm secretary, and his father's mistress, since it opened. Long past retirement age, tiny and white-haired, she moved so deliberately Paul thought he could hear her bones creak. She was in the office before Paul arrived for work and still at her desk when he left, fixing him with a judgmental stare as he passed by her.

Father was not practicing anymore, but he still owned the firm. His doctor had advised him to retire after his third heart attack. His latest wife, who had been his personal secretary and outmaneuvered the Hag for the privilege of becoming the next Mrs. Lewis, dragged him down to live in Cabo San Lucas. She knew the score. She needed to keep him away from the kittenish secretaries and cougar clients if she wanted to secure her inheritance as his widow.

Now the Hag was at the front desk stuck with Paul, and he was stuck with her. Despite his father's betrayal, her loyalty was unquestionable. She was his father's spy.

"What do you think you're doing?" the Hag repeated.

Paul didn't know. He didn't answer.

"Get that cleaned up before you bleed on the carpet." With that, she marched down the hall and out of sight.

Chapter Nine

I SAT IN A courtroom at the defendant's table, not the side of the room I usually occupied. In most cases, I represented the plaintiff, so I would take the table nearest the jury box. The box was empty today – there was no jury to persuade – but sitting on the opposite side of the room had a disorienting effect on me, as if I were Alice Through the Looking Glass. Everything was reversed.

Esme was by my side, dressed for court in a blue shirt-waist dress and her hair braided behind her back. Hanging from her neck was the Our Lady of Guadalupe medal. The purpose of the hearing was to have the judge set aside the restraining order and to restore Esme to the board of directors of Esme Inc.

A couple of days after Esme was served with the injunction, Tanzini's attorney sent over an offer. Ten thousand dollars for her shares, but the non-competition clause would become permanent. When I called Esme to convey the offer, her response was a profanity, followed by "no."

We were going to fight it out in court.

On the bench, Judge Sharon Rediger perched above the courtroom, hawk-like, gazing down upon the participants as if they were tasty fat rodents. In her fifties, she had short dry brown hair and wore a narrow pair of reading glasses.

Alfred Tanzini was on the stand. It was the first time I saw the man in flesh. He wore a black suit as expensive as his lawyer's but cut more generously to cover his girth. His hair was unnaturally black for his age, thin, and slicked back. His black tie, embroidered with tiny gold fleurs-de-lis, was unfashionably wide but accommodated his size. A heavy, gold-plated chain bracelet dangled from his left wrist.

When he took the stand, Yolanda, who was sitting in the front pew wearing a natty gold tweed suit, passed me a note saying, "He looks like a movie mafia don." I nodded and tucked the note into my pocket.

His attorney, Paul Lewis, stood at the lectern. I felt useless as Tanzini and his lawyer steamrolled over us.

Tanzini had just testified in a self-congratulatory tone about how he formed Esme Inc with my client for the purpose of expanding Esme's Casa de Galletas into a nationwide brand. When asked what his profession was, he said "entrepreneur."

"What shape was the business in when you formed the corporation?" Lewis asked.

"It was a wreck," Tanzini said. "Ms. Castillo owed tens of thousands of dollars in taxes and insurance premiums. If I hadn't come along, she would have gone under within a matter of weeks."

Esme leaned into me. "I paid those myself with my credit cards."

I nodded again. I knew, or believed I knew, all the facts before we walked into the courtroom as the result of several meetings with Esme. She had maxed out her cards paying off the company debts, figuring that the future profits she'd been promised by Tanzini would cover her payments. But there had been no profits. Now she struggled to make her minimum monthly payments, while her debt ballooned from the heavy interest rates.

"Then why bother, Mr. Tanzini?" Lewis asked. "What made you think you could turn this business around?"

"You have to understand, Esme is an artist. She created a line of baked goods that are so inviting to the eye and with such unique flavors that no one thinks about the calories. When office workers stop off at their favorite coffee shop on the way to work, they see her brightly colored cookies and rolls in the display, and they want one. It's the perfect impulse buy. A little bit of happiness, small enough to put in your pocket or purse. And the next morning, they come back and buy again. The shop sells out by ten every morning. She couldn't keep up with demand."

I would have objected since he didn't answer the question, but everything he said was true.

Tanzini unbuttoned his blazer, sat a little straighter, pulled in his gut, then buttoned it again. "I saw right away Esme's could be a going concern. It just needed to be managed. God bless her, Esme may be an artist in the kitchen, but she has no head for business."

Esme whispered to me, "I don't rip off my workers so I can line my own pockets."

I patted her forearm reassuringly, something I had learned from Yolanda, then held my forefinger to my lips, asking her to be quiet.

Esme had an employee-centered business model. Her plan was to pay her workers fairly, which would make for dedicated long-term employees, and in the long run, there would be profits that could be shared with everyone who worked in the business. She had hoped for a loan from the San Francisco City Office of Small Business to see her through the early stages, but it had been months since she applied with no word. She tightened her belt as much as she could. She sold her personal car and drove the delivery van when it wasn't in use. She moved back in with her grandmother. The bakery was one small crisis away from collapse. If her customers' payments were late, she wouldn't have enough money to both pay wages and buy baking supplies.

Lewis asked his client, "What steps did you take to salvage the business?"

"Objection." I was on my feet.

Judge Rediger peered over her glasses at me. "Nature of the objection?"

"Mr. Lewis' use of the word 'salvage' implies the business was a disaster. It wasn't. It was a going concern in the early stages of growth."

Lewis threw up a hand in disgust. "Your Honor!"

"Counselor, this isn't a jury proceeding. I'm perfectly capable of distinguishing hyperbole. Objection overruled."

Lewis turned back to his client. "You can answer the question, Mr. Tanzini. What steps did you take to salvage the business?"

"First off, I injected a huge infusion of cash from myself and another investor. Then I began organizing the business to make it profitable. The bakers were being paid far too much. We reduced their wages commensurate with other bakeries."

"Minimum wage," Esme whispered loudly. The judge looked up from her notes, frowned at my client, gave me a warning look, then turned her attention to Tanzini.

Tanzini waited for the judge's attention, then said, "We couldn't justify having a delivery driver on salary and making payments on a van when he only worked three hours a day. We hired a delivery service for a much more competitive rate, sold the van, and laid off the driver."

Esme leaned over to me. "I found out he sold the van when Jojo didn't bring it back to my grandmother's place. The van was my personal car, too. With it gone, I had nothing to drive so Grandma lets me use her car. Besides, he didn't save anything. The van would have been less expensive in the long run when we had a few more accounts. The whole point of getting rid of JoJo was that he was my cousin."

I patted the air, gesturing for Esme to lower her voice.

Tanzini went on. "Fortunately, the other investor, Mrs. Osteen, is a certified public accountant, so we didn't need a bookkeeper on salary. Esme's records were a shambles when we took over. I get that Ms. Castillo wanted to run a family business, but her aunt, the bookkeeper, was way over her head. That's probably why the Small Business loan was delayed."

Esme leaned into me. "That's bull. There was nothing wrong with the paperwork. The city loan process is a mess, and everyone knows it."

Judge Rediger heard her. "Ms. Castillo, you will have the opportunity to testify. Meanwhile, please refrain from commentary."

Paul Lewis lowered his head to hide his smirk. Tanzini gloated.

"Mr. Tanzini," Lewis said. "Why did you ask the Court to order Ms. Castillo from contacting you or coming to the premises?"

"Because she's disrupting the business. It all started when she visited the bakery. She hadn't been there in a few weeks. She said she was busy signing accounts, but we never saw new business."

Esme slapped the table. "He's lying!"

Judge Rediger's voice was sharp. "Counselor, I will not warn you again. Your client is dancing very close to contempt of court."

Tanzini cleared his throat. "She went into the bakery one day and saw the changes we'd made. Shelf-stable ingredients at a lower cost. A time clock. Apparently, the bakers told her about the wage reduction and that we had eliminated overtime. She hit the roof. She talked the bakers into going on strike. We had to shut down for a few days while I hired new employees. Then she started calling me day and night, demanding I change everything back. So, the board had an emergency meeting, and we agreed that she was damaging the business, in violation of our agreement, and we terminated her. We had no choice if Esme's Casa was going to survive."

Judge Rediger studied Esme for a reaction. My client was slumped in her chair – the fight had gone out of her. Everything Tanzini had said was more or less true. In our meetings, she confessed to persuading the bakers they could make more money elsewhere. She didn't want to see them go, but she didn't want them to take a pay cut out of loyalty to her. She had vowed to them she'd fight to make things right.

Lewis asked, "After you obtained the injunction, did she violate the order?'

"That very night. She called me over and over again. I finally had to turn my phone off to get some sleep. Then she showed up at my apartment the next day. The concierge let her into the building, not realizing there was a problem. She banged on my door for an hour. I had to call building security to have her removed."

This was new.

Behind me, Yolanda had suddenly grown quiet. If she knew Esme had violated the order, she would have told me. I didn't want to telegraph a reaction to the judge, so instead of wheeling on Esme for an explanation, which I very much wanted to do, I took notes. I could feel the judge's eyes on me.

Lewis tapped his legal pad a few times as he reviewed his questions, then asked, "Mr. Tanzini, are you asking the court to continue the injunction?"

"I am."

Lewis stepped back from the lectern. "No further questions for this witness."

Judge Rediger turned to me. "Counselor, do you have any questions?"

I stood. "May we take a quick break?"

The judge looked at the clock. "Very well. Ten minutes." She stood and walked out of the courtroom as the clerk scrambled to her feet and called, "All rise."

The clerk left through her door as Tanzini strode past us, snickering and elbowing his lawyer. When we were alone, I spun my chair to face Esme. "What were you thinking?"

"I didn't know that I couldn't call or go to his apartment."

"Actually, you did. I told you. I explained the terms of the injunction to you very clearly. And you had a copy of it that you took with you. All you had to do was read it if you were confused. Or you could have called me."

I heard Yolanda rustling behind us. I had spoken too harshly and felt bad about it. Clients don't retain a lot of information from their first legal consultation. They simply don't have the mental framework to store and organize legal terms and procedural explanations. Which is why I say the same thing at least three times before they leave the office.

"I'm sorry, Maureen. Please don't be mad at me. I just thought if I could get Al alone, talk to him privately, we could work this out. It's that she-devil that's causing all the problems."

I softened my tone as a half-hearted apology. "Do you mean Rita Osteen?"

"Her. We were doing fine until she showed up."

Once a party violates an injunction, the court rarely dissolves the order. Putting Esme on the stand wouldn't help. But letting her testify wouldn't hurt either. It was her choice.

"I have to be honest, Esme. You're not giving me a lot to work with. It's pointless to cross-examine Tanzini, he'll only repeat everything he just said. I can put you on the stand and you can tell your side of the story. But don't get your hopes up."

"I need to make the judge understand," Esme said.

Cases belong to the client. It was their story and their lives on trial. While I thought I could fashion a more effective strategy than the ones my clients sometimes insisted on, my job was to advise them and to present the story they wanted to tell.

"Then you're going on the stand next," I said.

The clerk stepped into the room, caught my eye, and tapped her watch. She remained standing, expecting the judge to enter any minute. The courtroom door behind me whooshed as Paul Lewis and Al Tanzini entered, their conversation trailing off. The judge's door opened, and the clerk called, "All rise."

"Please be seated," Judge Rediger said. "Ms. Gould, do you have any questions for Mr. Tanzini?"

"I do not, Your Honor. I wish to call Esme Castillo to the stand."

Esme crossed the courtroom, her ankles wobbling in the pumps she wasn't accustomed to wearing. She took the stand and was sworn in.

"You may begin," the judge said.

I touched the Shaughnessy pearl necklace around my neck for good luck. Lizzie always said, "You're as smart as any of them, and smarter than most." On this day, I was afraid that being smarter wasn't going to help my client.

I took my place behind the lectern and began the examination of my client. "Ms. Castillo, please explain to the court what inspired you to open your business, Esme's Casa de Galletas."

Esme turned to face the judge, as I had instructed her before the hearing. The judge would need to be convinced that Esme should be allowed back into her business. She was the same judge who had signed the order throwing Esme out.

"The Casa is a tribute to my grandmother. She is the fountain of our family. All life flows from her. She taught me how to bake. She instilled in me the customs and traditions of our people. From her, I learned the importance of family and how our beautiful culture sustains us. The recipes I used are hers. I gave them a modern twist, but the heart of my business is my grandmother."

Judge Rediger watched Esme closely.

"Thank you, Ms. Castillo," I said. "Please describe for us how the dispute arose at the bakery."

"When the corporation was formed, Al said that I was the face of Esme's Casa, so the best use of my time would be in signing new accounts, instead of baking. So that's what I was doing. He wanted me to focus on bigger vendors, like trendy grocery stores, and café chains. So, I spent all day making telephone calls, setting up appointments, and visiting prospective accounts. One morning, I went into the bakery and found one of the bakers in tears. She said she couldn't afford to live on what I was paying her since I cut her wages."

"Had you cut her wages?"

"No, I had not. That was Al's work. He went to the bakers and told them we couldn't afford to pay them so much and that Esme's, the company – not me, was reducing them to minimum wage and cutting out overtime. Then the baker showed me a time clock they were required to punch in and out of. My bakers were insulted, like I didn't trust them anymore."

"Did you encourage them to go on strike?"

"I told them that I'd do my best to get to the bottom of this and make things right, but if they needed to quit and find another job, I understood completely."

"How did they respond?"

"They cried and they hugged me. Then they all walked out. There I was, alone in an empty kitchen that used to be my bakery. I was stunned. Everything had been going so well. I didn't understand what had happened. I felt like I didn't belong there anymore. I thought that bringing Al on as a partner would make things better, not just for me, but for my bakers, too. He promised we would become a stronger business with his help. While I was sitting there, I realized the smell of the baked goods was off. So I went into the pantry and saw that he had bought different ingredients. There were gallons of cheap vanilla. Mexican vanilla is very different from what you get from wholesalers. It is one of the things that lends such a unique character to my products."

Judge Rediger took notes. Out of the corner of my eye, I could see Tanzini shifting around in his chair uneasily.

Esme said, "I called him and asked him what was going on."

"What did he say?"

"He said that he was in the middle of something, and he asked if he could get back to me that afternoon."

"Did he?"

"No. And he didn't answer any of my calls. So, I started calling my old accounts, to see if they noticed the difference in the quality of the goods. They said they had and that they were having trouble selling them. It used to be that everyone sold out every day. Now they were cutting back on their orders. He was destroying my business."

"Did he ever get back to you?"

"There was a shareholder meeting. It was Al Tanzini, Rita Osteen, and me. They told me I was off the Board. The next day he sent me an email with a letter attached, written on my own letterhead, telling me the Board had terminated my services because I was damaging the business. Me! I was trying to save the business. The letter said I wasn't allowed in the bakery anymore."

"But you were still a shareholder, is that right?" I asked.

Esme replied, "What good that is. The letter said they had the right to cash out my shares because of my malfeasance – that's what he called it – when they said I'd instigated a strike, but the shares were worthless because of the company's heavy debt load. I didn't get it. Why were we in debt? I had paid the taxes and insurance with my credit cards. The day we signed the agreement, there was no debt."

"Did anyone give you notice of the directors' meeting before it was held?" Under their agreement, all directors had to be notified of a meeting beforehand. If they weren't, the action taken at that meeting would be illegal. This argument was the basis of my motion to vacate the injunction. The directors didn't have the legal authority to throw her out.

Esme shook her head. "The first I heard about it was in that letter."

"What did you do?"

"I tried calling him, but he didn't take my calls. I went to his apartment, but he never answered the door. He ghosted me. And I kind of gave up."

"Did you start a new business?"

"I figured, I did it once, I can do it again. So, I started baking in my grandmother's kitchen and selling my goods at pop-ups around the city. I wasn't competing with Esme's Casa, because the bakery had never sold from pop-ups before. It was a whole different market. In fact, Al said he wasn't interested in pop-ups because it was too labor intensive for a minimal profit. He kept telling me Esme's Casa was going to be big. It was going to be nationwide."

Esme had told her story. Now the judge would decide what was fair, either to let Esme back into the business or to lock her out.

"Thank you, Ms. Castillo. I have no further questions."

Judge Rediger looked at Lewis. "Counselor, any questions?

"None, Your Honor."

"Very well. You may step down from the witness stand, Ms. Castillo."

Esme grabbed a tissue from a box kept on the stand and walked across the room to our table. Before she sat down, she reached over the railing to squeeze Yolanda's hand. After she had settled, the judge said, "I'm prepared to rule from the bench."

The judge then slid a piece of paper out of her file and began to read the decision she had written before the hearing began. "It has been established to the satisfaction of this court that Esme Castillo, Alfred Tanzini, and Rita Osteen formed a corporation named Esme Inc. for the purpose of manufacture and distribution of baked goods nationwide. To this endeavor, Mr. Tanzini and Ms. Osteen contributed cash. For her contribution, Ms. Castillo signed over to the corporation her recipes, her brand, her likeness, and her goodwill. In addition, all the parties executed a non-competition clause that forbids any of the shareholders from engaging in a competitive enterprise. Further, it is the duty of each shareholder to refrain from taking any actions or failing to take any action which would cause harm to the corporation."

The judge flipped to the next page. "Ms. Castillo admitted that she encouraged the bakers to quit their jobs, which damaged the business. Whether they went on strike or walked out is immaterial. She admitted that she began a competing business, another violation of the corporate agreement. And she admitted that when she was served with the restraining order, she immediately violated it by attempting to contact Mr. Tanzini.

"Accordingly, the court rules that the injunction shall remain in place for the duration of the litigation. Ms. Castillo is specifically forbidden from engaging in any baking enterprise and from contacting any employees or shareholders of Esme Inc except through their attorneys.

"This hearing stands adjourned."

The clerk called, "All rise!"

We stood as the judge swept off the bench, disappearing into the door behind her throne. Esme stared straight ahead as the courtroom emptied. The clerk tapped a couple of buttons on her machines, then left through her door. As Lewis packed his briefcase, Tanzini said, "Can I buy you a drink?"

Yolanda, who was seated behind me, tugged on my blazer. Annoyed, I pivoted to face her. She locked eyes with me, then slid her eyes to her left. I followed the direction and saw a well-dressed, large, dark man with black curly hair standing in the last pew. I hadn't heard him come in.

As Lewis led Tanzini down the aisle, the man lifted his hand, pointed a finger gun at Tanzini, and snapped his thumb down. Tanzini stutter-stepped, trying to position Lewis between himself and the stranger. Lewis was apparently unaware of what had taken place. The man smirked as Tanzini pushed his way past Lewis to get out of the courtroom quickly.

After the courtroom door closed behind them, the stranger walked up to me. "Ms. Gould, my name is Bruno Fernandez. I have some information about Alfred Tanzini you might find interesting."

His complexion was Mediterranean and pock-marked. He smelled of soap and freshly starched and ironed cotton. His accent was East Coast, but I didn't know enough to pinpoint exactly where.

"Such as?" I asked.

"Perhaps we could meet in your office an hour from now."

As the saying goes, my enemy's enemy is my friend. "Okay." I reached into my pocket to retrieve a business card.

He held up a hand to stop me. "No need. I know the address."

When we were alone, I said to Yolanda, "I'm sorry."

"You did your best," Yolanda answered.

Esme fell into her chair, crossed her arms on the desktop and lowered her head to rest on them. "What's the point of going on? I'm out of business. They've taken everything from me, even my name."

Yolanda came around the railing and squeezed Esme's shoulder. "Don't think like that. We'll come up with something. What I want to know is if he's got so much money, why's he wearing cheap jewelry?"

I raised my hands for attention. "I don't want you two to get excited. It may be nothing, but it might be something. Esme says the bills were all paid up when the corporation was formed. Tanzini said she owed tens of thousands of dollars that he paid off with his investment. If all the bills were paid before the corporation was formed, and if Tanzini and Rita Osteen invested a chunk of cash, where did the money go?"

Chapter Ten

BRUNO FERNANDEZ ARRIVED TEN minutes before our appointment. Yolanda didn't like the looks of him, so she rushed back after dropping Esme off at her grandmother's house to be with me.

I was in my back office with the door open when I heard Mr. Fernandez introduce himself again to Yolanda. She buzzed me to see if I was ready – to give me a chance to close down my computer. It was never good law office practice to leave a client's file open on the monitor when someone was in the office, because of confidentiality, so I made it a habit to shut down completely when I had a visitor.

The page that was open when she buzzed was a news article about how Alfred Tanzini, then a practicing attorney, had embezzled from a Newark, New Jersey, butcher Bruno Fernandez and his wife, leading to his disbarment. I very much wanted to know what this man could tell me.

I pressed the intercom button on my landline. "Please show him in."

I stood, tucked in my blouse and buttoned my blazer.

When Yolanda appeared at my door with Mr. Fernandez, I came around the desk, with my arm extended. "Thank you for meeting with me," I said.

When we shook, he gently held my hand in his own dry, beefy hand. He was a man who because of his looming size had learned to make an extra effort to appear harmless. His black eyes looked directly into mine, glistening with excited anticipation. He wanted something from me.

I swept my arm towards the conversation nook, where an oxblood-colored leather chair and couch were positioned for interviews in an informal setting. The desk was good for maintaining distance and my authority. But there were times when I wanted the atmosphere to feel more intimate, which would either encourage the other person to openly share with me or feel exposed. How he or she reacted was as important as the information exchanged.

He took in my office. The antique partner's desk. A computer hutch I'd commissioned to match the desk. The heavy bookcases. Hardwood floors covered with oriental rugs. The corner windows overlooking brick buildings and rooftops, with Coit Tower in the distance.

Compensating for the fact that I had just opened my practice and had no experience whatsoever representing individuals in court – unlikely to inspire confidence in prospective clients – I'd purchased the office condo with the last of my inheritance and filled it with big heavy furniture to signify that I was a permanent installation.

He nodded his approval and moved to stand in front of the couch.

I sat down in the adjacent chair as Yolanda pulled one of the visitors' chairs from my desk to form a triangle with myself and Mr. Fernandez. She sat with a legal pad on her lap and a pen poised for notetaking.

He hiked his pants legs for comfort and sat.

"How much do you know about Alfred Tanzini?" he asked.

He was the one who said he had information to share, not that he was interested in pumping me.

"How much of the hearing did you sit through?" I responded.

"Just the last few minutes."

The truth was I didn't know much, but I didn't know this man well enough to confide that to him. Still, it couldn't hurt to give him the broad brushstrokes that anyone would have ascertained had they bothered to pull the court file.

"He entered into business with my client, Esme Castillo, to form a corporation for the purpose of manufacturing and distributing baked goods. We are now in litigation."

He nodded, waiting for me to go on. I didn't.

He shifted forward, placing his elbows on his knees, and shuffled his feet impatiently, apparently eager to share his news. He clasped and unclasped his hands. He wasn't quite ready. And I wasn't going to impart any more information about my case to him. For all I knew, he was planted by Tanzini as a spy, and the little drama at the courthouse was pure theatre.

"I'm sorry," I said, intending to outwait him. "Where are my manners? Would you care for something to drink, coffee or tea?"

I looked up at Yolanda, who stood in anticipation of being sent to the kitchenette for refreshments.

He held up his hand. "Nothing for me, thank you. I don't want to take up too much of your time."

Yolanda sat again.

I shifted in my chair to focus on my guest. "At court, you said you had information for me."

He paused as if to consider his words. Then he said, "I've known Alfred Tanzini all my life. We grew up in the same neighborhood, went to the same school. I was married to his sister. I am here to tell you that Alfred Tanzini is a liar, a cheat, and a fraud."

"Where are you from?" I asked.

"Newark, New Jersey."

"Did you come all this way to tell me that?"

"No, ma'am, I came to find Al." He scooted close to the edge of the couch. "Ever since he skipped town, I've been watching the Internet for news. Your local paper ran a story about up-and-coming small businesses, and that's where I saw his name. I came here to see for myself if it was the same man."

Mr. Fernandez left his life behind on a moment's notice to trace Alfred Tanzini. That sounded a lot like revenge.

"Are you satisfied that the Alfred Tanzini you knew and the man I am litigating against are the same man."

"It's him. I'd know him anywhere."

I sat back in my chair. He started talking. And Yolanda started taking notes.

"My wife, Al's sister, was badly injured in a car accident a few years ago. She was paralyzed. Broken neck. She died not long ago from complications as the result of her injuries."

"That's horrible," I said. "I'm sorry to hear about her accident."

He continued. "She insisted on hiring Al to handle the case, against my advice. But she said they were family. Al had always been a loser. Couldn't hold down a real job so he went to law school."

I heard that a lot and I couldn't argue. The truth was a lot of people went to law school because they were unemployable.

He went on. "He flunked the bar a bunch of times, I lost count how many. Finally, he got a job with a law firm. When he landed my wife's case, they were so excited they made him partner."

I didn't know much about personal injury law, but I knew that severe injuries didn't necessarily mean a big money case. Most people drive around with minimal insurance so often even the most tragic cases result in a low settlement. "How did they come to realize the case was worth so much?"

"I know how you lawyers think," he said with a jerk of his head.

He was a grieving widower. I decided to let slide the implied insult that all lawyers measure human life in dollars. To be honest, some do.

"You want to know what kind of insurance was involved. It was a city garbage truck that ran a red light and T-boned her car."

His wife's case was worth tens of millions. Maybe even more. Not that a big settlement would fix her, but it would have made her more comfortable.

"It's not about the money," Fernandez said.

I heard that a lot too. And sometimes it was true, but not often.

"It's about betrayal. We had no idea what was going on with the case while my wife was slowly dying. Every time I called Al, he said he was working on it. So, one day, I went to court and found out the case had been dismissed because of a stipulation. Turns out, he'd settled the case not long after we hired him. He told his partners that he'd transferred the money into a trust account set up for my wife."

Fernandez scoffed. "He'd made himself the trustee so he could make withdraws without anyone knowing. Blew all the money on gambling. Meanwhile, like I said, he told us the case was ongoing. So, I took a copy of the court file to his partners and showed it to them. When everyone got talking, that's how we found out he was lying – his lies to us and his lies to his partners just didn't add up."

He paused for dramatic effect. "Ms. Gould, my wife died knowing that her brother stole from her. She was heartbroken."

Then he pointed a finger at me. "You need to talk to this Mrs. Osteen person. See if she knows who she's dealing with. That's my advice to you."

Yolanda had been writing furiously on her pad. Her pen came to a rest a few moments after he stopped speaking.

Tanzini's history of burying his thefts under a blanket of false paperwork was good information. His testimony didn't add up with what I knew about Esme Inc's finances. Where did the money go that she and Tanzini said they'd contributed to the business? Had they ever contributed to it? Or did they spend it all, and if so, how? I needed the paperwork before I was prepared to take depositions, Tanzini's or Rita Osteen's, under oath in the presence of a court reporter who would transcribe every word they said. If Tanzini lied to me, then I would make sure that his lies were documented for the court. When we eventually went to trial, his word wouldn't be trustworthy.

"Thank you, Mr. Fernandez. I'll take that into consideration. Is there anything else I should know?"

"That's all?" he asked. "Aren't you going to do something about it?"

"There's no quick fix in the law, Mr. Fernandez. Building a case properly, assembling the evidence, trapping the liars, takes months, even years."

He stood and plucked at his trouser legs again. "That's all I had to say. Please tell Ms. Castillo that I am sorry for her troubles, and I hope everything works out for her."

A few weeks later, Alfred Tanzini was murdered.

Chapter Eleven

THE DAY AFTER THE hearing, I was at my desk, absorbed in writing a motion to compel Esme's Inc to produce its books. The question of where the money had gone nagged me. I hoped the answer would be the key to dismantling Al Tanzini's hold on Esme Inc.

Yolanda was out running personal errands on her lunch break, so the front desk was empty, and the door was unlocked. We never had a reason before to lock it during business hours. Leaving it open allowed the mailman and couriers to drop deliveries on Yolanda's desk without disturbing me.

My back was to the door while I pounded away on the keyboard, absorbed in my work, so I didn't hear the man come in.

An image drifted across my screen, but I dismissed it as an optical illusion.

He slammed his fist on my desk. I jumped out of my chair and spun around, my hands raised in a boxer's pose.

He cackled. "Does the little girl want to fight?"

I scanned my desktop for a weapon. A pen rested on a legal pad. He hadn't moved. If he had planned to attack me when he came in, he would have by now. If I reached for it, I would put myself within his arm reach, and I was afraid he might grab me.

It wasn't Dixon Vaughn. It was someone else. Smaller, younger, solid from lifting weights, tanned with his face a deep maroon color from high blood pressure. Wearing black jeans and a black T-shirt. The veins in his neck stood out. He thrust a pointed finger at me. "We know who you are! And we know what you do. You better watch your back, bitch. A mighty battle is coming. Your female privilege will be vanquished. And then you'll be back where you belong."

He swept his arm across my desk, sending the pen, paper, and books flying. He threw over one of my visitor's chairs. Still not satisfied, he picked up a crystal paperweight my mother had given me and threw it through the window, shattering the glass.

A horn blared from the street below. In an instant, his expression switched from rage to fear. When he ran out of my office, I noticed his high-top Converse shoes. The front door banged shut. I looked out onto the street and saw the man jump into a red Mustang with a white racing stripe that was double-parked in front of my building. It pulled out into traffic and disappeared around the corner, too far away for me to read the license plate number.

It was the same car Dixon Vaughn had escaped in when he tried to force his way into the mansion.

I ran into reception and locked the front door. My hands shook, but I managed to text Yolanda that she needed to use her keys to get in. I called Jake and told him what happened. He told me to keep the doors locked until he could get there.

I threw up in the trash can.

Twice in the past few weeks, an angry man had confronted me, and I had resorted to self-defense moves learned years ago. I was lucky. Both men ran away. But I had no idea what would happen if they were committed to hurting me. I wasn't confident that I would execute some long-forgotten kung fu moves well enough to repel an attack.

I didn't want to buy a gun. I hated them. A gun protects you only if you're holding it. I read a news story once about an office worker who came home for his lunch break, only to surprise teenagers that had broken into his house and were playing with his gun. They shot him and stuffed his body in a closet. I made Jake get rid of his sidearm when he moved in with me.

Yolanda arrived a few minutes later. She started the tea kettle, bagged up the contents of the trash can and took it out to the dumpster in the alley, then came back and made me a cup of sugary tea.

When Jake and Gerry arrived, Yolanda let them in. Gerry stopped to squeeze her arm and exchange a discreet tender look with her while Jake sat down on the couch armrest next to me where I clasped a tea mug, trying to force my hands to stop shaking. Yolanda settled on my other side. Gerry pulled Yolanda's chair out from behind the desk and sat opposite us.

"You're sure it wasn't Dixon Vaughn," Jake said.

"I'm sure. I got a pretty good look at him. This guy was much younger. But he drove away in the same car."

"How many cars like that in San Francisco?" Gerry asked.

"How many cars like that in San Francisco used for a getaway after they attacked my wife?" Jake said. "Red, we need to file a report."

"For what? It wasn't burglary. He didn't break in. It wasn't trespass. The door is open to anyone who wants to enter."

Yolanda said, "Jake's right. If a report is filed, SFPD could find out whose car it is."

"He just tried to frighten me. The police don't have time to investigate non-violent crimes."

Gerry said, "Jake could find the vehicle owner on the DA's database."

I shook my head. "It's illegal to use the state's resources for personal reasons. I don't want him getting into trouble."

"This guy must be a friend of Vaughn's," Jake said. "I don't like the thought of them coming back again. We need to take this fight to his door."

"Metaphorically, you mean," I said, patting his thigh. "Because you, an assistant district attorney sworn to uphold the law, cannot go pound on a man's door and pick a fight with him because he frightened your wife. The law, i.e. your boss, takes a dim view of people taking the law into their own hands. Let's find out everything we can first and then go from there. I love you, but there's no reason to lose your job over this."

Before I'd finished that sentence, Yolanda was on her feet, whisking her hands at Gerry so he'd relinquish her chair, which she dragged behind her desk. She logged onto the computer. While we waited, Jake got on his phone. "I'm calling a security company to come install cameras. And I'll get a window guy in here to replace the glass."

"Got it!" Yolanda said. "Dixon Vaughn has a podcast. He also has a business license and a limited liability company, with a physical address listed." She hit a couple of keys, and the printer began grinding out paper.

Jake finished his call. "The security guys can be here tomorrow."

"That quick?" Yolanda said.

"I put a rush on it. Now tell me, what's this about a podcast?"

Jake, Gerry and I huddled around Yolanda's monitor while we watched episode after episode of the same screaming diatribe from the stony-faced man with a buzz cut. Vaughn's favorite catchphrases included "Enough is enough," "Men are the real victims," "A mighty battle is coming," and "Female privilege will be vanquished." The last two had been spoken by the intruder in my office.

As we watched the programs, Yolanda worked in my back office, using my computer to find more information on Dixon Vaughn. She came back into reception as the printer hummed to life. I paused the video.

"Here's the deal," Yolanda said. "Dixon Vaughn's wife filed for a divorce and custody case. She got a restraining order against him last year. He violated it a couple of times. Got charged with criminal violations, but it doesn't look like that case is going anywhere." She shot Jake a dirty look.

Jake held up both hands. "Hey, it's not my department. And I couldn't get involved if I wanted to, now. He'd claim I was using the office to push a personal dispute."

She pulled documents from the printer and handed them to me. "I still don't recognize the name," I said. "Is she one of the Foundation clients?"

"Nope," Yolanda said. "Never heard of her."

Gerry stroked his beard. "So why's he claiming his wife's in there?"

"A ruse to get inside," I said. "See what we're doing for himself. Maybe get a chance to terrorize the women and kids."

I passed the papers to Jake. While he read, I glanced at the podcast menu. One of the episode titles was, "Maureen Gould, Femicult Queen."

I hit play.

Vaughn stared into the camera. An expensive microphone hung near his face. He flexed his jaw muscle and pointed at the camera, just like the intruder had pointed at me. "This is what you need to know, men. Your ex-wives and their castrating lawyers treat you like a stock animal. Enough is enough. So much for 'to death do us part.' When the little woman's got what she wanted, you're out the door."

He slammed the desk, just as the intruder had. "You know what that is? Your semen. Your life force. She used you for breeding stock. And now she wants half of everything you made, your home, your retirement. She wants to take your kids, your legacy, away from you so you'll never see them again, but guess what! You still got to pay child support! Enough is enough!"

"Brothers, we have a new enemy. Maureen Gould, Femicult Queen." A picture of me taken surreptitiously as I left the courthouse, flashed on the screen. He pointed to it. "This woman. Remember her face. She's helping your wives run away from their homes and duties and kidnap your children." The Shaughnessy mansion labeled with its address now appeared. "And here is where she's hiding them. Want to know where your women and your kids are? They're here.

"This is Dixon Vaughn, doing right by my brothers. Carry on." With that, he saluted the camera.

A window popped up on the screen, providing a link for supporters to contribute money.

Jake reached across me, hit a couple of keys, and shut down the computer.

My hands had stopped shaking. My own anger was setting in. This man had declared war.

I had started the Foundation because my mother suffered in a bad marriage to a pedophile. She felt like she couldn't get out. She abandoned me to a girls' school rather than leave her husband. My own daughter was taken away from me. Generations to come in my family, if they did, would be molded by what Frank had done.

"I'm not going to let him scare me out of helping women."

Chapter Twelve

AL TANZINI THREW THE sheet off one of his legs to cool himself while Rita crawled out of bed. She wasn't bashful as she walked naked to the ensuite. She kept herself trim, but even under the soft glow of bedside lamps, her age showed in the sagging dimpled butt cheeks that rolled away from him with every step. She was making a point, by the way she sashayed across the room, that she was in control of the moment as she had been the entire night. That was alright with him, as long as she knew it was only in the bedroom. In the boardroom, The Great Tanzini was boss.

Earlier that evening, they had a videoconference call with the man from DKI, Samuel Porter. Porter wore an expensive suit and was so lean, Al would bet that he ran on the treadmill every day for exactly one hour. Because that's the kind of guy he was. Precise.

If Al was the king of the hill, Sam was an ambassador from a neighboring world power. Al knew he was being absurd. He wasn't a king of a hill, but he had just taken over a thriving bakery with a hip brand that, if handled right, could be leveraged into a multi-million-dollar concern.

Rita had set up the franchise deal. She said she'd known Porter through her late husband, the poor sap that left her all that money.

Samuel Porter was a senior vice president from Dahlberg Kemp International, the baked goods distributer with a dozen brands to its name, including Della's Delights – the 1940s-era cookie company started by a stay-at-home mom in her kitchen who then mismanaged the company and had to sell it, eventually dying in poverty. She didn't have the head for business and paid the price. Sorry, Della, but it's a dog-eat-dog world.

And The Great Tanzini was a big dog. A very big dog indeed. Sam should appreciate how Al scooped up Esme's Casa de Galletas. He stole his strategy from Dahlberg Kemp's playbook. After all, imitation is the sincerest form of flattery.

"Is everything lined up for the airport venue?" Sam asked.

"Contract signed and safely tucked away in my safe," Al said. "There's no going back now. Our builder is ready to start on the first. The grand opening is scheduled for two months after construction begins."

"There must be some way of moving up that date."

"Sure, Sammy."

"It's Sam."

"Right. Sam. We can move up that date for you. If we throw some extra money at the contractor, he'll put his crew into overtime. And we have a guy in the city office who could get the inspections done as soon as needed. No problem. But here's the thing, we haven't seen a commitment from DKI yet."

Al was running out of money. Or to be more accurate, the cash flow from Rita had slowed to a dribble. His share in Esme Inc had been fronted by her. If he didn't pay her back in time, he'd forfeit his shares to her. He'd be out on the street. No more fancy car. No more fancy condo. Starting over again.

He needed the DKI deal to go through – fast.

It wasn't fair that he should be scrambling to make this thing go through. Rita might have found Porter, but Al was the one who found Esme, the goose who laid the golden eggs. He had stopped in at a coffee shop one morning and saw people lined up for her cookies. The next morning, he came back before the shop opened and waited for her to make her delivery. He bought her dinner that night, told her he could make her into a star. She just needed someone with a business head like his.

Then Al took the deal to Rita Osteen, who'd been a regular with her husband at the North Beach restaurant he'd managed. It served Italian food but was owned by Koreans. They needed someone who looked and sounded Italian. He laid the New York wise guy accent on thick when he interviewed for the job. Played up the charm. The Great Tanzini was their man. He was hired on the spot because his personality was an asset.

Like Rita's money. Like Esme's recipes. Al Tanzini's contribution to Esme Inc was just being there. People liked him. Talking them into deals was his gift.

"So, Sam, when do you get the final verdict from your bosses? In or out?"

"Get the airport venue opened, and we'll watch the receivables for a few months. Then we'll let you know."

The screen went blank.

Al reached over and gave Rita's thigh a squeeze. "Sorry, babe. Looks like we're going to need another cash infusion."

"We'll see," she said. "And don't call me 'babe'."

He didn't like the feel of that, her teasing him about money. He was the brains. She was the bank. That was the deal.

And a deal is a deal.

What she didn't know was he had leverage. He knew her little secret. The one that she shared with Paul Lewis.

Al had found her husband's will. Not long after he hooked up with Rita, they spent the afternoon at her mansion, drinking champagne and rolling around in bed. Rita and her husband had separate bedrooms. When the time came for romance, she led him to the dead guy's room. Her excuse for not taking him to her own bed was that she didn't want to sleep in filthy sheets that night.

When she went to the bathroom, Al rooted around in the bedside drawers and found the old man's cell phone. He took it home, charged it, and found the email. The old man had sent Paul Lewis a signed handwritten will with instructions to type it up, so it was legal.

Al knew the story about the lawsuit with the old man's kids and how they believed there was a new will, but Rita and Paul Lewis denied it. The will never turned up. The kids got nothing. Rita got everything.

Al had gone to law school. He knew a signed handwritten will was enforceable. Not only had Lewis lied to the court when he said there wasn't a new will, he must have destroyed both the handwritten and the formal wills. Paul Lewis could be disbarred. He might even go to jail if some smart prosecutor made a case against him for defrauding the old man's kids. Rita would lose big, too. Half her fortune – at least. Maybe jail for her, too.

Life was good for Al Tanzini. Hot broad in his bed, even if she was older. Fancy apartment. Nice clothes. Wine brought up by a waiter from the restaurant downstairs. Al pushed himself up on one elbow, emptied what little was left in the bottle into his goblet, and poured it down his throat.

He heard the shower start. She was fastidious, that woman. He'd join her, but he had tried that once before, and she screeched at him to go away. That was when he learned that once she hit the shower, she was done with him.

He grabbed a remote from the end table and flicked on the late news. A pretty young news anchor read a story about corruption in the city Building Inspection Department.

Several businessmen had ratted out city employees and gotten plea deals. The city guys were going to jail.

Her Highness returned to the bedroom, showered, and dressed in the clothes she had worn when she came over.

Al grabbed the switchblade resting on a platter of cheese and meats and speared a chunk of cheese. He put the food between his teeth and slowly pulled the knife out. The vein in her neck began to throb quickly, even though she pretended not to notice. She never mentioned the knife, but she reacted when it was brandished. She was afraid of him. She should be.

"Did you see the news?" he asked.

"The Building Inspection scandal," she said, nonchalantly. "So what?"

Al threw off the sheet. Her face registered disgust as she turned to pick up one of the high heels she'd carefully placed at the foot of the bed earlier that evening.

"Look, Rita, we're sitting pretty. We have the lease. The contractor is ready to build. Your DKI guy is happy. Esme's out of the picture. There's nothing to worry about."

"Did you sleep with her?"

She had never wanted to know before. After all, they were both grown-ups. He used her. She used him. Win-win. No one said anything about them being boyfriend and girlfriend. Still, what Rita didn't know didn't hurt her – or him.

"No way. She's just a girl, not my type. What I like is a real woman." He reached for her wrist. She jerked out of his grasp.

"You're not jealous, are you?" he teased.

She snorted. "Certainly not. Esme's volatile. Blew this whole thing out of proportion. If she feels like you took advantage of her, she could become vindictive, make problems."

"Look, she doesn't know anything about the airport lease. I kept her away from all of that."

"What about that little county paper pusher. Can you trust him?"

"Henry? He's my man! We're like this." Al held up two fingers crossed. "Besides, he's got as much to lose as we do. He ain't talking to no one."

As Rita walked away, Al slapped her on the ass. "We're going to be rich, baby. Just stick with me and you'll be farting in silk shorts."

She stopped in her tracks, turned, sneered, then gave a little laugh, and walked out without saying good-bye.

Chapter Thirteen

WHEN THE MAID SHOWED the visitor into the white-on-white Victoriana sitting room, Rita Osteen rose politely from her throne-like chair to greet him. Although it was mid-afternoon, the curtains had been drawn against the gray day that hid her view of the Golden Gate Bridge from her Presidio Heights mansion. There was no point in looking out if you couldn't see anything.

"Good afternoon, Mr. Fernandez. Please make yourself comfortable. Would you care for something to drink?"

The man who stood before her was larger than she'd expected. He clearly worked with his body. Wide shoulders, broad chest, thick arms. His complexion was dark and pock-marked. Rain droplets sparkled in his thick curly hair. In contrast to his rough physicality, he was neatly dressed in a pressed shirt, slacks, and a blazer. The open neck of the shirt revealed a mat of thick curly hair.

"No thank you, Mrs. Osteen," he said. "I appreciate you making the time to meet."

"I must confess. Your call this morning was intriguing."

Intriguing, but not surprising. Rita had been waiting for Bruno Fernandez to show up. Al thought he'd hidden his past. Al was an idiot. When he first came to Rita with his idea for taking over Esme's business, she had Paul Lewis do a background check.

It only took a day for the report to come back.

Al was a disbarred lawyer. He had stolen the multi-million-dollar personal injury settlement that he had negotiated for his own sister, a woman crippled in a car accident and slowly dying from her injuries. Al didn't tell her that he'd settled the case. Instead, he used the money to cover his own gambling debts.

Her husband was Bruno Fernandez. After his wife's death, Fernandez had discovered the theft and reported Al to his partners. They took care of the rest. Paid out a generous settlement from the malpractice insurance. Fired Al from the firm. Turned him over to the bar association for disciplinary action.

And now Fernandez, who had no reason to be in San Francisco, was standing in her living room. Bruno Fernandez, who owned a successful butcher shop. His heavy musculature no doubt was the result of dismembering cattle. He had come here to tell her something. She wanted to know what that was.

"Please, take a seat." Rita swept her arm towards the couch as she lowered herself into her chair, her legs crossed at the ankle like the Queen of England. "How may I help you?"

Fernandez perched on the edge of the couch like an uneasy supplicant. "How much do you know about Alfred Tanzini?"

Knowledge is power. Secrets are gold.

Rita inhaled deeply as if she needed to search her memory. She decided to repeat the story Al had told her. She shrugged. "Not much really. He was from New York City. He worked in the restaurant industry. He came to me with a good idea."

Fernandez smirked. "Ha! Al's not from New York. More like Jersey. And restaurants? My –," The man stopped before he said a word that might offend a lady. He cleared his throat, then went on. "He was a lawyer. And he embezzled my wife's settlement. My wife, his own sister. She died heartbroken, knowing that her brother had stolen her money."

Rita put on her surprised look. "I am so sorry, Mr. Fernandez. I had no idea."

"You should keep an eye on him, Mrs. Osteen. He'll steal you blind."

"Thank you, Mr. Fernandez. I will do that."

A silence developed between them. Rita could hear the drone of tires as traffic passed her mansion. If Fernandez had nothing newsworthy to share, it was time for him to leave. "Is there anything else I can do for you?"

"I wanted to warn you 'cause you seem like a nice lady."

Bruno Fernandez had never met Rita Osteen before this afternoon. There is no reason for him to believe she was a nice lady. He had some other motive.

"I'm listening, Mr. Fernandez. What do you wish to warn me about?"

"I intend to get what is owed."

"And what is that, Mr. Fernandez?"

"Revenge."

Rita let the word hang in the air before she spoke again. "And how do you hope to accomplish that, Mr. Fernandez?"

"I'm going to ruin his life."

Ruining Al's life wasn't on her to-do list. She had merely intended to use him until he outlived his usefulness, then she'd discard him. But she was curious. "How do you intend to do that?"

Bruno stood. "That's all I have to say, Mrs. Osteen. I'll show myself out."

After Fernandez left, Rita called for a cup of tea, then relaxed in her chair as she processed the new information. Fernandez had come to San Francisco to exact revenge on Al Tanzini. He didn't need Rita for his plan, or he would have enlisted her. The purpose of his visit was to distance her from Al, to ensure that if Al called her for any kind of assistance, she would turn her back on him.

It was unlikely Fernandez had a plan. He was waiting for an opportunity to present itself.

He was a simple man. If Rita Osteen could feel compassion, she would have felt sorry for him.

Chapter Fourteen

Henry Watkins stood on the sidewalk, conscious of how cold and wet his feet were. His shoes were drenched. When he wiggled his toes to circulate his blood, his socks squished with rainwater.

The walk from the Market Street bus stop to 123 Baywater Street was only a couple of blocks, but just as Henry had stepped off the bus, rain began pelleting down. By the time he arrived at his destination, his hair was plastered to his head, water trickled down his back, and his pants legs were soaked halfway to his knees.

Henry told the valet he was meeting Tanzini for lunch. A lie. The man said Tanzini had just called for his car to be brought around and that he should be out any minute.

Henry was scared. Anderson and Sinclair had never returned to the office. The day after they left, all their personal items had been cleared out. The word among the worker bees was they had quit. That same day, a memo was emailed to everyone in the department stating that the chief had been put on administrative leave. Someone from another department would be taking over in the interim. The department was to be audited. The employees were asked to give their full cooperation.

When the database was audited, they would find the unsigned contract sitting in Anderson's email box. They would find repeated emails from Henry asking Anderson to finalize the document. They'd ask questions. They wouldn't find a copy of the forged contract. Henry was careful not to save it. But, if they contacted Tanzini, they would find the signed version. Tanzini would tell them that Henry had delivered it. The authorities would realize that Henry had forged Anderson's signature. It wouldn't take long for them to figure out he was bribed.

Henry would lose his job. If he was charged with a crime, he could be sentenced to ten to twenty years, according to the Internet. It might as well be a life sentence. Or a death sentence. Henry was soft. He'd never last in prison.

He needed to get that contract back.

The glass front door of 123 Baywater Street blasted open as Tanzini barreled through. He gave Henry a quizzical look, like he couldn't place him.

"It's Henry Watkins, Mr. Tanzini. Remember me?"

"Right, Henry. What are you doing here?"

"I'm sorry to have to tell you this, sir. But the department is being investigated."

"What's that got to do with me?"

"All contracts are frozen – for the time being." That wasn't exactly true, but it might as well be. As far as the department was concerned, there was no contract, and without a contract, there would be no building permit.

Tanzini's face went slack. He looked like a basset hound. "What do you mean, frozen?"

Henry never told Tanzini that Anderson's signature was forged. For all Tanzini knew, the contract was genuine. "I mean, sir, that the city can't go forward with your project – just for the time being – while everything is under review. And I'm afraid I need to ask for the contract I gave you back. There may be some irregularities."

"Irregularities."

A silver Cadillac pulled up to the curb. A valet got out and handed the keys to Tanzini.

"Mr. Anderson, my supervisor who signed the contract, resigned recently under a cloud, I'm afraid. So, as I said, I really need to get that contract back. Just until things settle down."

"No can do, little man. A deal is a deal." Tanzini poked his finger into Henry's chest. "I don't expect any problems from you – or anyone else. I paid you good money. The builder is starting on the first. Everything's lined up. You get me?"

Tanzini had often hinted about his underworld connections, drugs, gambling, other illicit activities. He'd talked about what happened to people who snitched out or double-crossed the wrong people. Tanzini reached into his pants pocket, where he kept his knife. Henry could see Tanzini's knuckles pressed against the fabric, working as if they were turning something over and over.

Henry's voice shook when he answered. "I understand."

Tanzini gave Henry a little shove. "And don't show up here again. *Capisce*?"

"*Capisce.*"

Chapter Fifteen

QUINN SLOTTED THE YELLOW BMW into a compact car space in the school's parking garage and pushed the button that made the car's trunk open. Quinn got to drive the car because Maureen was stuck in the office all day.

Mechanical arms clunked and ground as they lifted the convertible top up and dropped it into place. Quinn raised the door windows with a push of another button, then grabbed her book bag and climbed out of the low-slung car.

"Nice wheels," a young man's voice said from behind her. She spun around.

"Sorry," he said with a sheepish laugh. "Didn't mean to scare you." It was the guy who sat a couple of rows below Quinn in the tiered lecture hall. Whenever the professor called on someone in her vicinity, he would turn around in his chair and his eyes would scan past her in a poor pretense of nonchalance.

Outside the classroom, he seemed to be everywhere. The student cafeteria between classes. The library. On the lawn, sitting under a bench.

He was cute enough, bordering on becoming handsome when he matured. Six-two at least, light brown hair and eyes. Square jaw. Perfectly straight gleaming white teeth, too perfect not to have been the product of orthodonture. This was a child born of money.

Quinn's adopted family wasn't poor, but her parents needed both incomes. Fortunately, she didn't need braces on her teeth. They wouldn't have been able to afford it. When it was time for her to go to college, she had to rely on student loans.

Quinn pointed the key fob at the BMW and pushed the lock button. The car beeped in response. "It's my mom's," she said.

"Your mom's Maureen Gould, right?"

What business was it of his?

Quinn swung her hair around to look at him, in a gesture meant to convey she was affronted but may have unintentionally appeared flirty, her subconscious undermining her.

He seemed confused by her mixed messages. "I'd heard that somewhere. Your name is Quinn, right?"

"Quinn Brennan."

"Different name than your mom's."

"That's right." She hiked her bookbag up on her shoulder and began heading to the stairs. Quinn didn't want to talk about her family. Everyone knew Maureen was her mother. And everyone was curious about why she had a different last name and who her father was. When exactly in the development of friendships, did you share that you were the product of an incestuous rape, that your mother was fourteen years old when her own father accosted her, and then you were given up for adoption?

Did he know about what Frank had done?

The professors called him, "Mr. R-something." She really hadn't been listening closely enough to learn names, too busy taking notes.

When she glanced up to see if he was keeping pace, she saw a bashful, crooked smile. Butterflies fluttered in her stomach.

No law school romances. That was one of the maxims recited in her study group, a ragtag collection of ambitious early-twenty somethings who constantly struggled with the terror that they weren't good enough to get through law school. "Equity aids the vigilant." "Let justice be done though the heavens fall." And "No law school romances." The last maxim might not have been penned by a bewigged seventeenth-century Lord Somebody, but it was given the same reverence as if it had.

"Not being nosey or anything," he said. "I just thought since we're going to spend the next three years in the same classes, it'd be nice to meet. My name's Adam."

He was confident, compared to the students in her study group. Mr. Straight Teeth knew he wouldn't flunk out of law school. As if it was his destiny.

Quinn took the downward stairs at speed, lightly touching her feet on each tread. Back in college, she'd run stairs for exercise when the weather was bad. He followed right behind her.

He wasn't going to go away. Quinn gave up. When she stepped out of the garage onto the winding concrete path through the law school courtyard, she slowed so he could catch up. "Right, you're Mister..."

"Rediger. Adam Rediger."

No way.

"My parents know your mom," he said.

Absolutely no way.

"From court."

Quinn stubbed her foot on a crack in the sidewalk. He caught her elbow. She thought about jerking it away, but by the time she decided to, he'd let go.

"They're judges," he said. "My parents, that is."

Shit.

▼

AFTER THE PROFESSOR DISMISSED their class, Quinn hurried past Rediger, head down as if she was on a mission, while their classmates collected their things and began chatting, thus preventing another awkward social encounter. She found a cubicle, shielded on three sides by tall wooden partitions where she was hidden and where her eyes wouldn't meet with those of anyone else. She pulled out her laptop, set it on the desk, and dumped her bookbag at her feet.

It was like everyone in San Francisco knew more about her than she did.

She signed onto the library Wi-Fi. In the search window, she typed "Shaughnessy" and "San Francisco."

Quinn had always known she was adopted. Her adopted parents loved her, but their extended family was cool. Stories about the family history and heritage were never shared. As a small child, it felt like they didn't quite accept her, and that feeling lingered. Perhaps they were trying to spare her feelings because there would be no comparing her to one of their ancestors the way that families do – "you have your grandmother's eyes" or "you're just like your great aunt Tilda."

As she grew older, she had yearned to discover who she looked like and whose character traits she'd inherited.

That's why, after her adopted parents had died, she signed up on an DNA website. She got a close match with a woman named Mary Margaret Gould. Margaret, as she preferred to be called, messaged her, "I'm so glad I've found you. I am your grandmother."

Margaret said she'd recognized Quinn from her profile photo – that she was the image of her mother, Margaret's daughter, Maureen Gould. Margaret was clearly very proud of Maureen, who was a lawyer. In the letters that followed, she'd sent newspaper clippings about the trials Maureen had won. Quinn studied the photos. She did look like this woman.

Quinn could have gone on as she had been, living on the East Coast and getting her teaching certificate as she'd promised her adopted parents, both educators, although her heart wasn't in it. Teaching was a noble profession, and she knew that the value of caring, committed educators in the lives of their students could not be underestimated. But it didn't feel right for her. She'd toyed with the idea of law school, but when she brought it up one night over dinner, she could tell by the looks on their faces that they were disappointed. They must have felt like she was rejecting them. She didn't mention it again.

The next thing Quinn knew, Margaret offered to fly her out to San Francisco in May to meet her mother.

That was last year.

Now Quinn was in San Francisco, living with Maureen and Jake, going to law school, working in Maureen's office in her free time, and sitting in a law school library wondering if she couldn't bear to admit to strangers that she was part of her new family, did that mean she was ashamed of them?

The search engine did its magic on the slow-moving Wi-Fi, and a list of links rolled out onto the screen.

Quinn clicked.

Chapter Sixteen

PAUL LEWIS WAS TRAPPED behind his desk. His ears rang like fire sirens. Across from him, Alfred Tanzini sprawled across the visitor's chair with a smug self-satisfied grin.

Tanzini glanced at Paul's knuckles, pink with newly formed skin, and smirked. Tanzini would know Paul had not been in a fight. As macho as he was, Tanzini had quickly sized Paul up as a chicken when they first met. He had tried to intimidate Paul ever since. He would have suspected Paul punched a defenseless wall. Even chickens have a boiling point.

Paul hid his hands beneath the desk. He flexed his fingers and made fists, trying to loosen the tight new skin.

On the desk between them was a copy of the handwritten will Old Man Osteen had emailed to Paul. The will that would have restored the Osteen children their inheritance. Millions of dollars. The will that Paul swore to the court never existed.

Every lawyer's first line of defense is denial.

Paul lifted an arched eyebrow. "I've never seen this before in my life."

The fat man snorted. "I thought you might say that."

He reached into the blazer pocket from where he had produced the will and pulled out another sheet of paper. He unfolded it. Read it silently. Head to one side with an eye on Paul, he tossed it across the desktop. Then he relaxed back into the chair again.

When Paul didn't react, he said, "Aren't you going to read it?"

Paul didn't have to. He knew what it was. Heat rushed into his face. Sweat prickled on his cheeks, his forehead, beneath his collar. He wanted to jump out from behind his desk, run out the door, and never come back.

The document on his desk was the reply email the dutiful Paul had sent back to Mr. Osteen acknowledging receipt of the handwritten will. The message from Mr. Osteen asked Paul to "write this up to make it legal." Paul's response was he would visit the next day to obtain Mr. Osteen's signature – and a request that someone attend the signing as a witness. The formal will required two witnesses. Paul would serve as one. Mr. Osteen would need to supply the other.

And so it came to be that Mr. Osteen signed the will in front of Paul and Geraldine Evans, the old man's nurse. For less than twenty-four hours, two virtually identical wills had existed: the handwritten will that was legally enforceable, and a formal will, padded with legalese, equally enforceable.

When the formal will was destroyed by his father, Paul had covered for him. Misguided loyalty to the man who promised him wealth and status. Trying to protect his own inheritance, the law firm.

"You have a problem, Pauly" Tanzini said.

Paul winced at the Italianized version of his name. Tanzini enjoyed playing the goombah. Like he was a big man. Dangerous.

And Tanzini was now dangerous to Paul. If he turned that will over to the Osteen children, Paul would be disbarred. He could be prosecuted for fraud. His father and Rita Osteen could both deny they knew of his actions. It would look like he had destroyed the will on his own and lied about it to curry favor with Rita. Prosecutors may suspect she put him up to it, but there would be no evidence unless he confessed.

"Here's what I want you to do, Pauly," Tanzini said. "You're going to get me the money I need to pay back Rita."

"You want me to *give* you a hundred thousand dollars," Paul said.

"That's right."

Paul had used his entire salary every month to finance his lifestyle. He'd saved nothing.

"I don't have that kind of money."

Tanzini shrugged. "Cash out your retirement."

"There is no retirement." His father had strongly encouraged Paul to put away a portion of his salary, but he barely got by on what the cheapskate paid him. Paul was banking that he would inherit at least the law firm and half his father's estate if the new wife held on long enough. If she got tired of his crap and divorced him, Paul could get everything. The new Mrs. Lewis had signed an ill-advised prenuptial agreement, hoping she'd outlive the scoundrel.

If Paul was being honest with himself, that was why he stayed, too – for the inheritance. How long would he have to wait with the way his father drank, ate, and slept around? If a heart attack didn't kill him, a jealous husband, or his own wife, might.

Tanzini paused. The ringing in Paul's ears obliterated the noise he usually heard from the street below.

"Then you'll just have to take it out of the firm's accounts."

"There's no way. I don't have access. I'm not an authorized signer. I don't have the passwords. Besides, even if I did, they'd find out, and what would I tell them? You blackmailed me?"

Tanzini stood. "Figure it out. You have forty-eight hours."

He headed for the door, stopped, and turned. "You can keep those. I have copies," he said, indicating the documents on Paul's desk with a jerk of a head. "*Arrivederci*!"

Paul could still hear Tanzini's bellowed laughter long after the fat man had gone.

Chapter Seventeen

PAUL DIDN'T KNOW HOW much time had passed while he considered his alternatives. He could ask his father for the money, tell him it was a membership fee to an exclusive country club where Paul was bound to make connections with the rich and powerful. But Father knew he hated golf.

He could break into the Hag's desk.

She probably thought she could hide the bank account passwords by locking them in a drawer that could be picked with a paperclip. But they'd know who had taken the money. Then he'd have to tell them why he stole it. He was no good at keeping secrets.

Was it better to ask for forgiveness than for permission? It would have to be. Father would never give Al Tanzini the money to outwit his good old friend, Rita. But then they would know Paul was a liability. He wouldn't be useful to them anymore. Father could shut down the firm.

Paul had no way of supporting himself. He couldn't even wait on tables like Marigold Osteen or bake cookies like Esme Castillo.

He had to keep Rita Osteen happy. There was only one way to do that. He hit the speed dial on his cell phone. When she answered, he said, "We have a problem."

Chapter Eighteen

I WAS HAVING A late lunch in the Coit Tower Café with Mickey Wong, my best friend, if I had one. A news reporter, she dressed comfortably in a sweater and slacks, her most striking feature her blue-black shoulder-length hair that shimmered when she moved. Currently, she was unwrapping a beef sandwich that looked, and smelled, enticing. I'd settled on a hummus wrap in case I was subjected to cross-examination later by my daughter.

The café was down the street from my office. It was the place I went into on my way to work if I craved something large, gooey and baked, and where Yolanda would pick up muffins and mochas for our office meetings. I'd quit sending Quinn because she kept bringing me green tea that tasted like grass clippings instead of the raspberry mocha with a double shot of espresso that I'd wanted.

If you stood on the sidewalk in front of their windows on a good day, you could see the tip of Coit Tower peaking above the surrounding nineteenth-century brick buildings. Inside, the establishment was a mash-up of hip and Coit Tower kitsch that worked. Above the counter, the menu was handwritten in colorful chalk on an oversized blackboard. Bright acrylic paintings of various views of the tower itself hung on the walls.

Mickey and I met in the women's studies program at UC Berkeley. From there, she went on to journalism, and I went to law school. After graduation, both of us worked insane hours, so we saw each other less often, but we tried to meet up for lunch or a drink from time to time.

On this occasion, I'd called her and offered to buy lunch. We made small talk as we ate.

When Mickey finished eating, she wadded the paper her sandwich had come in, deposited it in a wood-clad garbage can across the room, then came back and sat. "So, what's really going on with you?" she asked.

"I need your help," I said.

The last time I'd asked, Mickey produced a series for her TV station on sexual abuse. She interviewed me, along with a few of my clients, about our experiences. I talked about how the abuse by a trusted male family member had shattered me. How recovering from it had been the inspiration for my desire to help women and children. I didn't talk about bearing a child as the result or the fact that Frank was the abuser, as that would have invaded Quinn's privacy.

"Anything you need is yours," Mickey said. "Tell me, what's going on?"

I pulled my laptop out of my briefcase, set it on the table between us, logged on to the café Wi-Fi, and opened Dixon Vaughn's latest podcast targeting me. I spun the laptop around for her to see and handed her a pair of earbuds, glancing at the other diners. "You'll need these."

She watched, eyes widening, occasionally glancing up at me in horror, as I sipped the raspberry mocha I planned to lie about if asked.

Eventually, she pulled the earbuds out and handed them back. "Wow. That's some pretty heavy shit."

"There's no point in engaging him. That would only fuel the fire."

"Never, ever feed the trolls," Mickey said.

"Right. I have a plan. I'm going to do a very big, very public campaign putting out a positive message – a message of hope and compassion. Our goal is to empower women. I want to produce public service announcements for TV and radio and posts on social media sites."

"Gotcha." Mickey pulled a small tablet out of her messenger bag, flipped open a portable keyboard and started typing.

I stashed the earbuds and my own laptop and pulled out a legal pad where I'd scribbled some notes. "Listen to this," I said reciting to her the statistics I'd found online. "More than one in three women have experienced rape, physical violence, or stalking by an intimate partner in their lifetime."

Mickey nodded as she typed.

"Nearly half of all women in the U.S. have experienced psychological aggression by an intimate partner in their lifetime."

She typed.

"Women ages 18 to 34 experience the highest rate of intimate partner violence."

When she finished typing, Mickey looked up from her monitor. "Images. What did you have in mind?"

I pulled out a silhouetted graphic of a woman holding a child's hand that Quinn had created.

"Where'd you get this?"

She didn't mention copyright infringement, but I figured she was thinking about it.

"Quinn designed it. It's from a photo of her with her adopted mother."

I had complicated feelings about this image. It represented losing my daughter. At the same time, it represented a kind family who rescued her from the hell I'd grown up in. The latter was exactly what we hoped to do for more women and children, so it was perfect to represent Lizzie's foundation.

"Very nice," she said. "I can build on this. Overlay that with text. I'll do the voiceover."

"Every video should end with our help line number. We have volunteers answering twenty-four seven. Beneath that, our logo and our name, the Elizabeth Shaughnessy Foundation for Women and Children."

"Do you have a log line?"

"A what?"

"A motto."

"You're not alone. We're here to help."

Chapter Nineteen

HENRY WATKINS SAT IN a dark, seedy bar off Market Street drinking cheap beer. The only décor was a much-pierced dart board. Despite the smoking ban, the place reeked of tobacco that had soaked into the fake-wood paneled walls, no doubt the reason why the bar's door was open to the street, letting in a cold, wet breeze that carried the smell of rain and dirt and car fumes. A drunk at the end of the bar nodded off over his half-finished beer. Henry watched him, fascinated, to see if he'd fall off his stool.

He couldn't go back to work. What if detectives showed up to take him away for an interview, like they'd done with the chief?

Henry needed an air-tight story. He could blame the whole fiasco on Anderson, who wasn't around to defend himself. The way Anderson quit, right after the chief was taken in, made him look guilty. He was probably doing something illegal, anyway. Something Henry didn't know about. It was only a matter of time before the authorities discovered it.

No one would blame good old dependable Henry, the tortoise. Unless they found the forged contract.

Getting that contract back was the only thing Henry could think about. If he got it back, there was no way Tanzini could claim Henry was involved. If he didn't get it back, it was going to all blow up on the first of the month when Tanzini's builder showed up at Concourse C to start the remodel. The badges he would need to get through security wouldn't be waiting for him. No one at the airport would've heard about the lease. There would be angry phone calls.

There would be questions.

The contract had to be in Tanzini's apartment. Henry needed to break in and steal it.

He left a dollar tip for the bartender, who whisked it away with a dirty side-eye while Henry was still untangling himself from the stool.

When he arrived at his apartment, Henry stripped off his drenched shoes and socks, draped the socks over the radiator to dry and set the shoes on an old newspaper spread on the entry's linoleum. He pushed his icy feet into the old pair of slippers he wore around the house.

The book he was re-reading about the Second Punic War waited for him in his chair, a bookmark neatly peeking from its pages. Henry returned it to the shelf, set up a TV tray table, retrieved the used reconstructed laptop he'd bought on sale, and began his search on "how to break into a key card lock." What he got back was a lot of technical stuff he didn't understand. He would just have to convince the concierge that he needed to go into the apartment. Henry wasn't good at lying, but he'd have to learn. Fast. That was his only hope.

Before Henry climbed into the Uber, he brushed his teeth, hoping to get rid of some of the beer stink, and changed into gym socks and trainers, his only other pair of shoes. He couldn't face sitting on another bus squished between tired, grumpy, wet office workers. It was more expensive than riding the bus, but if Henry didn't solve his problems soon, money was not going to be one of them. At least he would be dry when he arrived at his destination.

The valet he spoke to earlier that day was not on the street. Henry took a deep breath, then pushed open the glass door into the vestibule.

"Good evening, sir," a young man at the desk said. He was in his twenties and wore a baggy uniform. It looked like the regular concierge hadn't shown up that day, and they had grabbed a busboy to fill in.

"Good evening. Is Mr. Tanzini in?"

"No sir, I'm afraid he isn't."

Huzzah! Henry said, "Oh, no, this is terrible. I left something in his apartment the other night and I need to get it back."

"I'm very sorry, sir. I'd be happy to leave a message for Mr. Tanzini."

"That won't do." Henry had seen on the old Columbo TV series that the best lie is one that is a version of the truth. That way you don't look like you're lying. "Here's the thing. I need it back tonight. My boss wants it. I can't go back to the office without it." He looked at the kid at the desk with his most apologetic look, the one he used on Nancy when he didn't want to spend an hour in the break room listening to stories about her cats. "If you check, you'll see my name on the list of approved visitors. I was just here the other evening."

The boy in the uniform chewed his lip. "I don't think I can help you."

"I'll lose my job if I don't come back with the contract." Damn, he didn't mean to say "contract." But once Tanzini found it was missing, he'd accuse Henry of taking it anyway. Besides, he couldn't unsay it. "Please. Just take a look at your list. Henry Watkins. W-A-T-K-I-N-S."

"Well, okay." The boy tapped on the screen in front of him, frowning. After a few moments, he nodded. "It's here. ID please."

Henry pulled out his driver's license and handed it over. The boy looked at the screen and the license, then squinted at Henry. He handed the card back. "Follow me, sir."

When they arrived at Tanzini's apartment, the boy receptionist used his key card to open the door. He held it while Henry went in.

"Thank you," Henry said. "I'll be okay. It should only take a few minutes."

The boy leaned against the door, holding it open, as he watched Henry. Drat!

So much for rummaging through drawers and closets or looking under the bed.

"It was right over here, last I saw it," Henry said. He walked to a sideboard upon which were crystal decanters on a silver platter. The view from the floor-to-ceiling window caught his eye. Clouds hung so low that the tops of tall buildings disappeared. Condensation streaked down the dark glass. When Henry looked down on the street, a silver Cadillac turned the corner and headed this way.

Tanzini was back.

He couldn't catch Henry here.

"Hell's bells," Henry said. "I guess I'll just have to ask Mr. Tanzini to find it for me when he returns." He looked at his watch. "Got to go. I'm running late as it is."

"But your job," the kid said. "Won't you get into trouble?"

"I'll think of something. Better get you back to your post before you lose yours."

Henry followed the kid to the elevator banks, praying that when the door opened, Tanzini wouldn't be staring back at him. He was in luck. The carriage arrived empty. They stepped inside, turned around, and the kid hit the button. Just as he did so, Henry saw a maid push a cart out of the service elevator down the hall.

Drat! He should have bribed her to let him in. That's what Tanzini would have done.

The elevator doors began to close as a bell from the next lift rang. Its doors whooshed open, and Tanzini appeared, his back to Henry as he walked towards his door.

Henry took a step sidewise, hiding behind the closing door.

Chapter Twenty

BRUNO FERNANDEZ LEANED AGAINST a mirrored column, smoking a cigarette, across the street from 123 Baywater St. He was pleased when he caught his reflection, that of a dangerous, sinister man. Tall, beefy, with dark, curly hair and pock-marked skin. A full-length raincoat over a black turtleneck sweater, black slacks, and black wingtips. A man needed to look sharp.

His clothes were damp, his hair wet. He had heard that San Francisco was cold, but he wasn't prepared for the bone-penetrating rain. As he waited, the clouds lowered hour by hour, swallowing tall buildings. Soon, he wouldn't be able to see the building across the street.

Bruno had been watching all afternoon since Tanzini drove away in his Cadillac. Now, Tanzini was back. He handed the keys off to a valet, like he was the man about town, and strolled into the all-glass modern structure.

The little balding man from the county, Henry Watkins, exited the building a few minutes later. Bruno had seen Watkins and Al argue earlier in front of the building. Neither Al nor Watkins had noticed Bruno. While they argued, Bruno took a photo of Watkins. He ran the photo through his phone app and found that Watkins worked for the county office in charge of airport concession contracts.

Bruno quickly dismissed the possibility that they were friends. Al was a parasite – he didn't have friends. Most likely, Al had enlisted this little county man to help him with an airport concession. And since Al had his fingers in only one business, Esme Inc, advancing the bakery had to be his reason for the concession.

Bruno's Plan A had been to approach Maureen Gould and tell her the truth about Al. She seemed to believe him, but she didn't jump on his information like Al's law partners back in Jersey did. Bruno didn't know what he expected from her. His Plan B had been to meet with Rita Osteen and tell her the truth. He figured once she knew what Al was, she'd cut him out of the business. When she faked surprise to the news that Al was an embezzler, Bruno realized she had already known.

Bruno's plans hadn't worked. Now that he'd met Rita Osteen, he knew she was the one calling the tunes. And Maureen Gould played by the rules. She might use his information someday when it suited her, but not quickly enough to give Bruno satisfaction.

Bruno took another hit of his cigarette, tossed it to the sidewalk, and ground it out with his shoe. When he was satisfied that the ember was dead, he bent over, picked up the stub, and flicked it into a nearby trash can.

Bruno didn't leave garbage lying around.

And, if there was one thing Bruno Fernandez knew, Alfred Tanzini was garbage.

Chapter Twenty-One

THE NEXT MORNING, BRUNO told his Uber driver to cruise past 123 Baywater on the way to the airport.

The weather had broken. High clouds raced across the sky, leaving behind ever-growing patches of blue. The air smelled fresh and clean and a little salty.

The police were there. Marked and unmarked cars lined up along the sidewalks and filled the alleys. An ambulance was parked directly in front of the building. Cops wandered around distractedly. No lights flashed. No one was in a hurry.

Someone must have died.

Chapter Twenty-Two

ON THE MORNING OF Al Tanzini's deposition, before anyone came into the office, I rocked in my desk chair and perused my questions one last time.

The books from Esme Inc, had not been produced by Paul Lewis yet, so one of the questions I had for Tanzini was why. They should be readily accessible. Rita Osteen, the other shareholder, was the treasurer and took care of the books.

The big question was, "where did the money go?"

I had the records kept by Esme's aunt, Bebe, Yolanda's youngest sister, up until the time the corporation was formed. Bebe worked as a bookkeeper out of her home office while raising school-aged children. Her husband was a self-employed building contractor, specializing in finish carpentry. Her clients were small businesses, like Esme's, mostly run by Hispanics. Janitorial, daycares, handyman services, landscaping companies.

I also had copies of Esme's receipts for the payments she'd made for taxes and insurance. The records proved the bakery didn't owe any money because Esme had paid all the debts, but its income barely covered its expenses.

Yet, in the letter Tanzini sent to Esme when they ejected her from her own business, he claimed that the company was still in the red. I wanted to know what had happened with all the money Tanzini and Rita Osteen paid into the corporation.

Yolanda rolled in shortly after I did. I heard her moving around the outer office as she made coffee and boiled water for tea, and ferried carafes and coffee paraphernalia to the conference room. She greeted the court reporter who arrived about thirty minutes early to set up. Esme and Quinn came in at the same time, stuck their heads into my office to say hello, then went back down the hall to settle in. Five minutes before the scheduled time, I heard Lewis show up at my office alone.

At 9 a.m., I gathered my scripted questions and stack of exhibits, then headed down to the conference room to take my place, which Yolanda had saved for me by placing a legal pad and pens at the head of the table.

I glanced at my watch as if I was checking the time, then caught Paul Lewis's eye.

"My client should be here in a few minutes," Lewis said. "Probably stuck in traffic."

Alfred Tanzini never arrived.

But the police did. Detective Dobson, the African American woman with short hair and dressed all in black with comfortable shoes. The younger detective, Chong, an Asian American man in jeans and a stylish haircut. When I greeted them in my reception room, Detective Dobson asked, "You're all waiting for Alfred Tanzini, is that correct?"

"We are," I said. "He should be here any minute."

Dobson shook her head. "I'm afraid Mr. Tanzini won't be coming. His body was found this morning."

Esme, who had been standing behind me, fainted.

Chong herded Lewis back into the conference room while Yolanda hovered over Esme. I went into the kitchen for a glass of water. By the time I returned, she was sitting up.

"Esmeralda Castillo, I presume," Dobson said, watching the scene impassively.

After I handed the glass to Yolanda, I turned to Dobson. "We can wait in my back office, if you like."

"I'm fine here," she said.

"Would you like to sit?" I motioned to the couch.

"I'll stand."

We stood in awkward silence for several minutes waiting for Esme to pull herself to her feet. Tanzini was dead, making Esme the majority shareholder. Mentally, I scrolled through a list of actions I would need to take to restore Esme Inc to her: obtain the death certificate, file a motion to change the interim management back to Esme, ask for a hearing. Would Rita Osteen drop out of the suit at this point or would she hang on?

Through the conference room's glass wall, I saw Lewis in his chair, checking his watch and texting. Detective Chong leaned against the windowsill, arms crossed, eyes on Lewis. The court reporter had packed up her wares and was waiting for the okay to leave. Quinn had scooted into my chair at the head of the table where she could work on her computer without Chong looking over her shoulder. Smart girl.

Yolanda helped Esme to her feet.

"Are you ready to talk?" Detective Dobson asked.

Esme nodded.

Yolanda led Esme to my back office and settled her in the corner of the leather couch I sometimes napped on when I pulled an all-nighter. Yolanda sat close to her niece, taking her hand. I offered a chair to the detective again. She again declined. I took the side chair adjacent to Esme, so she was protected by Yolanda on one side and me on the other.

Dobson remained on her feet. She flipped open a notepad and began her questions. "Ms. Castillo, what exactly was your relationship with Alfred Tanzini?"

Esme's head was in her hands, a curtain of hair hanging loose and hiding her features. She looked up at Dobson and shook her hair out of her face. "We were business partners." She shrugged. "That is, until they forced me out."

Dobson wrote in her pad, then asked, "You were aware there was a court order against you contacting Mr. Tanzini?"

"Yes, I was."

"Did you call Mr. Tanzini or visit his apartment after you learned about the court order?"

Esme was curled up, almost in a ball. She rubbed her eyes. "What does this have to do with anything?"

"We need to understand what was going on in Mr. Tanzini's life before his suspicious death."

Esme's head snapped up. "Suspicious – you mean like murder?"

I'd assumed someone had killed Tanzini. Two detectives wouldn't show up unannounced to investigate a natural death. But with the cops watching us, I didn't have the time to take Esme aside – which is exactly what Dobson intended.

Dobson fixed her gaze on Esme. "The evidence suggests he did not take his own life."

Esme made a guttural sound, something primordial, and haunting.

Yolanda pulled her in and rocked. Dobson observed, then made a lengthy note in her pad.

"Are you okay to continue?" Dobson asked.

"Sure." Esme choked on the word. "Anything I can do to help."

"Did you contact Mr. Tanzini after the court ordered you to stay away from him?"

How did Dobson know about Esme going to Tanzini's apartment? She didn't hear it from Tanzini's lawyer, Paul Lewis. She hadn't talked to him yet. She must have already interviewed Rita Osteen, who would have filled her in on the case, and would have known the deposition was scheduled for this morning at my office.

"I'm sorry," Esme said. "It was impulsive. I wish I hadn't done it."

And I wished my client hadn't just told a homicide detective that she was impulsive.

"Why did you contact him?" Dobson asked.

"I just thought if I could get him alone, we could talk and work it out. I thought we had a good relationship."

"Speaking of which, was your relationship more than just business?"

"What do you mean?" Esme asked.

"Is there any reason why we would find your DNA in his apartment?"

Now I was worried. Dobson seemed to know something I didn't. "Detective, is my client a suspect?"

"No, ma'am, she is not."

I stood, taking up the space between Dobson and Esme. "Is she a person of interest?"

Dobson ditched the question. "Just trying to get some background on Mr. Tanzini."

So Esme was a person of interest.

That term, "a person of interest," came about after the Supreme Court strengthened the rights of suspects. Some smart prosecutor cooked up the term "person of interest" to avoid providing suspects with their constitutional rights.

Suspects are entitled to Miranda warnings before they are questioned. They are entitled to be told that anything they say can be used against them. They are entitled to an attorney.

Most importantly, suspects are entitled to a warning that they have the right to remain silent.

But when the cops interview a "person of interest," they don't have to give them the Miranda warnings. So the "person of interest" doesn't know they have the right to remain silent, the right to an attorney, and that anything they say can be used against them.

The only reason a detective wants to interview a "person of interest" is to get that person to make incriminating statements – and then charge them with a crime.

Not on my watch.

"Great," I said. "We would be happy to help. Ms. Castillo is obviously distraught upon suddenly learning that the man we all expected to appear this morning was murdered. She's in no fit state to provide information. I suggest if you require another interview, you arrange it through my office."

"She looks okay to me," Dobson said.

"I'll show you out," I said as I swept my arm towards the door. Dobson left my office, hesitating for a moment on the threshold to glance at Esme, and I pulled the door closed behind me. When we entered the reception, we could see the conference room had emptied. Detective Chong was lounging on the reception room couch, hands dropped between his splayed legs, tapping on his phone with his thumbs.

Chong jumped to his feet and dropped his cell into his coat pocket. "Mr. Lewis said he had another meeting at his office, and we could contact him there. The court reporter left her card. The other young lady, Ms. Gould's daughter, said she had a lecture to go to."

"My daughter is employed by my office."

"Right," Dobson said. She got the drift of my message. She would not interview Quinn because my attorney-client privilege protected anything my employees knew.

Dobson turned to me. "We'll be in touch."

I thought about Lewis lying to Detective Chong that he had to leave for an appointment as I held the door open for them and they silently walked out of my office and into the hallway. I'd warned Lewis that the deposition would take all day. He shouldn't have scheduled another meeting.

My head was spinning. I woke up that morning, fired up, ready to dissect the weasel who swindled Esme out of her business. It wasn't even noon, the weasel was dead, and my client was now a "person of interest" (translation: suspect) in a murder investigation.

My phone buzzed with a text. Quinn sent me a link to a news article about a man's body discovered in his 123 Baywater Street apartment earlier that morning. The reporter promised to provide details as they became available. There was a photograph of a modern glass-sided building with police cars swarming around the entrance and the alleys next to it.

I returned to my back office and found Esme and Yolanda huddled on the couch. My client wore a distracted stare, as if she wanted to magic herself into a different reality.

"We need to talk," I said.

Esme startled. She hadn't heard me come in. "What, did you say something?"

Chances were, Rita Osteen told Detective Dobson that upon Alfred Tanzini's death, his shares would be split between the remaining shareholders. That meant Esme Castillo was now the majority shareholder of Esme Inc. The judge would have no choice but to return the business to her. Some might consider that sufficient motive for murder.

"The business is yours now that Tanzini's dead. I'll just have to file a motion, and you can start operating it again."

Esme jumped up so quickly, Yolanda was thrown to one side. "How can you talk about the business at a time like this? A man is dead!"

She stormed out of my office. Yolanda scrambled to pull herself off the couch and followed.

Firecracker Esme. Impulsive Esme. Secretive Esme. Could she have murdered Alfred Tanzini in a fit of rage and then appear at my office as if nothing happened?

Chapter Twenty-Three

THE DOOR SLAMMED WITH Esme's departure. I listened for movement. Silence. Yolanda must have followed her niece out to the street.

I wandered into the reception room and opened the bottom drawer of Yolanda's desk. Her massive cherry red patent leather purse was still tucked away. She hadn't taken her car. Or her cell phone. She'd be back, soon. I unlocked the door so she could let herself back in.

I grabbed my empty coffee cup, swung by the carafe to give it a couple pumps, and settled behind Yolanda's desk, then cruised through the Internet looking for updates on Tanzini's murder. Nothing new. Just a body at 123 Baywater St. Victim and cause of death not identified. So far, I knew more than the reporters did.

The doorknob twisted slowly, and the door drifted open. Yolanda appeared, shiny from physical exertion with melted mascara dotting her cheeks. I wiped my own face as a signal for her to do the same. She simultaneously slid fingers across each cheek, then examined both hands for smudges. I pushed her box of tissues across the desktop. She stepped forward and pulled one tissue out and scrubbed her hands.

"Aren't we supposed to keep that door locked?" she asked.

"I'm sitting right here watching out for bad guys. Take a load off," I said, pointing to the couch.

We needed to talk. And when we did, I wasn't going to allow her to slip behind her desk, her sanctuary, invoking her authority as office mom. Right now, I was the lawyer, and she was the difficult client's aunt.

She sank into the couch. From that point of view, she examined the room as if it was her first time, then pointed to a copy of a Diego Rivera painting hanging over her desk. I had sold Lizzie Shaughnessy's original to finance the foundation. But before I did, I commissioned a local artist to copy it.

"It's crooked," she said. Stalling.

I turned, saw that she was correct, and adjusted the painting.

"We need to talk," I said.

"Esme's frightened, that's all. You would be, too, if someone accused you of murder."

"Granted." I settled on the pressure-by-silence technique police are so fond of. Most people can't stand the uncertainty of time passed in silence. They need to take charge, make things happen. Yolanda was one of those people.

She cracked in seconds. "This whole thing has been hard on her. She started the company as a tribute to my mother. Esme adores her. That little old Mexican lady worked night and day to keep clothes on our back and food on our table after my dad died. When my sister got a divorce, she moved back home with Esme. You'd think my mom would have wanted a break by then, but she was delighted. My sister, Gloria, started the night janitor business. My mom still worked days, cooking at the elementary school. Esme would go to school with my mom in the morning and come back home with her after school got out. In the afternoons and weekends, they baked. That's what got Esme started."

I took a sip of my coffee. It was cold again. How was it I was always walking around with a cup of coffee, but by the time I got around to drinking, it was cold? Is this the kind of stuff cops think about when they use pressure-by-silence?

"We have to help her," Yolanda said.

"As I recall, when Tony Paredes was accused of murder, you argued that we weren't in the business of helping accused killers. Quite forcefully, I might add."

When I first hired Yolanda, I told her my mission was to help abuse victims get their lives back. She was bored working in the back office of a big law firm, shuffling paper, and welcomed the opportunity to interact with clients, to personally make a difference.

Tony Paredes had been an abuse victim. We took his civil case against his teacher and the school to trial and won millions. But the judge set aside the verdict because of jury misconduct. Then the abuser turned up dead, and Tony was charged with murder.

Yolanda didn't want to take the criminal case. I did. We came very close to parting ways, and I would have missed my office mom. But my compulsion to help people in need, whatever their circumstances, was stronger than my attachment to her. It drove me. It was the thing that carried me through the grief of having my baby taken away. Helping people was who I was. One of those people was Tony.

"I was wrong," Yolanda said. "I'm glad we took Tony's case. And I shouldn't have questioned your judgment." She winced.

It must have been difficult, even painful, for her to admit she was fallible. She'd suffered enough.

"You're forgiven," I said.

"I took advantage when I asked you to take Esme's bakery case. It's not like the freebies law office employees expect, like a will or a landlord-tenant thing. You've put so much work into it and you haven't even tracked your hours."

I was doing the case on a *pro bono* basis, meaning "for free." Esme didn't have the money for an attorney. If we lost the case, she'd have to start over with nothing. If we won, her prize would be a bankrupt business. Either way, she wasn't going to earn much money for a long time, no matter how hard she worked.

Helping people without expecting something in return is good for the soul. Business had been brisk since I won my last criminal trial, so income wasn't a problem.

I was committed to her case, but I was worried about where the truth lay. "Here's the thing, Yolanda. Esme is behaving erratically. She's reacting to questions that most people wouldn't. I'm not sure what's going on. How can I help her if I don't know what the truth is?"

Yolanda took a deep breath. "You're right. I watched that kid grow up. I know her like my own daughters. She's hiding something."

Chapter Twenty-Four

HENRY WATKINS SAT IN an old chair, leather cracked with age, left behind in his apartment when he moved in. Its seat cushion was so flat, it felt like he was sitting on wood. He stared dumbfoundedly at the television, conscious of his aching rearend, afraid to move, with the ghost of his own image blinking back at him. Middle aged. Balding. Dumpy. Pathetic.

The morning news reported the police were investigating a suspicious death at 123 Baywater St., the building Alfred Tanzini lived in.

Before anyone would have arrived for work at his office, Henry left a message on the missing Anderson's voicemail stating that he was sick, knowing no one would check it, but he was required to report his absence to his supervisor. Anderson was still his supervisor, if in name only. If Henry missed more than three days, he'd have to get a doctor's note.

Three days! A blink of an eye. If Henry didn't have a solution by then, he was lost. Go back to work and face the investigators. Or quit his job, too young to draw his retirement, and his only savings was that envelope of cash from Tanzini stashed in a book. Neither option was workable.

Henry pulled his inhaler from a pocket and took a hit, watching the ghost in the screen mirror his movements.

When the cops searched Tanzini's apartment, they'd find the contract. They might take it as evidence, stick it into a bag, and file it away, a time bomb that could blow up when someone finally read it. Or they might look at it immediately, call the department and ask for Anderson. Who had vanished. That would look bad for Anderson, disappearing at the same time one of his vendors was murdered. The police would search for him.

Anderson didn't kill Tanzini. He didn't even know who Tanzini was.

But someone did.

Tanzini had hinted at his Mafia connections back in New York City. Would the police learn about his past? Was Esme's Casa a front for drugs or human trafficking? A slot on Concourse C of San Francisco International Airport would be quite the advantage, with access to travelers, flight crews, and aircraft. Surely, there must be organized crime in The City.

Would it be a breach of protocol for an out-of-town crook to show up and start his own enterprise? The West Coast Mob might have killed him over that.

Was Tanzini even his real name? He could be on the run from someone in New York, someone who wanted him dead. He'd often warned that bad things happened to snitches and double-crossers.

Henry was small and insignificant. No one but Nancy would miss him for days if he disappeared. What if Tanzini was murdered by some Mafia hitman, but before they killed him Tanzini told them where to find Henry? But why would a Mafia hitman want to kill Henry? He didn't know anything.

It didn't matter what he knew. What mattered was what they thought he might know.

He could take the train. He wouldn't need to show his ID card so he couldn't be traced. The money he had would go much further than if he flew out. But where would he go?

Henry's brain felt like it was being squeezed. Tanzini, forged contract, bribe, hitman, murder. The only thing Henry knew was that he didn't know what to do.

Get murdered or go to prison.

He leaned out of the chair to pull the curtains closed against the blinding daylight. He didn't want anyone looking in.

The television screen flickered, and his ghost image disappeared. He turned up the volume with his remote. One of the businessmen charged in the building permit scandal had cut a deal. He wasn't going to jail at all in exchange for his cooperation.

That was Henry's only choice. Cooperation.

Henry texted Nancy. "What is the name of the DA investigating our department?"

Chapter Twenty-Five

DIXON VAUGHN SAT IN the spare bedroom of his rented Emeryville house. A shaft of sunlight heated the air as it drifted across the floor.

A laptop was open in front of him, to which he'd hooked up an auxiliary camera and a ring light for a more professional look. He flicked a switch. Light on. He tapped the keyboard. Camera on. He watched himself in the monitor as he jerked down on his sweatshirt to smooth out the wrinkles and then wiped a hand across his buzz cut. Check. He reached up and pulled the foam-encased microphone into the frame – again for the more professional look. Sound testing, one, two, three. Check.

He was good to go with five minutes to spare.

This was the room that he had prepared for the overnight visits that never happened. Emeryville was miles away from San Francisco, but he needed to make a proper home so he could see his boy after the divorce. Then, without a word, the bitch, his ex-wife, disappeared, taking Dixon's son with her. Dixon only found out about it when he went to McDonald's for the changeover. When she didn't show up, he called the police to do a welfare check. They went to the bitch's house – used to be Dixon's home – and found the place empty. Furniture, clothes, pictures, toys, everything gone.

In his new home, he had painted the boy's bedroom blue. Bought a brand-new twin bed. Covered it with a Superman bedspread, the boy's favorite hero. He even got a desk for the boy's homework, which is where Dixon was now sitting.

Dixon Vaughn, digital creator.

This podcast wasn't just his way to spread the message – it was his new career. He couldn't go back to working as a cop. The bitch lawyer saw to that. The so-called "severance package," really a don't-let-the-door-hit-you-on-your-way-out pay-off, that the city gave him was dwindling away. He needed to make this podcast work if he didn't want to end up a night guard on minimum wage.

In the last few minutes, he glanced at his social media feed. There it was again, Maureen Gould's happy crap ad to runaway wives. "You're not alone. We're here to help."

The ad was everywhere. You couldn't turn on your cell phone, laptop, or TV without seeing it. The bitch. He felt his heart pounding in his neck. He needed to get control.

Deep breath in, deep breath out.

Dixon Vaughn, in control – a man who harnessed and wielded power. The lawyer bitch had no idea who she was playing with.

He bent his head to one side, then the other, like a fighter getting ready to go into the ring.

The second hand on his glow-in-the-dark military watch swept upwards.

Showtime.

He tapped a key on his laptop. The camera's red light began to glow.

Dixon slowly raised his flattened hand to his brow. "Hail, brothers in arms. Join me in our holy quest to restore the natural rights of men." He snapped the salute and lowered his arm.

"Greetings, brothers. My name is Dixon Vaughn. In the Rights of Man, you and I together will explore the systematic suppression of our sex by the feminist cults that are insinuated into every aspect of American life." Dixon had paced the floors for several days memorizing that last sentence. He'd delivered it perfectly, and smirked, pleased with his accomplishment.

"At work, at home, and in public. How many men lost a promotion to the less-qualified candidate because she was a woman? How many men went to jail for defending himself against a hormonal wife in the privacy of his own home? Not to mention if you should use the wrong words in public. Sorry, buddy, the PC cops will crawl up your backside."

The chatroom comments were flying now. In an online podcast marketing class, he'd learned that viewers love to see their name, so he made sure the chatroom was visible.

They loved it even more when they heard their names. "I see a few old friends in the chatroom. Sarge, Mad Dog, Tank, welcome back! Everyone, post your comments and questions and we'll come around to them at the end of the show."

The word "Booya!" floated up the screen, in caps with fireworks emojis.

"That's right, brothers. Booya!" Dixon held up a power-to-the-people fist. "Now, down to business. We've met her before."

He tapped a key. A split screen appeared with a photo of Maureen Gould leaving her office building. Long red hair. Red raincoat. In good shape. She'd be hot if she wasn't such a bitch.

"That's right! We're talking about the extreme privilege of one of the queens of the Femicult, Maureen Gould Kuhn. My bad! *Ms.* Gould only uses her maiden name. Another blow against the natural order. When did women become ashamed of their husbands? That's a topic for another day."

"Bow down, bros. Attorney Maureen Gould is a member of the San Francisco aristocracy. She comes from old money. Grew up in one of the biggest houses in Pacific Heights. A palace, really. Her grandfather was a justice on the California Supreme Court. Her father is the attorney, Frank Gould, now serving time for money laundering. By the way, she had a hand in sending him to jail. Can you say 'patricide,' anyone?"

Someone typed "manhating bitch" in the comments. A flurry of thumbs-up emojis appeared on the screen.

Dixon tapped a key again, this time posting a photo of Maureen standing next to her yellow BMW M-5, holding her hair out of her face while she watched for traffic to pass before she crossed the street. A briefcase, traditionally a male symbol of authority, hung from her shoulder. Hot. Dangerous. She knew it and she loved it.

Dixon gave the viewers a moment to take in the photo, then continued. "In two recent cases, Attorney Gould struck heavy blows against the natural order. You should remember the trial in *Navarre vs Cleville.* It was all over the news. That was the case where a young woman, I won't say 'lady,' went to the hotel room of her Hollywood producer boss in the middle of the night after drinking with him and his cronies in a bar and was shocked – shocked, I tell you, when he naturally expected sex. By the time Ms. Gould was done with him, his company was bankrupt, his brother went to jail, and he had to leave the country. Nice job, Counselor!"

Another tap. Another photo. This on the courthouse steps during an impromptu press conference. Microphones aimed at her. Cameramen shoulder-to-shoulder, focused on her. The warrior queen basking in her glory.

"And who could forget Anthony Paredes? That was where she got her client off for murdering his *alleged* male lover – only after they humiliated the dead man in a prior lawsuit. They got a multimillion-dollar verdict with a corrupt jury. Mind you, I'm not saying she tampered with that jury. I don't have any proof, so if I said she tampered with the jury, she could sue me for defamation. So let me be clear, I am not saying she tampered with the jury. I'm just saying the jury was tampered with, and the judge had the good sense to set aside the verdict."

In another on-line class, this one on persuasion techniques, Dixon had learned that you must deliver your message over and over for it to sink in. People have the attention span of gnats. Three times is good. He said "tamper" four times, just to be on the safe side. The fact that he disclaimed the term didn't matter, what they heard was the word, "tamper." He couldn't be blamed if the viewers jumped to their own conclusions.

Tap. A photo of the Pacific Heights mansion filled the split screen.

"Which brings us back to the mansion. As we discussed in earlier podcasts which you can view when you visit my page, *Ms.* Gould has a pet project, a foundation for so-called 'abused' women and children. She uses the house she inherited – as the result of hardworking male ancestors, I'd like to point out – to hide women from their husbands and children from their fathers.

"This, brothers, is a woman who has privilege. She has money. She has connections. And she uses it all in her campaign to oppress men.

"Which now brings me around to the county's building inspection bribery scandal. Guess who we find sitting smack dab in the middle of it!"

Tap. A close-up of the bitch lawyer hit the screen, a smile on her lips.

"None other than *Ms.* Maureen Gould.

"Turns out, brothers, she used her connections to slide through an inspection in a matter of months. Brothers, you and I both know, even if you want to build something as small as a deck, us peons would wait years to get the permit – if ever."

The comments were flying even faster. Dixon couldn't keep up.

"Brothers, you are on fire! I can see you guys have a lot to say. I'll get to your comments in just a moment. But first, we got to pause for the cause. I want to thank each and every one of you who've supported this podcast. Together we will accomplish great things. You can show your commitment to our crusade when you click the link below. By becoming a member of our brotherhood, you will get exclusive content from me, including newsletters and invitations to members-only zoom meetings."

Dixon pointed downwards, directing the viewers to the link that said, "JOIN NOW!" all in caps with an exclamation point. When someone clicked, they'd see another link at the form's bottom, inviting them to add merchandise to their purchase, including coffee cups, T-shirts, hoodies, and baseball caps, all printed by a website after the order was placed. No major outlay of cash for Dixon. No storing unsold stuff. The merch had more than doubled his podcast income, but he was still a long way before he could make a survival income.

Dixon Vaughn wanted to be a media star. He needed something big, something that made his podcast go viral. Sooner or later, the bitch lawyer would slip up and he'd be right there for a final showdown. An epic winner-take-all battle.

"Booya!" floated up the chatroom screen again.

Dixon held up his fist again, higher this time. "Booya!"

Chapter Twenty-Six

IT WAS JAKE'S NIGHT to cook, but he was still working overtime at the DA's office, so I picked up pizzas on the way home. A meat-eater for Jake. Veggie for Quinn and me, deferring to her commitment to vegetarianism. I suspected it was a cultural thing as well as a sensitivity to animals. The tribe she found for herself in law school was politically aware, had strong beliefs, and was judgmental in a way reserved for the young and idealistic. To be honest, I loved a good steak, but to bridge the gap between us, I joined in, grateful that at least vegetarians ate bread.

When I arrived home, Quinn was parked at the breakfast counter with her laptop open, her wild red hair pulled back with a scrunchie, and focused on her screen. She had a desk in her room, but she preferred to work in the common area, where she could interact with Jake and me.

I set the pizza boxes on the dinner table and began rummaging through a drawer for placemats. In this episode of All American Mom, I settled on eggplant-colored napkins on grass-woven placemats coupled with chunky stoneware that would evoke an earthiness I thought complemented the aroma of warm bread and melted cheese. "Wine or beer?"

Quinn didn't answer, absorbed in whatever she was looking at.

I spread the placemats on the table, folded the napkins, and positioned them. "Something bothering you?"

"I've been doing genealogical research."

It sounded like she was warming up to a sensitive topic. "Okay."

"You know how you said the Shaughnessys got rich with a silver mine?"

I returned to the kitchen for the plates. "That's what Lizzie told me."

"Remember the guy that Jack Shaughnessy won the mine from? After the mine started making money, that man sued, claiming Jack had gotten him drunk and taken advantage of him. By then, Jack had money and could afford a lawyer. The other guy couldn't. Jack won. Not long after that, the other guy hung himself."

I set the plates on the table. "That's awful. Where'd you find all this stuff?"

"Old newspapers. There's more. The mine used indentured Chinese for labor."

My father, Frank, had mentioned Chinese workers every time he went on a drunken rage about my snobbish Shaughnessy family. I thought he was making things up for the sake of being obnoxious. He claimed the Shaughnessys allowed him to marry into the family to improve their societal position, but never did they let him forget that they had the purse strings. I was fairly certain Lizzie hadn't approved of the marriage at all – it was her son and daughter-in-law who fancied the match – and I didn't doubt she reminded Frank often where the money came from.

"America was built by immigrants," I said. "The hardships they suffered are unimaginable."

"Doesn't it bother you that the workers were housed in filthy tent cities, that the mainstay of their diet was rice, that they were charged room and board that equaled their wages, and that work safety was deplorable? Workers died in those mines. Even more died of cholera."

"It was like that for everyone. The Irish, the Italians, the Jews. African Americans had it even worse."

"But Jack Shaughnessy got rich exploiting the Chinese. That's the fortune that built the mansion. And supported the family for generations." She looked around the room pointedly. I had bought the condo with the funds that Lizzie had left me in trust until I was twenty-four years old. It was also the money I used to buy my office condo.

"Frank squandered most of the family money."

"Except what you got. Doesn't it bother you that you grew up with all this privilege because your ancestor exploited vulnerable people?"

When I had driven home after a long day at work with her preferred veggie pizza to bond with my daughter, who was still a stranger to me, I hadn't expected to be hit with a demand for an apology for something I hadn't done.

"Sure, it bothers me. I am truly sorry for their difficulties. But what can I do about it?"

I'm a fixer. When there is a problem, I find a solution. What could I do to make up for my ancestors? Give away the money? It's already gone. Establish a nonprofit for charity? Done. Say a novena? I didn't even know where the rosary Lizzie gave me for my first Holy Communion was. Maybe my bedside table.

Hoping to change the subject, I returned to the kitchen, grabbed a bottle of beer out of the fridge, and wagged it in Quinn's direction. She shook her head. I popped the cap and chugged a third of the bottle down. This might be a good night to get tipsy. Beer tonight. Novena tomorrow. Maybe, maybe not. I'll see how ashamed I felt in the morning.

"*Mangia*!" I commanded as I swept my arm towards the dinner table. "Eat, eat."

"No, thanks. I'm not hungry." Quinn dropped the lid on her laptop, tucked it under her arm, and shuffled to her bedroom.

Chapter Twenty-Seven

HENRY INSISTED ON MEETING with Assistant DA Kuhn that evening after hours. Whoever killed Tanzini could have seen Henry going in and out of 123 Baywater Street. They might target him next. He had to be careful. He had an idea, again from watching cop shows, that he was less likely to be seen if it was dark out. On the other hand, it'd be harder to detect someone following him.

He recalled when he'd talked to Tanzini in front of his apartment building, across the street was a big, beefy man who leaned his shoulder against a building and smoked a cigarette. He was dark, Spanish- or Italian-looking, with wiry hair, and wore a raincoat. Henry didn't think much of the man at the time. But now that Tanzini was dead, he thought about the stranger a lot.

As Henry pulled the hood of his jacket over his head and started for the bus stop, he felt eyes on his back. When he boarded the bus, he turned to see if he was being followed. The sidewalk was nearly empty. The man was nowhere to be seen. Henry's imagination was playing tricks with him.

At the DA's building, Henry had to give his name to a security guard who then made a call, all the while watching Henry closely. He waited for his escort in the glass-walled foyer, scanning the streets for the scary man. He was reminded of the time when he was a child, his father had taken him to the pet shop where he watched in horror as a greasy, pimply-faced store clerk reached into a glass-enclosed cage, picked up a pink-eyed white mouse by his tail and dropped it into an aquarium with a snake.

Henry shut his eyes. He could still see the clerk's shadow cross over the mouse's cage and the quivering little mouse inside. He could hear the latch click. He saw the big hand descend.

"Mr. Watkins?" A woman's voice made him jump. "Sorry. Didn't mean to frighten you."

"I wasn't frightened," Henry protested in a high-pitched voice. He took a breath and lowered his tone with effort. "Just preoccupied. You know how it is."

From her appearance, she must have been a secretary, thirty-something, plain narrow skirt and plain white blouse with very high heels, shoulder-length thick brown hair, and wearing as much make-up as a cover model. Around her neck was a lanyard from which a card dangled. She smiled coolly at him. "Please follow me."

She swiped her card across a detector on the elevator bank. The doors hissed open, and they stepped onto the carriage. The elevator clunked, then shuddered, before it began its climb. They rode in silence as Henry fixed his eyes upwards, to the floor numbers lighting up in turn.

The carriage bumped to a halt. The doors squealed, opening to an empty reception area. A large black-and-gold State of California seal hung over an empty desk. The secretary led him to a secured entrance and swiped another detector. The lock clicked. She pushed her weight into the door, forcing it open. "This way."

He followed her down a hallway, turned a corner, and walked several yards before she showed him into a conference room. "Have a seat. Mr. Kuhn will be with you in a few minutes."

A long table was surrounded with cloth-covered rolling chairs, like the ones sold in office stores. On the far wall was a white board, wiped but smudged with black marker tracks. The room had no windows. Henry felt trapped. If he left now, he could find his way back to the security door, but could he open it? Was he locked in this maze?

He picked a chair near the head of the table. When he sat, the chairback fell away and he nearly tumbled out. Why would they keep a broken chair? Was this room hardly used?

Henry moved around to the other side of the table, taking the seat one down from the end. He assumed Mr. Kuhn would sit at the table's head, the power position. Better to have some distance between them, but close enough to talk confidentially.

The clock on the wall was broken. With every tick, tick, tick, the second hand lurched, then fell back again, pointing downward.

He had no idea how much time had passed, but it was long enough for his insides to start shivering from the cold. He stood, rubbed his hands together for warmth, and began walking around the room, just as the little white mouse had circled around his cage in those last moments before the store clerk's shadow crossed over him.

The lights flickered. Henry flinched. An earthquake? Lifting his arms for balance, he looked to the ceiling for signs of movement. Was this building earthquake-proof? Would it collapse into a pile of twisted metal and broken glass? A moment passed. The lights brightened.

A power surge, that's all. What a scaredy-cat!

Henry laughed at himself, even though the thought of being crushed by a falling skyscraper wasn't funny.

The little mouse had screamed when the snake attacked, and Henry jumped behind his father, who then hoisted him by the upper arm to his toes. "Boy, what kind of scaredy-cat are you!" The pimply store clerk cackled.

Henry rubbed his arm. He could still feel the bruises his father had left.

The doorknob clicked, and the air pressure dropped. Henry turned to find a man standing on the threshold.

"Sorry to keep you waiting, Mr. Watkins. My name's Jake Kuhn. I'm an assistant district attorney."

He was dark-haired, tall, and broad-shouldered. Women would say he was handsome. He wore dark slacks and a wrinkled white shirt with sleeves rolled up to reveal hairy muscled forearms. His tie had been pulled loose and the top button of his shirt was undone.

He scooted around the table and sat, not at the head but along the side, facing the door, then dropped a file folder on the table. "Please take a seat. Anywhere you like."

It was a test. Henry was certain of that. Kuhn was evaluating Henry to see if he'd sit far away or close, at the head of the table, beside him, or across from him. In the leadership training Henry had taken to bolster his qualifications when he applied for Anderson's job, he'd learned that proximity and position were critical in asserting power in a conference room. The place Henry chose would tell Kuhn what Henry believed about himself, whether he was in charge, or not, if he felt friendly to Kuhn, or not.

Henry chose the seat closest to the door for a quick escape. Let Mr. Kuhn think what he liked.

From his file folder, Kuhn pulled out a lined yellow pad with a pen clipped to it. He pulled off the pen, and clicked its button, making the tip appear. "Can I get your full name?"

"Henry William Watkins."

"Date of birth?"

Henry told him.

"Do you have ID?"

"Yes."

"May I see it?"

"What do you need that for?"

Kuhn looked up from his legal pad, taking Henry in, evaluating him, judging him. "To verify who you are, sir."

The lights flickered again, making Henry wince.

"Are you alright, Mr. Watkins?" Kuhn asked.

Henry's necktie felt tight, and he tugged at the knot. "I don't know," he said truthfully.

"Is there something I can get you? Coffee, tea, water?"

"No, please, don't go to any trouble."

"You sure?" Kuhn sounded genuinely concerned.

Henry nodded.

Kuhn made check marks on his notepad as if he was ticking off a list. His head lifted again. "Your identification, may I see it?"

Henry couldn't be too careful. If he didn't strike a deal, he didn't want any evidence that he had been there. What if the mob had spies in the DA's office? Everyone was on the take. Why not the prosecutors?

"I don't understand why you need that," Henry asked.

"Just crossing the T's and dotting the I's, sir." Kuhn watched him with narrowed eyes.

"Can't we just talk about why I'm here?"

"After I verify who you are." Kuhn glanced at his expensive gold wristwatch. "Look, Mr. Watkins, it's late."

Kuhn spun his gold wedding ring with his thumb. The man had a wife waiting for him. Maybe even kids. And here Henry was, keeping Jake Kuhn away from his family. All because he was too chicken to come to the office during normal hours.

Henry reached into his back pocket and pulled out his wallet. He flipped it open to his ID card and passed it to Kuhn.

"No driver's license?"

"No car," Henry said.

"Is this your correct address?"

"Yes."

Kuhn compared the photo to Henry, copied some information from the card, closed the wallet, and handed it back.

"I understand you're employed by the county transportation department."

"In the airport division."

"So, what brings you in today?"

"I want immunity."

Kuhn took a beat while his eyes appeared to glaze over. He massaged his forehead, then the bridge of his nose. When he redirected his gaze to Henry, spidery blood vessels stood out in the whites of Kuhn's eyes.

"I need a little more information," Kuhn said.

Henry wasn't going to give up his secrets without protection. Everywhere was danger. The contract he'd forged. He could go to prison just for that. The money he'd taken. More prison time. Someone killed Tanzini. They might want him dead, too. But he knew he had to give Kuhn something to prove he had important information to share, something the DA would want to know.

"How do I know I can trust you?"

"The truth is, Mr. Watkins, you don't. You took a gamble when you called my office. I have no idea what your situation is, so I can't predict if my bosses will agree to immunity." Kuhn shrugged. "It's up to you, whether you want to go forward with this interview." Kuhn put his pen down, sat back, then rolled his neck, stretching the muscles.

Henry said, "I must have something you need to know. You arrested the chief of the department. The next day, Anderson and Sinclair went to see a lawyer. Anderson's my boss. Sinclair is another manager. No one's seen them since. They must have come back during the night and cleared out their offices."

"Okay."

"That building permit man got immunity in the corruption scandal. It was on the news."

"I can't comment on an ongoing investigation."

The image of the man lurking outside Tanzini's apartment building was stuck in Henry's mind. "I need immunity and witness protection before I talk."

Kuhn took a deep breath and sighed. "Here's my problem, Mr. Watkins. Immunity and witness protection are big asks. I don't have the authority to give that to you. I'd have to talk to my bosses. When I ask them, they're going to want to know what information you have. Think of it as a contract. You give us something. We give you something."

The lights flickered again as Henry felt Kuhn's eyes look deeply into his soul. What did he see? A frightened little mouse quivering under the shadow of doom.

Henry cleared his throat and opened his mouth to speak, not knowing what he would say.

Kuhn leaned forward, raised his pen, clicked it twice, then pressed it to the legal pad.

"If I tell you what I know, how do I know you'll give me a deal?" Henry asked.

"I'm sorry, sir. That's how it works. You give us a proffer, which means you tell us what you would testify to. It's not testimony so we can't use it. If the information is useful, the DA may agree to immunity. But I can't make any promises."

Kuhn wanted Henry to give up everything he knew without any guarantee. But he knew what happened to snitches in jail – Tanzini had told him. Henry's lungs suddenly felt they were filled with cotton. He pulled in air, but he couldn't get oxygen. He patted his pockets. No inhaler. He'd left it at home.

The room's pressure dropped again as the door behind Henry opened. He jumped to his feet.

It was the secretary. She glanced coolly at Henry. "Sorry to interrupt. I wanted to let you know I'm leaving for the night, Mr. Kuhn."

"I'm sorry," Henry said. "This was a big mistake." He pushed his way past her. The security door opened from the inside without a badge. The elevator opened, too. Minutes later, Henry was out on the dark street, running to the bus stop.

Chapter Twenty-Eight

When Henry returned home, he found his inhaler on the table next to the door where he kept his keys. He scooped it up and put it to his mouth, drawing deeply. Within seconds, his lungs filled with fresh air and his head had that happy dizzy feeling.

He fell into his old, cracked chair. Everything had gone wrong. His department was under investigation. The chief had already been arrested. Anderson and Sinclair had disappeared. It was only a matter of time before Henry was found out.

He needed that contract. No one could ever see it. If the police got hold of it, they would figure out he'd taken a bribe.

He googled Esme's Bakery and found a phone number listed for orders. He called and tried to ask the woman who answered about the contract without sounding suspicious. She didn't know what he was talking about.

There was only one person he could talk to. He made the call and left a message on the voicemail.

Chapter Twenty-Nine

PAUL LEWIS STARTED THE clock on his computer billing program, then touched the intercom button. The Hag answered.

"Show her back," he said. While he waited, he spun his chair around to take in the view from his seventh-floor office.

On a nice day, Paul would walk down to the Ferry Building, pick up a roast beef sandwich from the deli, and sit on a bench by the pier as he ate his lunch, watching the boats bob in the water, listening to the seagulls caw overhead, feeling the cool breeze on his face and tasting the salt in the air, maybe tossing breadcrumbs to the birds who hopped along the concrete pad begging for food.

Ironically, it was Paul who discovered that Esme Castillo was operating a pop-up after she had been ousted from Esme Inc. He saw her booth in front of the Ferry Building on one of his lunchtime visits. He even bought a selection of cookies from her, but she didn't recognize him. They'd only met once when she came into his office to sign the papers. All guys in suits probably looked alike to her. When he had returned to the office, he called Mrs. Osteen.

He heard his door open. He spun around and leapt to his feet.

The Hag, ancient, bent, withered, and perpetually angry, stood before him. "Mrs. Osteen," she said.

The Hag moved aside to allow the client to enter, then disappeared into the hall, pulling the door until the latch bolt snapped into place. When anyone else closed that door, you could barely hear it. But when she did it, the sound was like a gunshot. She'd held the doorknob open until the perfect moment to suddenly let go, shooting the bolt into place. He may be the man behind the desk, but she was the woman at the door, and it was she who decided who entered and left. Paul was her prisoner.

He came out from behind his desk, graciously, as he had seen his father demonstrate when the old man made him clerk for no pay one summer in law school while his classmates partied.

He extended his hand. "It is so good to see you again, Mrs. Osteen. You're looking well."

A woody perfume reached him as she accepted his hand.

She was elegant despite her age, which he knew from the file was fifty-three years old. Her face was a glossy mask, the neck smooth. He wondered if her skin was so tight she couldn't smile or frown, even if she wanted to.

"I just returned from a holiday," she said.

Her moss green silk blazer matched her skirt. The lapels met between her breasts, and she wore no blouse, so that if one were so inclined, he – or she – would be able to see down into her bra and view its contents. She was coming on to him. Paul could feel it. But he wasn't interested. He'd sooner crawl into bed with a viper.

Father, however, would've had her on top of the desk. For all Paul knew, he had. All the old man would say is that they were "old friends."

Paul gestured toward a visitor's chair. "Would you like to take a seat? We have some developments to review."

Paul felt her energy withdraw from him. Job done. He sauntered back to his chair, dragging a fingertip along the desk edge as he did so. In no hurry because he was on the clock. Dad would be so proud.

"We have a couple of issues in the Esme Inc case." Paul handed Mrs. Osteen a copy of a document, then held his copy in both hands. "If you look at request number one, Maureen Gould is asking for copies of all contracts, agreements, invoices, proposals, and any other document relating to the existence of a lease in the San Francisco International Airport." Paul laid the papers down and folded his hands on top of them.

He never understood this woman. Was she really going into the café business, standing behind a counter and serving up lattes? No way. She had something else planned. Did it matter to Paul? His job was not to decide what the truth was or what was fair. His job was to advocate for, and protect, his client. If she wanted to keep secrets from him, that was her business. As long as she kept paying the bill, his father and the Hag would be happy, and Paul would continue to draw his salary, live in his ultramodern Castro neighborhood condo, and party with his friends.

"Let's look at the remaining requests. They want to know about several unexplained expenditures. You were the business treasurer, so you're the person best situated to answer the questions. Perhaps you should take this request home with you and review it. Then we can meet again in a week or two and draft some responses."

"How long do we have before we answer the questions?"

"The rules say thirty days, but we can string that out."

Mrs. Osteen rolled up the document and began tapping it against her open palm. "Again, how long do we have?"

Paul felt like a puppy who was about to get whacked for peeing on the carpet. "Several weeks? Maybe a few months. Eventually, Maureen Gould will file a motion to compel answers. We can get a routine continuance to respond to her motion which will give us a few more weeks. The judge could take a couple months or more even to decide the motion. How much time do you need?"

Her voice took a sharp tone. "Is that the best you can do?"

Paul had seen his father string out litigation for years, throwing up one hurdle after another to slow down the opposition. They were paid by the hour, the old man kept saying, no matter if it was the first hour or the hundredth. "I could claim that the business plans are trade secrets and ask for a protective order against releasing that information."

"How much time would that buy?"

"If the judge grants the motion, months, maybe even years."

"Do it." Mrs. Osteen neatly folded the document in half and slipped it into her purse. She rose to her feet.

Paul stood. "There's something else."

She had been reaching for the door. "What?"

"Esme Castillo filed a motion to take over the business."

Mrs. Osteen frowned. "Can she do that?"

"Here's the thing. When Tanzini died, his stock was split up pro-rata in relation to your prior percentage of ownership. So she's the majority stockholder now. Unless we come up with some reason against it, the judge will grant her motion."

She snorted in disgust. "Pay attention. I'll go slowly for you. Remember that side deal with Al? His shares became mine if he couldn't pay back the loan on time. He's dead. So, he can't repay the money. His shares are now mine, and I'm the majority shareholder. Tell that to the court."

He wasn't sure the court would enforce the side deal, but like his father always said, the customer was always right. "Yes, ma'am."

After Paul escorted her through the office of Lewis and Lewis, past the Hag's desk, and to the corridor, he opened his computer and recorded his notes of the meeting. He reviewed the entry to make sure it was complete and the grammar and spelling were correct. When he had spent as much time on it as he could, he hit "save," then went into his billing program and stopped the clock.

Chapter Thirty

A FEW WEEKS AFTER Tanzini was murdered, we were in my conference room seated around the table: myself, Yolanda, Esme, and Esme's aunt, Bebe, who had been her bookkeeper. I'd cranked the windows open to let in the warm sunshine and soft breeze.

Bebe was an older version of Esme, but less intense. In her late thirties, her wild brown hair was cut shoulder-length. She wore jeans, a T-shirt, and big silver hoop earrings. Her brown eyes were large, framed with a thin layer of black eyeliner and a heavy coat of black mascara on long, curly eyelashes.

I was keenly aware of Quinn, in my back office on a Zoom meeting with her study group preparing for an upcoming exam. Since the night she'd scolded me about Chinese laborers, she hadn't spoken to me except to be polite.

We each had our laptops open. In the center of the table were stacks of paper files with so many colored stickies protruding from the pages that they looked like a bad haircut a child had given to her doll. That was my handiwork.

Because of Tanzini's death, I had filed a motion to have the civil case dismissed. Esme was now the majority shareholder of Esme Inc, and she no longer wished to pursue the case against herself. The judge would have no choice – or so I'd thought.

Rita Osteen, the minority shareholder, objected. Her attorney, Paul Lewis, filed a brief arguing that because of Tanzini's death, his stock had reverted to her by virtue of a side agreement. She claimed she had loaned him the money for his investment and that when he didn't repay her on time, his shares became hers.

The court denied my motion. Judge Rediger said she needed a full trial to resolve the ownership issues. Meanwhile, the court appointed a business management firm to run the bakery.

But we had one win. The judge ordered Rita Osteen to turn over the corporate books immediately.

I had combed through the files, evidenced by the stickies. Bebe had gone over them, too. She sat to my immediate left so we wouldn't need to shout across the table.

"On a day-to-day basis, the bakery is barely getting by," Bebe said. "What I mean by that is, there is enough money coming in to make payroll and rent and to buy supplies, but that's it. Otherwise, it's in trouble. Its liabilities exceed its assets. Esme had paid off all the big debts before she turned the business over, but no one is setting aside money for next year's insurance premiums, and the employee taxes haven't been paid."

Esme pulled her braid over her shoulder and began unraveling it. "But what about all that money Al and Rita put in?"

"Gone," Bebe said. "They paid it into the general account, and it's been bled dry. Rental payments on Tanzini's condo and his car, payment to his credit cards, and large cash withdrawals." Bebe tapped her computer mouse and studied the monitor a moment before she went on. "And there was a payment for ten thousand dollars and a later payment for forty thousand made out to Hughes Fisher Inc."

Esme straightened in her chair. "Who's that?"

"An architectural firm," Bebe answered. "I looked it up."

"Architect?" Yolanda asked. "Why would he pay all that money to an architect?"

Bebe shrugged. "Did you get a copy of all the board minutes and business files?"

"Looks like we did," I said. "There was nothing about an architect. I would have noticed." I had to pay an architect to draw up plans for the extensive refurbishment of the mansion before we obtained permits to do the work.

"Okay, then," Bebe said. "What I want to know is, why is Rita Osteen fighting so hard to keep a business that is virtually bankrupt."

Good question.

Chapter Thirty-One

I CRUISED BY THE mansion on my way home with the top down because of the warm weather. I wanted to make sure Lizzie's home was okay since Dixon Vaughn had made it a target with his podcast.

As the mansion came into view, I saw the color red peaking from behind the monkey puzzle tree on the front yard. Words had been spray-painted on the front wall. When I got closer, I read, "FEMICULT BITCH" in big block letters.

My hands started shaking. I pulled into a parking place and hit speed dial for Jake. *Pick up, pick up, pick up. Please, pick up.*

He didn't. I texted, "Call me ASAP."

I got out of the car and ran across the street. When I stood in front of the bloody scrawl, the noxious fumes clinging to the mansion wall made me queasy. That paint was fresh.

I punched in the code for the door, Quinn's birthday. There was no one in the mansion that day because we didn't have any events planned. I powered up the computer at the reception desk and accessed the security files. Less than half an hour before I arrived, a scrawny man dressed in black wearing a ski mask and high-top trainers had quick-stepped up the walkway and disappeared off the frame when he crossed the lawn heading for his destination. A moment later, he reappeared again as he jogged toward the street.

I didn't see the muscle car with the racing stripe. Nor could I see his face. So I couldn't be sure if it was the same man who had trespassed in my office and broken my window. But both had the same build and wore high-top Converse sneakers.

My phone buzzed. It was Jake. "What's up?"

"The mansion was vandalized." My hands were shaking with adrenalin. Until now, I was hoping Dixon Vaughn would get bored with me.

"When did this happen?"

"In the past hour."

"Red, I don't like the sound of this. I told you before about this guy. Doesn't give up, like a terrier. This is the third thing he's done. I'd feel better if Gerry was with you."

I wanted to feel like I could handle Dixon Vaughn by myself. I was a grown woman. But the truth was, I'd gotten lucky when he tried to bully past me into the mansion. If he had not spotted the security camera, I don't know what would've happened. And now his henchmen had violated my office and vandalized my family home.

Jake spoke, interrupting my thoughts. "It's great you're taking self-defense classes, but you're not a black belt. Vaughn had a lot more training in the academy and on the force than you can pick up in a few afternoons."

I didn't want to feel like I needed a man to protect me. But I knew Jake loved me enough to tell me what I didn't want to hear.

"Okay, fine," I said, echoing my daughter's juvenile adage. "Just until this is over."

Chapter Thirty-Two

MICKEY WONG WAS CALLED in to man the evening news desk that night. She hated reading stories. The field, talking to real people, was where the news was. Let someone else stare into a television camera pretending it's a human being. But the anchor was on vacation, so here she was.

Words crawled across the teleprompter and Mickey read them aloud.

"This just in. A body has been discovered under what police describe as suspicious circumstances. The victim was found in his apartment following a police welfare check. He had not gone into work for several days and his coworkers called the police out of concern. His identity will be released after his next-of-kin is notified."

Chapter Thirty-Three

ESME AND I SAT in a district attorney's windowless conference room that I knew well. I'd given Gerry the morning off.

I'd always hated this room. Stagnant air. The smell of dust and paper overlaid the astringent stink of synthetic furniture and carpet. Light glowed from milky ceiling tiles. Where one light bulb was burned out, the plastic tile beneath it was gray, reminding me of a gapped tooth smile. Another tube light flickered and sizzled.

Across from us were Detective Dobson, wearing a black suit, the younger Detective Chong, in a pressed cotton dress shirt and jeans, and Vivian Thandi, a prosecutor I knew from my time with the DA's office.

Vivian was British African. Slim and with a shaved head, she spoke with an expensive accent and wore a tailored beige suit and a white silk blouse. She was famous for her win-loss record. Formidable and ambitious, she had won every case that went to verdict before the Tony Paredes trial. It was rumored throughout the office that she had her eye on the DA's job as a launchpad to the bench.

I had gone up against her in Tony's case. I'd won, so there was a feeling in the room that Vivian needed to tread carefully around me. But winning one trial does not mean winning the next one. Every case is unique. She and I both knew that.

"The reason I called you in is that there has been another homicide," Vivian said, matter-of-factly. "We have reason to believe that it is connected to the murder of Alfred Tanzini."

With the eyes of Detectives Chong and Dobson on Esme and me, I felt like a zoo animal. Everything that she and I said or did, or didn't say or didn't do, would be noted with interest by them. I had cautioned Esme before the meeting that we would be neutral and say as little as possible. At least we weren't being videotaped. I knew from my time working at the DA's office that they didn't permit any recording in the office, just in case some wily defense attorney got their hands on it and made them look bad.

I waited for Vivian to continue.

She looked at me. "Did your client know a man named Henry Watkins?"

I gave Esme a nod. "You can answer that."

"I don't recognize the name," Esme said.

I could hear my phone, stashed in my briefcase, buzz with an incoming text. I ignored it.

Vivian took a photograph out of the file folder in front of her and passed it across the table to us. Esme examined it. "Oh, yeah, I know that guy. He was a friend of Al's. I saw him at Al's apartment when I dropped off some cookies that Al had asked for."

"Why was he in Mr. Tanzini's apartment?" Vivian asked.

My phone buzzed again.

"They didn't say," Esme said. "I just thought he was a friend. I didn't hang out long. Actually, I didn't feel welcome. Al acted like I was just the hired help. So I left after a few minutes."

"What does this have to do with us?" I asked.

"Henry Watkins worked in the County Department of Transportation. He was involved in issuing vendor permits at the airport," Vivian said.

"You mean like the restaurants and kiosks?" Esme asked.

"Just so," Vivian said.

My face warmed as I felt the detectives watching me. I focused on Vivian.

"Worked, as in past tense," I commented. My phone buzzed again.

"Should you get that?" Vivian asked, glancing down at my briefcase.

Yolanda can handle anything that might come up at the office. Quinn was at the mansion babysitting while some mothers used a classroom and computers to take an online class in office software. Jake was at work. For all I knew, the texts were spam. "I'm okay. Please continue."

Vivian took a deep breath. "Yes, to answer your question: 'worked' as in the past tense. Mr. Watkins was discovered in his apartment this morning. The police were called for a welfare check by one of his coworkers. He had not been into the office for several days, and he had quit answering his phone."

Esme's hands were in her lap, clasped so hard her knuckles were turning white.

"Why do you believe this murder is connected to that of Alfred Tanzini?" I asked.

"For a couple of reasons. First, they had business dealings. Mr. Tanzini was in the process of obtaining a permit to open a café and bakery outlet at the airport. The enterprise was in the name of your client's business. He was working with Mr. Watkins towards that end."

"How do you know that?" I asked.

"It was in Mr. Tanzini's text messages," Vivian answered.

"Did you find a contract?"

"Unfortunately, we did not." Vivian addressed Esme directly. "Perhaps you could help us with that."

Esme's body stiffened as Vivian gazed at her.

I interceded. "I don't know anything about a contract." I looked at Esme, a cue she could respond.

"News to me," she said.

I said, "Vivian, you said there were two reasons why you believe these murders were connected. What's the second?"

"The unusual modus operandi." Vivian paused for dramatic effect.

The faces of the two detectives were blank. I couldn't tell if they were breathing. "And that was?"

"They both had their throats slit."

Esme gave out a little cry, and her hand flew to cover her mouth.

Vivian leaned across the table ever so slightly. "I need to ask your client. Where were you yesterday, Esme?"

The detectives still weren't breathing.

Here we go again. "Is my client a suspect?" I asked.

"Not at present," Vivian said. "We would like to rule her out so that we can focus our investigation."

"I was at home," Esme said, blurting out her answer despite my cautions before we had come to the DA's office. She might have told the truth, but if they caught her in a lie, they would zero in on her as the prime suspect.

"Is there anyone who can verify that?" Vivian asked.

"I live with my grandmother, but I don't want you bothering her. She worries."

"You do understand how important it is for us to verify your alibi, Ms. Castillo. This is a murder investigation."

Esme turned to me. "Can they do that? Just go around harassing my family like I was a criminal or something? I had nothing to do with this. I'm just a baker. Why can't everyone just leave me alone?"

I opened my mouth to advise my client to stop blurting things out, but before I could speak, Esme jumped up from the table and ran out of the room.

Vivian picked up her file. "I don't have time for this drama, Maureen. You know the drill. Someone murdered these men. Someone who hasn't been identified and is free to kill again. We will keep pushing forward until we find this person, with your client's cooperation or not."

Chapter Thirty-Four

WHEN WE CLIMBED BACK into Sunny, my yellow BMW M-5, Esme got out her cell phone, placed a call, and spoke rapidly in Spanish, which I did not understand. Esme was deep into the conversation, and it didn't sound like she was going to finish anytime soon. When I pulled my phone out of my briefcase, it rang with a call from Yolanda. I didn't know who Esme was talking to, but it was obviously not my paralegal.

I hadn't started the car yet, so I got out and stood on the sidewalk while I spoke with Yolanda. I wanted to tell her about Henry Watkins' death, but I didn't get a chance.

"Are you out of the DA's office yet?" she asked. Her tone was urgent.

"What's going on?"

"Someone called in a SWAT alert about the mansion. Quinn was there babysitting for some moms who were doing online classes. The next thing she knew, the place was surrounded by sharpshooters and there was a guy with a bullhorn shouting for everyone to come out with their hands on their heads. Moms, kids, everyone!"

"What the –,"

"Everything is okay now. Gerry went over there, and he's with them."

"Who? And why?"

"We don't know. It was an anonymous call to 911. They said there was someone in the building with a gun acting crazy and threatening to kill all the children."

"I'm on my way." I jumped back into my BMW and started the car. Esme was still on the phone. She shot me a frown because she would not be able to hear the person on the other end as my engine revved. I ignored her.

I dropped the gear into reverse and backed up until the alarm sounded, warning that I was going to hit the car parked behind me, and then I backed up a few more inches. I threw the car into first gear, cranked on the wheel, and hurled myself into traffic, tires squealing. A horn blared. I shifted into second and then up into third, putting several yards between me and the angry driver behind me, and then glided through a yellow light before I turned right and headed towards Pacific Heights.

When we arrived, a SWAT truck was double-parked in front of the mansion. Gerry stood on the sidewalk talking to a guy wearing a bulletproof vest with a helmet tucked under one arm. I parked behind the truck, blocking in someone's SUV that had two children's car seats strapped into the second row. Across the street in the park, several young moms with babies in their arms and clutching toddlers' hands clustered together watching the drama unfold.

When we parked, Esme was still talking. I jumped out of my car and ran over to Gerry.

He patted me on the shoulder. "Everything's okay. The house has been cleared for intruders and devices."

"And Quinn?"

"She's inside with them. She did great – called me when the team got here. I came straight over." Gerry slapped the man next to him on the vest. "I know Bill from the old days. He worked the same shift with me and Jake when we were on patrol."

To the SWAT guy, he said, "Bill, this is the good lady who rescued Jake Kuhn from his miserable bachelorhood, Maureen Gould."

Bill stuck out his hand, and I shook. "It's nice to meet you, but I'd like to talk to my daughter right now."

"Understood," Bill said.

They stepped out of my way, and I jogged up to the mansion and began to input the security code when the newly repainted door swung open.

Quinn stood in front of me, breathing so heavily, I thought she was going to hyperventilate.

"Where is everyone?"

"In the kitchen having milk and cookies." Quinn burst into tears and fell into my arms, shaking as she cried. It was a long time before she could speak again.

"I was so afraid that something bad would happen to the kids," she said. "Can we do another self-defense lesson? If anyone came after the children, I'd hurt them."

Chapter Thirty-Five

My husband took the rest of the day off and met us at the condominium. When he arrived, he went straight to Quinn, who was sitting in her usual perch at the breakfast bar with a cup of tea. "Are you alright?"

She slipped off her barstool and buried her face in his chest, with a new surge of tears. Gerry took his beer over to the sliding glass window and looked out onto our little patio, giving them privacy. I stood by numbly. I didn't know what to do.

Jake stroked Quinn's hair and whispered that everything was going to be okay. I wished I had his parenting skills, but he had grown up in a loving family. And I had the legacy of a pedophile father and a mother who was so emotionally remote, I had sometimes wondered if she was mentally ill.

I regretted that Jake and I did not have children of our own, but it was a decision that we made together. When we married, I had just opened my own practice, and my workload varied erratically. There were days on end when I had nothing to do, but times when I slept in my suit on my office couch because I didn't have time to go home. His job was sixty to eighty hours a week. We couldn't take care of a baby. Instead, Jake bought the Siamese kitten for me, Germaine Greer, who was now yowling in front of her empty food dish.

I might be a deficient mother, but I could feed a cat.

I opened a can of cat food, filled the dish, and put it on the floor. Germaine sniffed, then turned her back and drifted out of the kitchen, settling in the hallway where she could watch the humans, her tail twitching. She was not accustomed to sharing Jake with others.

Later, the four of us, Jake, Quinn, Gerry and me, sat around the dinner table with a collection of empty beers as Quinn peeled off another label from a bottle.

"This can't go on, Red," Jake said. "Someone's going to get hurt. This has got to be the work of Dixon Vaughn."

"The police have the video of him the day he tried to blow past me into the mansion," I said. "They have the video of the graffiti artist. I sent them the links to Vaughn's podcast. What does that show? Unless they can figure out who called in the SWAT alert, we can't prove that all three things are connected."

"For the time being, it would be safer if no one was at the mansion," Jake said.

"You mean I should just give up and quit? That's what he wants."

"I get that. But someone is going to get hurt. It could be one of the mothers or one of the kids. Do you want that on your conscious?"

Gerry pushed his chair back from the table, distancing himself from his foolhardy friend.

"Jake, are you accusing me of putting the mothers and children in danger?"

Quinn's hands froze, a paper petal between the tips of her fingers about to be dropped onto the growing mound of moist shards.

I had not been this angry with my husband for a couple of years. Shortly after we were married, we fought all the time. He left me for what he said was a cooling-off period. I was so furious that I filed for divorce. Eventually, I came to understand that when Jake was critical, he was trying to support me. We made up and renewed our vows. Since then, when he said something that offended me, I tried to interpret his comments as loving concern even if they were awkwardly phrased.

But right now, I wanted to throw something at his head. Something soft, but still I really wanted to see it bing off his noggin.

Gerry had sat quietly through the exchange until now. He shifted his body weight to get Jake's attention. When Jake looked over at him, Gerry raised an eyebrow. Clearly, he understood that Jake was getting himself into trouble.

Jake took Gerry's warning. "Maybe I put it the wrong way. What I meant to say is that there's nothing more important to me than the safety of you and Quinn."

Frowning, Quinn dug her thumbnail under the label of another empty beer bottle. "I hate it when you guys fight."

I turned to her. "We're not fighting, sweetie. We're kicking around ideas."

"Sounds like fighting to me."

For all I knew, Quinn's adoptive parents never argued. Perhaps if they disagreed, they spoke quietly among themselves out of her earshot. But what I did know is that when she sensed tension in our house, it made her feel insecure. We were her newly found family.

She needed to know that we were stable. I might be a crap mother, but I could figure out that much.

I said, "Jake's right. He usually is. We need to be extra careful going forward. I'll send an email out to the mothers telling them that we will arrange for classes and babysitting in another location, and that we will resume in a few days. Yolanda could find us a couple of hotel conference rooms, and we'll set up there."

"Can you afford to?" Jake asked.

The foundation had some money left. Not enough to finance our long-term goals, but if we didn't get a grant soon, I didn't know how we could go on operating anyway. Jake didn't know how bad it was. He was too busy with his job lately for me to bother him about it.

I patted his hand. "We're okay."

"Meanwhile, back to business," I said briskly, signaling a topic change. "Esme and I met with Vivian Thandi today. There's been another murder."

Chapter Thirty-Six

I WAS AT MY desk at the office, reviewing the judge's order, while Yolanda watched me from a visitor's chair. Out in the reception room, Gerry was reading a Detective Byron paperback.

"You have got to be kidding me," I said to myself.

"What?" she demanded.

I held up my hand. I needed a moment to make sure I had read it correctly. I had.

"You have got to be kidding me," I repeated. "Remember that discovery request we sent over to Paul Lewis about an airport contract?"

"Sure. You thought that because Vivian Thandi had questioned Esme about that airport guy's murder, and Esme Inc had paid some architect a lot of money, Tanzini might be planning to open a location at the airport."

"Right. And Rita Osteen's response to my discovery request was to file a petition for a protective order to block me from asking those questions. She did not admit there was a contract or proposal for the airport, but she claimed that if there was, that information would be a trade secret, and she should not be required to release it to Esme given Esme's recent history of opening a competing business."

Yolanda scoffed. "By competing business, do you mean that little pop-up stand she had at the Ferry Building?"

"That's the one."

"That's ridiculous. How is she going to go from a little pop-up to a multimillion-dollar shop at the airport? She doesn't have any money. They made sure of it."

"I get that. And I answered their petition stating that she had no such intention. I also pointed out that she was still one of the owners of the business and, in fact, the majority shareholder. So she was entitled to know how the business was being conducted."

Yolanda crossed her arms over her chest. "And the judge said what?"

"Our old friend, Judge Rediger, ruled that the information we were seeking was a trade secret and that given the hostile relationship between Esme and the remaining shareholder, she would not be entitled to that information until there was a trial to determine who was entitled to run the business."

"But Esme is the majority shareholder now, right? What's there to decide?"

"Not until the trial, she isn't. The judge needs to decide whether that side deal was legal. And, get this! Lewis claimed that even if Esme is the majority shareholder, which he refused to concede, that she violated her good faith duty to the remaining shareholders when she urged the bakers to quit, so she shouldn't be allowed to run the bakery."

Yolanda was now perched on the edge of her chair. "And the judge bought that?"

"The judge already ruled, twice if you'll recall, that Esme opened a competing business and urged the bakers to quit. And as to the alleged side deal, the judge ruled that there are so many factual issues that need to be resolved, she wants a trial before she decides who will ultimately gain control of Esme Inc."

Yolanda's voice was loud enough to carry to the nosebleed seats. "Meanwhile, the business management company she appointed to run the bakery will be paid from the proceeds, which if Bebe is right, means what little profits there are will be eaten up."

"Yelling at me won't fix anything."

"Sorry," she said, then pushed herself back into the chair, her arms crossed again.

"There's more bad news. The trial date is set for a year from now."

"What is Esme supposed to do between now and then? How is she going to earn a living? Right now, she's helping out with my sister's janitorial service and living with my mother. But she is an ambitious girl. She needs to have a goal, to be building something. She'd hoped the business would provide for the family. It was her contribution to our heritage. She has a job, sure, but she has no purpose. And she needs that. She needs to feel like she's giving back."

I understood Yolanda's concern. But I was worried about a more pressing matter. It had been days since Vivian called us in to talk about the murder of Henry Watkins, and it had been even longer since Al Tanzini was murdered. There had been no news about an arrest. Until there was, I had to assume that Esme was a suspect.

I was right.

Chapter Thirty-Seven

LATER THAT MORNING, I got another call from Vivian Thandi.

"I will come to the point," she said. "I charged Esmeralda Castillo with the homicide of Alfred Tanzini based upon new evidence. If you bring your client in for processing and arraignment this afternoon, I will agree to bail."

I suddenly felt cold. "What new evidence?"

"I will be happy to release that to you after the arraignment."

Yolanda insisted on going along to pick up Esme. Gerry said he'd go, too. My BMW was too small for four people, or Gerry at all, so we took Yolanda's big red SUV. At first, she drove. But after she ran a red light nearly causing an accident, I demanded she pull over, and I took the wheel. Gerry sat in the back of the car, staring out the window, diplomatically keeping his opinion to himself.

Esme waited outside her grandmother's house, not dressed for court. She wore her skintight jeans, tank top, and bracelets. Arraignments aren't a fashion show, but we were in a hurry, so I reserved comment.

Gerry stepped out of the backseat and held the door open for Esme. He climbed into the passenger seat beside me, and I took off for court.

Esme was teary and her breathing was shallow. Her first words were, "I didn't do it. It had to be Rita Osteen.

"Is there anyone else you can think of who might have wanted Tanzini dead?" Yolanda asked.

"Everyone he ever knew," Esme said. "But it wasn't me."

"Did you ever meet this man, Bruno Fernandez, before court?" I asked. "He had a grudge."

"Never saw him, never heard of him," Esme said. "Maybe that county guy, Henry something, did it."

"Henry Watkins," I said.

Gerry slid me a side-eye. Henry Watkins was killed with the same M.O. as Al Tanzini, a knife across the throat. It was far more likely whoever killed Tanzini killed Henry, too.

"Butchers are good with knives," Yolanda pointed out, meaning Bruno Fernandez.

"Chefs are, too," Gerry answered.

Yolanda punched the back of Gerry's seat. "Hey, whose side are you on?"

He turned to look at her. "Esme's, of course. I know she didn't do it. I'm just pointing out what the prosecution is thinking."

"Gerry's right," I said.

"Rita did it," Esme said. "I know it. Everything was fine before she came along."

Before we were halfway to the courthouse, Esme began to hyperventilate. I pulled into a parking lot, went around to the back seat, and opened the door. "Esme, listen to me. Breathe in slowly through your nose. That's good. Now blow out slowly through your mouth. Perfect. In slowly. Out slowly."

Within a few cycles, Esme's breathing returned to normal. I closed the door and jumped back into the driver's seat.

"Where did you learn to do that?" Gerry asked.

"Law school." One of the other first-year students had panicked during an exam. When we were on break, she started hyperventilating at her desk. Another student, who had just graduated nursing school and was now going to law school with plans of becoming a medical malpractice attorney, talked her through it. I don't know what happened to the panicked student, but the nurse-lawyer had already made millions and retired.

When we arrived at the courthouse, Esme was calm enough to walk inside. The four of us found the courtroom. Vivian sat in the front row while another case was being processed. I walked into her field of vision to let her know I was there, and she nodded in acknowledgment. I returned to the pew where Esme, Yolanda and Gerry were sitting halfway back in the courtroom.

The case ahead of us finished. The judge signed some papers and handed them to his clerk. As the defense counsel stood, the defendant, a scraggly young man dressed in an orange prison jumpsuit, rose, rattling his wrist and ankle chains. A deputy took him by the elbow and steered him towards a small door to the side of the courtroom through which they disappeared.

"Where are they going?" Esme whispered.

"Back to jail," I said.

Esme turned on me, half-standing as she did so in an effort to escape, but I had her blocked in. "Am I going to jail? You said I wasn't."

Yolanda took Esme's hand and pulled her back down to a sit.

"You're not," I said. "The DA promised she would agree to bail."

The judge called, "Next case."

Vivian stepped through the gate. The assistant prosecutor at the table gathered his files and moved into a chair against the wall.

"If it pleases the court," she said. "We would like to proceed with State vs. Esmeralda Castillo."

"Very well," the judge said. The nameplate in front of him said, "Judge Matthews." I didn't know him. He was in his forties, with thinning dark hair and black-rimmed glasses.

I stood and motioned for Esme to follow. I held the gate open as she passed through and pointed her to the empty defense table. She stopped moving, paralyzed. I stepped into my place at the table. After she came around and stood beside me, she rested her trembling fingertips on the tabletop.

Vivian spoke. "The State of California charges Esmeralda Castillo with one count of manslaughter, to wit: Esmeralda Castillo caused the unlawful killing of a human being, Alfred Tanzini, in violation of Penal Code section 192. This crime carries a potential maximum sentence of eleven years."

Esme grabbed my arm so tightly I had bruises.

The judge turned to me. "Counselor, please state your name for the record."

"Maureen Gould for the defendant, Your Honor. Also present is my client, Esmeralda Castillo."

"How does she plead?"

"Not guilty," I said.

The judge made a check mark in the file before him. "What's the State's position on bail?"

"The State agrees to release the defendant on her own recognizance," Vivian said.

Esme leaned into me. "What does that mean?"

"You can go home after we're finished here," I whispered back to her. I had already told her this several times, but people in fear have difficulty absorbing information, so I'd learned to repeat myself.

"Very well," the judge said. "The clerk will issue a scheduling order. You may be excused."

A deputy came forward. Esme looked at him blankly.

"I need you to come with me," he said.

She grabbed my arm. "But you just said I can go home."

"They need to take your fingerprints and photo now," I said. "Don't worry. I'll go with you."

The deputy took a step back, allowing room for me to lead my client to the small door on the side of the courtroom. He came around when we reached the door, unlocked it, and pulled it open revealing a scuffed beige wall a few feet away. We were about to enter a narrow hall that immediately required us to turn left before we reached the door at the other end. I felt like a rat running through a maze.

Esme was just behind me. I heard a groan, then the sound of a body falling. When I turned around, she was on the floor, having fainted, as she had at my office when we first learned Tanzini was dead. Instead of catching her, the deputy had stepped out of the way.

"What is wrong with you?" It was Yolanda as she pushed her way forward through the gate.

The deputy turned to face her, reaching for his side arm. I held up my hand, signaling Yolanda to stop.

She did.

For a moment, we all froze.

"Yolanda, would you please get my briefcase and meet me downstairs in the lobby in half an hour?"

"But–"

Gerry came through the gate and gently placed one hand on Yolanda's arm.

"I've got this," I said.

Esme was coming to. "What happened?"

She pushed her hair out of her face. When she saw me and the deputy standing over her, she tried to scramble backwards.

I knelt beside her. "It's okay. I'm with you."

I helped her to her feet and together we went through the door.

Chapter Thirty-Eight

By the time Yolanda, Gerry, and I had returned to the office, after dropping Esme off at her grandmother's house, an email from Vivian Thandi was waiting for me. Attached to it were several documents and photos.

I called Yolanda into my office. Gerry followed her in. They stood behind me while we looked at the attachments on my monitor. Photographs from the crime scene. Alfred Tanzini in a pool of blood that had soaked into the white carpet beneath him. Evidence markers scattered about the apartment. Fingerprint-dusted surfaces. A disheveled bed with another evidence marker identifying stains on the sheets. The bathroom and more fingerprint dust. Close-ups of a shower drain that had been pried off.

The documents included a list of evidence taken from the crime scene. One entry was vaguely identified as business files.

"Look! Did they find the airport contract?" Yolanda said, bending over my shoulder.

If there was a contract for an airport shop space and Tanzini had kept the files in his apartment, it should have been found by the police.

I opened another pdf labeled "business files taken from scene" and scanned for the contract. "I don't see it. Did you?"

"Go through it again," Yolanda said. "More slowly this time."

I started from the top and clicked through ninety-seven pages. It wasn't there.

"Maybe there never was a contract," Gerry said.

Yolanda jumped in. "If there wasn't a contract, then why'd they pay that architect all that money?"

"Are you sure they did?" Gerry answered. "Did you trace the funds or are you just relying on an entry in a banking app? I could say I wrote a check to Humpty Dumpty. That doesn't mean it's true."

Gerry had a point. "Do you mean like a money-laundering scheme?" I asked.

"Could be," he said.

"Maybe," I said. "I'll keep it in mind. But that doesn't fit with what we know. Tanzini said he was going to turn Esme Inc into a national brand. According to Viv, there were texts between him and Henry Watkins about an airport lease. It's much more likely that the person who murdered Tanzini took it. Let's look at the rest." I clicked and scrolled.

Yolanda stepped around my chair to look directly at me, "But if it was Bruno Fernandez, why would he take the contract?"

"No idea. But why would Rita Osteen? Wouldn't she have a copy already?"

Yolanda muttered, "Maybe there's someone else we haven't thought of, someone who doesn't want that contract seeing the light of day."

I opened the forensic reports. It identified fingerprints from Alfred Tanzini, Rita Osteen, and my client, as well as three unknown persons. They could belong to maids or room service waiters. Or they could belong to the killer.

The DNA results from the shower drain identified only two different individuals. Alfred Tanzini and one other, a person who had a familial match with Esmeralda Castillo. They had accessed an ancestry website to match the DNA.

I looked up at Yolanda. "Did anyone else in your family know Al Tanzini?"

"You mean personally?"

"I mean so personally that their hair sample would be found in his shower drain."

"I'm going to run down the hall," Gerry said. My implication was obvious, and he didn't want to get embroiled in a family drama.

Yolanda paled. She shook her head slowly. There was only one person who would have used Tanzini's shower.

"Esme led me to believe that they didn't have a personal relationship," I said.

"That's what I thought," Yolanda said. "But did you really ask her in so many words?"

I had not. In fact, I had never asked her at all. Detective Dobson posed the question when she came to my office, and I had shut down the interview before Esme answered.

"I need to talk with Esme," I said. "In person."

Yolanda glanced at her oversized step-counting wristwatch. "Does it have to be today? We need to explain to my mother tonight about the murder charge. Can it wait until tomorrow?"

On the one hand, if I postponed this talk until tomorrow, that would give Yolanda a chance to tell Esme what we had learned, and to help her prepare an explanation, which might not be entirely accurate. Yolanda was protective. Having some experience in criminal law, she would be able to guide her niece in such a way as to hide incriminating evidence. I wouldn't put it past her. The maternal instinct to defend one's child, even if it's a niece rather than a daughter, was strong – especially in Yolanda.

On the other hand, there was no way of cooking up a story about why Esme's hair was in Tanzini's shower drain, other than the truth. She had been in the shower because she had been in his bed.

"Sure," I said. "I'll see both of you here first thing in the morning. Go home to your kids. Give them my love."

Yolanda lingered by the door. "Aren't you coming?"

I needed to get rid of her. "I want to check my emails and messages first. Make sure there isn't anything on fire. I'll go home in a few minutes. Have a good evening."

Yolanda shrugged. "I don't know if that's possible. My mother is not going to take this well. Esme is her favorite grandchild."

While I listened for the sounds of Yolanda shutting down her computer, then loading and starting the kitchenette dishwasher, I scrolled through my email.

Gerry came back into my office. "Yolanda says you're not leaving yet. Are you sure about staying behind? Jake will have my hide if something happens to you when I'm not around."

"It's late in the day. What bad guy is going to venture into this traffic?"

"Got a point. But don't make a night of it. I'll lock up on my way out"

"Promise. Now off with you." I commanded.

He gave me a two-finger Boy Scout salute and left. I scrolled through my emails, while I listened for them to leave. Yolanda and Gerry called "good night" from the reception room. The door finally clicked shut, and I pulled up the DA's evidence.

I was certain that Esme had not murdered Tanzini or anyone else. Jake thinks I am being fanciful when I say that when someone commits murder, it leaves a mark on their soul – unless they are a psychopath. The eyes of most murderers look inward even as they watch your reactions. Like chess players, they are always thinking two moves ahead and trying to steer the conversation away from themselves.

Esme wasn't like that. If anything, she blurted out too much, when she spoke at all. Fear motivated her, not guilt. And she wasn't a psychopath. She was a hardworking, kind, loving young woman who endeavored to support her family and her community.

TV mysteries ask the question: who had the most motive to kill? That's the wrong approach. There are plenty of people who have been wronged to a degree that could inspire murderous rage, but they choose to walk away. Some even forgive.

The real question was: Of the people who had motive to kill, who was most willing?

Certain that Yolanda was gone, I opened the forensic report again. The lab had iden-tified the DNA in the shower, but whose DNA was on those bed sheets?

Two individuals were listed. Alfred Tanzini and an unknown woman. Not Esme. So Tanzini had another lover while he deceived Esme into believing they were going to become the next power couple of baking.

Was he calling the tunes or was he dancing to someone's music?

Chapter Thirty-Nine

THE NEXT MORNING, I arrived at the office to find Yolanda behind her desk and my client sitting on the couch next to Gerry, who was back in his favorite spot. He was a good and faithful man. Yolanda could do worse.

"I printed off the discovery," Yolanda said. "It's in the conference room."

On the other side of the glass wall, three stacks of paper were neatly positioned, one before each chair.

After I had dropped my briefcase in my office and picked up a cup of coffee in the kitchenette, I took my chair at the head of the table. "Let's get to it, shall we?"

Yolanda and Esme sat on either side. Gerry was on the couch in the reception room, head buried in his Detective Byron mystery.

"Maureen, what's going to happen to me?" Esme asked.

"It's too soon to tell. I would love to say something encouraging and dispel your fears. But the truth is you're in a lot of trouble."

"I didn't do it," Esme said.

"That's the funny thing about the truth and evidence. You can't prove a negative."

"I don't get what you mean."

"The justice system depends on evidence. Evidence is something that was left behind after an event. If there was no event, there is no evidence. So you can't really prove you didn't do something. Your best defense is that you didn't have the opportunity."

"You mean like an alibi? Fine, I have an alibi. I wasn't even there."

"That's a great place to start. Where were you the evening that Al Tanzini was murdered?"

"Asleep in my bed at my grandmother's house."

"Can your grandmother verify that?"

"She went to bed before I did. When I got up the next morning, she was already making coffee."

"Let's look at this from the prosecution's point of view. How old is your grandmother?"

"Eighty-three years old. I don't see how that has anything to do with it."

"Would she have heard you leave the house?"

"Her hearing's fine."

Yolanda's face gathered in a frown. "Her hearing isn't what it used to be. You probably didn't realize it because she covers up the fact that she's nearly deaf. Esme, haven't you noticed that if she isn't looking at you, she doesn't know you're talking? She started losing her hearing when I was in school."

"I had no idea," Esme said.

"She hates wearing hearing aids. She says they're uncomfortable."

I looked at Yolanda. "So, if we put Esme's grandmother on the stand, she will have to admit that she couldn't hear Esme leaving or returning that night."

"True," Yolanda said.

"So, Esme doesn't have an alibi." I let that point sink in for a moment. "Not only that, but we also have another problem. The prosecution has evidence that Esme visited Tanzini's apartment the night he was murdered."

I didn't point out this evidence directly contradicted her denial of leaving home that she had just made a few moments ago, but by the looks on their faces, Esme and Yolanda got my meaning.

Esme paled.

"What evidence?" Yolanda asked.

"The doorman and the security video."

Yolanda looked at her niece, astonished. "You weren't supposed to go there. He had an injunction against you. You knew that. You just got done telling us that you were with Grandma all night. I don't understand."

"What I said was that I was in bed when he was murdered. I went out earlier that evening to his place to see if we could talk. Put this thing behind us. But he didn't answer when I rang his bell. The doorman said he had just come home. I waited a long time, thinking he was in the bathroom or something and that's why he didn't answer, and then I rang again. But he never came to the door. So, I figured he didn't want to see me. I left and went home."

"Did Yolanda discuss the forensic report with you?"

Yolanda said, "I thought it would be better coming from you."

Esme's head jerked up. "What did they find?"

I flipped through the stack of paper in front of me and found the report. "They took samples from the shower drain. The lab report shows the hair they found belonged to someone with your DNA."

"How can they possibly say that?"

"They found a familial match on a DNA website."

Esme stared out the window as her eyes brightened with tears. Yolanda reached out her hand, but Esme didn't seem to notice.

I said, "Here's the thing, Esme. If you tell me there is no way that hair can be yours, I will order an independent examination. Maybe the sample was contaminated. It happens all the time."

Her chin jutted forward. "It might not be mine."

"But it might be. Is that what you're saying?"

She was quiet for a long time. The only sound was from an unseen jet roaring across the sky. The atmosphere became heavy with silence. Yolanda clasped her hands on the tabletop, as we had seen judges do so many times.

I picked up my cup, not really wanting to drink but to distract myself while I waited out my client. The coffee's surface was shiny and reflected the overhead lighting. As I tilted the cup, the images distorted into long skinny trapezoids that floated across the ripples.

Esme swallowed, then took a deep breath. "Okay, fine. I had a thing with him."

Yolanda stiffened. "A thing?"

When Yolanda was involved in an intimate relationship, it was serious, exclusive, and committed, yet she understood that people made different lifestyle choices. But for her own family members, she had less tolerance.

Esme looked at her aunt. "It wasn't casual, if that's what you're thinking. I'm not like that."

"Then you admit that you were involved with him?" Yolanda asked. "If it wasn't casual, why did you keep it a secret?"

Through the glass wall that separated the conference room and the reception area, I noticed Gerry staring at his book as if he couldn't hear every word that was said.

"I wasn't keeping it a secret. I just didn't tell anyone." Esme looked at me for rescue. I was caught between my client and my paralegal. I needed accurate information, but I wasn't going to get it while Esme's aunt was in the room. "Yolanda, I really need to speak with Esme privately. Perhaps you could go down to the café and pick up some muffins."

Yolanda's face barely contained her rage. She didn't like being dismissed. "Fine."

She rose from the table and collected her purse from her desk drawer. She left, slamming the door on her way out. Gerry pretended he didn't notice.

I turned to Esme. "Exactly what was going on between you and Al Tanzini?"

"When we first met, he was charming. He took me out to dinner and told me that I was brilliant and beautiful and that my business would be the next hottest thing. He said he could help me take it to the next level. We would be partners. I would be the face of the business, and he would be the brains. I was fine with that. Running the business side was exhausting, and that's not what I was in it for. I'm a chef. I want to create food experiences."

What I really wanted to know was if they were sleeping together. Esme understood my question, given the context. She hadn't answered yet, but I had learned over the years that it's best to let the client or witness tell the story in their own way. Everyone organizes information differently. And if I became too surgical in my questions, I wouldn't get the whole story, aspects of which could be important. So, I listened.

She finally finished with her backstory and looked at me for a reaction. I nodded for her to continue.

"Anyway, we spent so much time together, we got close. I thought we were developing a serious relationship. Maybe even get married someday. So, yes, it is possible that they found my DNA in the shower drain because I showered at his place sometimes."

"Showered at his place after you had sex?"

"You make it sound so cheap. I thought he loved me."

Sitting before me was an intelligent, ambitious, attractive young woman who was easily bowled over by a middle-aged fraudster. I felt sad for her. And sadder that I would have to impart my next bit of news.

There was another woman. Her DNA was found in the bedsheets.

"How long did this go on?" I asked.

"Right up until the process server came that day at the mansion, I thought we were together. That's why I went over to his place so we could talk."

I made a show of studying the document in front of me although I knew what my next question was because I wanted her last answer to resonate. In the social contract between people in conversation, the last statement is accepted as truth unless the speaker modifies it or the listener challenges it. It felt like trapping my client through cross-examination, but sometimes I had to do that because if I didn't, the other attorney would.

"Prior to that day, when was the last time you had sex with him?"

"It had been a few weeks. I didn't think anything of it, at first. I was busy hustling new accounts, and he always seemed to be unavailable. He said he was meeting people, that he was exploring new opportunities for the business, and he didn't want to tell me about his plans because he didn't want to get my hopes up. Now that I think about it, he began to change right after we signed the paperwork."

"I have a difficult question for you. Could he have been involved with another woman?"

In the pause that followed, the air between us was electric with hurt, humiliation, and anger. I don't know if it was hers or mine or both.

When she responded to my news, Esme spoke quietly. "Are you saying that he slept with someone else just before he was murdered? How can they know that?"

"I'm sorry. There was DNA from another woman in the bedsheets. I was hoping you might know who she was."

"The maid? She came every day."

For all I knew, Tanzini slept with whoever was available. There are some people who engage in sex with strangers as casually as they would exchange small talk. "Could be."

The photos showed his body sprawled across the living room floor, wearing a suit. If his lover murdered him, she didn't do it in the aftermath of a liaison. He had dressed again for some reason. Perhaps he planned to go out. Then she killed him.

Or maybe the other woman didn't have anything to do with his death. Maybe after she left, someone else came to his apartment. I needed to watch the security footage from the foyer and building's back door to see who else had entered 123 Baywater St.

The expression on Esme's face went from confused to shattered. "I can't take any more of this."

She stood and walked out of the conference room, just as Yolanda returned from the café. Esme bent her head, hiding her face in a curtain of hair to stop Yolanda from asking her questions, and disappeared through the door. Yolanda dropped the bag she was carrying on her desk and followed Esme out.

Chapter Forty

RITA OSTEEN OPENED THE microwave door after the bell dinged. With her fingertips, she pulled the ready-made dinner from the rotating plate and set it on her white marble countertop. In the background, nighttime news droned from the small television mounted over the wet bar. There was an accident on the Bay Bridge. Protesters in Golden Gate Park were arrested. And a trial date had been set for yet another corrupt public official in the county's Department of Transportation.

Rita stopped what she was doing and turned to watch the story. What did this have to do with her? She had no dealings with the county, personally. They couldn't touch her.

As her dinner cooled, she set the table in the adjacent dining room. Whether she dined with others or alone, she was entitled to the best. Linen tablecloth. A linen napkin neatly folded. Silverware. Crystal goblets for water and wine. As she had done when she was married, she dressed for dinner wearing a smart suit or dress, high heels and freshly applied makeup. Just because she was alone now, there was no reason to reduce her standards even on the maid's day off.

She returned to the kitchen and peeled the plastic lid from the microwave dish. She spooned the contents onto a bone China plate. This was not the type of microwave dinner Rita ate every night as a young adult when she came home from the accounting firm, rubber chicken covered with a glutinous sauce accompanied by mushy vegetables. This was a gourmet meal, chicken Florentine with green beans and red peppers.

She carried the plate to the dining room. From the sideboard, she retrieved an opened bottle of white wine and refilled her glass. She slipped into her chair at the head of the table where her late husband once sat, the table his children had wanted to take from her, in the Victorian townhome they had tried to throw her out of.

But she was tougher than they anticipated, and she prevailed. The court upheld the will he had executed shortly after their marriage, leaving everything to her. Those children had been hateful, accusing her of being a gold digger. There were even suggestions she had murdered him, but they had no proof.

Rita deserved to inherit the entire estate. There were nurses, certainly, but he didn't want strangers tending to his personal care. It was too humiliating, he said. So she was the one who changed his diaper and cleaned him up while she choked down the urge to vomit.

His children got everything they deserved. Nothing.

She snapped the napkin open and draped it across her lap. She lifted a knife and fork and was about to cut into the chicken breast when she heard his name. Alfred Tanzini.

She leaned back in her chair so she could see the television through the open door. A studio photo of Al that had been poached from the business website was on the screen next to a one of Esme Castillo. That photo of Esme was not on the website. It must have been stolen from social media.

The reporter read from a script. "The DA's office announced today that it charged Esmeralda Castillo with the murder of Alfred Tanzini, her former business partner. Court records show there had been a falling out and that Mr. Tanzini had forced her from the business. No trial date has been set. And now, for the weather."

Al's murder had been solved. About time. Immediately after his body was found, the police came to inform Rita. She had merely told them the truth. The board of Esme Inc had been forced to remove one of the partners from the business because she had encouraged their employees to strike. The business was shaky already and now they had a crisis on their hands with no bakers. They had to hire unskilled labor on short notice to fill the orders. When Esme was removed, she began a competing enterprise, so they had no choice but to file a lawsuit against her. The court issued a restraining order, but Esme had violated it that very day. She was emotional, unstable, obsessed with Al, and Rita did not know what she was capable of doing. It was the truth.

Two birds, one stone.

Esme got what she deserved. Just like Rita's stepchildren.

Rita lifted her wine glass and took a long, slow sip. This was a very good vintage, paired perfectly with her dinner.

The cell phone next to her plate rang. Samuel Porter's name appeared on the screen. Rita set her glass down and picked up the cell. She pulled her clip earring off, put the device to her ear and pushed back into the armchair. "Samuel, good to hear from you. It must be late where you are."

"I just got out of a committee meeting. I'm sorry, Rita, but I'm following instructions. What is the status with Esme's Casa airport café?"

Rita toyed with her fork, contemplating the most diplomatic language she could use.

"As you know, we have the contract. However, Ms. Castillo has caused problems for us in court. As a result of which, the judge appointed a professional business manager to supervise the bakery until there is a trial to determine who will ultimately gain control of the company."

"How long will that take?"

"The trial date is next year."

"Can't you get the business manager to push the café through?"

Rita had considered the idea and dismissed it. Al had squandered all the money she'd put into the business, living the high life. There were no funds to pay a contractor for the airport café build-out. That would cost hundreds of thousands of dollars. Rita could put up her own money, but if Esme Castillo won control of the business, why should Rita risk her own capital? After all this litigation, Esme wouldn't be inclined to repay her. Then, there would be another lawsuit that would eat up the profits.

"Let me see what I can do. I'll get back to you."

"I'm sorry, Rita, but we only have two weeks. If we don't see progress by then, the committee has decided to drop the project and move on to something else."

"I understand," Rita said. "Time is of the essence."

"So it is. I hope you have some good news for me, soon. Have a good evening."

Rita looked at the phone's small screen as the call disconnected. Then she tapped the icon for young Mr. Lewis.

Chapter Forty-One

PAUL LEWIS WAS BELLY up to a bar, ordering a round of beer for his tablemates when the phone in his pocket buzzed. He had stopped off at his Castro Street apartment, took a quick shower, and changed into a beige silk short-sleeved shirt, faded jeans, and loafers, no socks, before he headed out to meet his friends.

The place had a hip vintage vibe, with an antique bar and tables, leather chairs and subdued lighting. On dark walls hung framed prints of old European masters that had been embellished amusingly. Mona Lisa with piercings. The little dog in Arnolfini's wedding portrait lifted his leg. Holbein's Henry VIII held a hamburger in his fist.

A great guffaw came from the table where Paul's friends waited for their drinks. He was missing the fun. The bartender had just finished uncapping the six bottles of beer he had ordered and was waiting to be paid. Paul slid his charge card across the countertop and the bartender swiftly concluded the transaction.

Paul stuffed the receipt and the card into one pocket as he pulled the phone out of the other. The caller ID said Rita Osteen.

Not now. I just got here.

Paul heard his name called. He turned and saw one of his friends gesture as if he was holding an imaginary bottle of beer over his mouth. They were impatient.

Rita Osteen had the firm on retainer. That meant she expected Paul to answer his phone any time of the day or night. That also meant when he answered, he could bill her for his time. It was clients like her, paying like clockwork, who financed his lifestyle and kept the Hag and his father off his back.

Paul carried the bottles over to the table, then shook his phone so his friends could see he had to take a call. These were the guys that he'd gone to school with. Two of them were now lawyers and the other three worked in the financial district.

"Sorry, guys," Paul said. "I've got to take this."

"Ka-ching!" One called out, pretending to pull down a cash register arm.

"At least I have a job." Not everyone did. Anderson and Sinclair, two of their gang, had walked out of their jobs and were hiding from the authorities. No one had heard from them in days.

"Working for daddy," his friend retorted, then slapped his neighbor's elbow as the boys howled with laughter.

Paul extended his middle finger, then stepped out into the street to return the call. When she answered, he said, "Sorry, Mrs. Osteen. I couldn't get to my phone in time."

"Have you seen the news?" she asked.

"Not today. Is there something I should know?"

"The police arrested Esme Castillo for Al's murder."

Paul felt like he was going to faint. He leaned against the cold stone wall to keep from falling. The aroma of gourmet baked pizza drifted on a warm breeze from a pizzeria down the street. It made him nauseas.

"Where are you?" she demanded.

She must've heard the street sounds, cars driving by, and people laughing.

Paul didn't like his clients knowing too much about him. If Rita Osteen had any idea that Paul enjoyed leisure activities at any time, she would accuse him of neglecting her business. "Just on my way home," Paul said.

"Am I interrupting?" she asked, sarcastically.

"Never, Mrs. Osteen. I'm at your disposal." That was his father's motto. He always said the clients paid a fortune for the fantasy that you were their servants.

"Good," she said. "But what I want to know is, how does this affect the shares? Isn't there some law that says murderers are not allowed to benefit from their crime?"

The buzzing noise in Paul's head blotted out her voice. "I'm sorry. I didn't catch that. A bus just drove by."

"Can't you go somewhere quiet?"

Paul peered into the pub window. His friends were on their feet, guzzling the dregs of their beers, getting ready to leave. If he ended the call and went inside to rejoin them, by the time he got home there would be a message from his father rebuking him for blowing off Mrs. Osteen.

"Let me call you right back," he said.

His friends filed out of the pub door, laughing, and pushing each other. Honestly, they had not matured much since school.

"We're grabbing a bite to eat," Andy said. "Are you coming?"

Paul shook his head. He didn't know if it was ethical to tell Andy about the charges. Rita was his client, so technically anything she said to him would be covered by attorney-client privilege. He couldn't even imply that a client had told him publicly known information. Since the charges were on the news, Andy would find out anyway.

"There's been a development," Paul said. "Look at the news and give me a ring if you want to talk later."

Paul had approached Andy on behalf of Rita Osteen about stalling the contract. Andy agreed, for a price. So the contract sat in the bottom of Andy's inbox, ignored until he got the word that it was time to let it go through. But then the District Attorney's Office came snooping around, and Andy got cold feet. He'd quit his job.

Andy was worried he would get busted for bribery, but Paul told him that because nothing had been done, he couldn't get into trouble – a lie. Paul was worn out with Andy's whining and told him the lie to shut him up.

"Have fun," Paul said.

He walked back to his apartment. When he was inside, he lit a joint, flopped into a chair, took a hit, and held his breath. The phone in his pocket rang again. When he looked at the screen, he saw that it was her. He needed to get into the right frame of mind before he answered, so he tossed the phone onto a side table, unanswered.

The smoke held in his lungs made him choke. He exhaled slowly, trying to capture every molecule of THC nirvana before allowing it to escape, then got a beer from the refrigerator.

He called Rita Osteen back. "Just got home. Run that past me again."

Her voice was sharp. Mrs. Osteen did not like to be kept waiting. "Remember the problems with my husband's estate? How his kids accused me of murder? They said that because I murdered their father, I couldn't inherit. There's some law, what did you call it, the Slayer's Rule?"

He remembered. The late Mr. Osteen's children had claimed she overdosed their father with his pain medication so that he couldn't change his will back after he disinherited her. Accusations are not evidence, and they had no proof. No proof of a new will. No proof that she killed him. The postmortem said the drugs in his system were not excessive. The old man died of cancer.

But because of the accusation, Paul had billed Rita Osteen for several hours for researching the Slayer Rule. The bill was heavily padded. He'd only needed thirty minutes to verify that what he'd learned in law school was still the state of the law. She read her bills carefully, so she had reason to believe he would be able to answer her question.

"So you want to know whether Esmeralda Castillo forfeits her shares in the corporation because she was charged with Al's murder?" Paul asked.

"I always knew you were a bright boy."

Rita Osteen was a skank. She had married that old man for his money and convinced him that his children were conspiring against him. Shortly after their wedding, she got him to leave everything to her.

"It doesn't apply in this case," Paul said. "The Slayer Rule only applies to probate law, when someone inherits money because of a death. It doesn't apply to corporate law."

"But Esme inherited Al's shares. It's the same thing."

"It isn't. I'm sorry, Mrs. Osteen. Esme wasn't Al Tanzini's heir either under a will or because of kinship. It's a business deal. She received the shares because of the language in the corporation agreement."

"And who's to blame for that?"

He closed his eyes and took a deep, slow breath. He had drafted the corporation agreement, using boilerplate clauses that are included in every corporate agreement.

The joint in Paul's hand had gone cold. He really wanted another hit, but he'd have to wait until he got her off the phone. She would certainly overhear him sparking a lighter and sucking on the doobie.

"You read the agreement before you signed it, Mrs. Osteen."

"How was I to know Al would get himself murdered?"

Paul stared at the ceiling. Could he convince Judge Rediger to set aside that clause in the agreement because of changed circumstances? Could he convincingly argue that Rita Osteen only agreed to the stock redistribution in the event of a shareholder's death because she didn't anticipate a shareholder's death? Yeah, sure, he could argue it. But even Judge Rediger, who had ruled for him at every opportunity, making Paul wonder whether she was another of his father's so-called "friends," would laugh out loud.

However, insulting Mrs. Osteen's idea would not be conducive to an amicable attorney-client relationship.

Paul said, "My feeling is that Judge Rediger has spent all the time on this case that she intends to before the trial. She's already ruled that there are issues of fact that need to be resolved. Besides, we can argue that Esme murdered Al, but it has not been established as a matter of law."

"What do you need to establish that?"

"She needs to be convicted."

"How long is that going to take?"

"Anywhere from a few months from now, if she insists on her speedy trial rights, until a year or two in the future, if her attorney stalls for time."

"Do you mean that I need to litigate who owns this company with the woman who killed my business partner? What exactly do I have to do to get rid of her?"

"Make her an offer," Paul suggested.

"She turned down the last one. What's the point?"

"People wear down over time. They get tired of litigation, the disruption to their lives, the hassle of lawyers calling them, the endless paperwork, and going to court. Sooner or later, they just want to get it over. She might be ready now."

All of Paul's friends were out partying. But here he was, alone in his apartment, straining his diplomatic skills to keep this woman happy, while the joint he kept staring at sat in an ashtray, luring him to a pleasant alternate universe where clients and cases did not exist.

"Mrs. Osteen, you made a very shrewd investment when you bought into Esme Inc, and that is because you're an experienced businesswoman and you understand how money works. If you want a quick resolution, I imagine that Esme could use cash right now. She's going to need to hire a criminal defense attorney. Or you could play the long game, continue to litigate this case, and see what happens."

"We'll see about that," she said, her voice icy. Then she hung up without saying goodbye.

Chapter Forty-Two

BRUNO FERNANDEZ WAS BACK in New Jersey, sitting at the small kitchen table he once shared with his wife. It was their first purchase after they were married. A simple wooden table, now scarred from years of use. Before him was a plate with two eggs, two pieces of bacon, and two pieces of toast lightly buttered. A six-ounce glass of orange juice was positioned within easy reach, next to a steaming cup of black coffee.

As he waited for his meal to cool, he opened his cell phone. A notification dropped onto the screen. There had been a development with Al Tanzini. The young woman who had been his business partner was charged with his murder.

That was too bad. She seemed like a nice girl.

Chapter Forty-Three

AFTER ESME LEFT, I went back into my office and began watching the building surveillance video. There were one hundred and eighteen apartments in that building, which meant a flurry of people went in and out of the foyer throughout the day. Alfred Tanzini had been murdered sometime after 5:45 p.m., the time when he'd returned to 123 Baywater St.

The most likely candidate for the other woman, and potential suspect, was Rita Osteen.

I found the video showing Tanzini coming into the building, stopping for a friendly word at the concierge desk, and then disappearing out of frame as he headed to the elevator bank. A woman with a small dog came in shortly after him, and she chatted cheerfully with the doorman. It appeared that she was one of the residents in the building. Although I noted her arrival, I needed to focus now on the most likely suspects. It would be someone who knew him from his business dealings in San Francisco or from his earlier life. I was looking for Rita Osteen and Bruno Fernandez, the only suspects I had at this t ime.

Esme appeared about five minutes later. As she walked across the foyer to the elevators, a small balding man with glasses strode past her on his way out. She appeared again approximately twenty minutes later when she left.

During the next couple of hours, no one entered the building through the front doors except for the small balding man who had been escorted by the concierge into the elevator and who left again soon thereafter. Several more people departed, some alone, some in pairs. It appeared they were going out for the evening.

It was possible that the murderer had hidden in the building during the day and left in the evening, falling into step with a resident as if they were on a date. But I didn't see anyone that looked like Rita Osteen or Bruno Fernandez.

I fast-forwarded through the video from the service door entrance in the back of the building. Throughout the day, maids, cooks, waiters, concierge, and maintenance men came to work through that entrance. The employees got in with a key card. When deliveries were made, the driver would buzz the doorbell, and someone would let them i n.

One thing struck me as odd. At approximately 6:35 p.m., a large man wearing a ball cap and coveralls, like a handyman or plumber or electrician, left through the back door.

That was late in the day for a repairman to be leaving.

He was the same size and shape as Bruno Fernandez.

"Got a minute?" It was Quinn standing in my office threshold, clutching a stack of paper to her chest. She had arrived at the office shortly after Esme left, following an early morning class, and set up in the conference room to review the evidence the DA had sent over the day before.

I tensed at first, the reaction that I'd adopted since the night she took umbrage with my family history. After a short moment of reflection, I realized she didn't have the tone in her voice that suggested an agenda.

Hopeful for a détente, I answered. "Sure. What's up?"

She put the papers on my desk and pulled a visitor's chair in close so she could sift through the pages for me. "Rita Osteen. It took a while for me to track her down, but this is what I found. She's a widow. That's where her money came from. She married a rich old guy a few years before he died. He left her everything and cut his kids out of the will. His kids sued, claiming that she had asserted undue influence over him. And they claimed there was another will that he had executed just before he died, leaving them the estate. But that will disappeared. They also claimed that she killed him, but the coroner said he died because of the cancer he had been battling for a long time."

"How long ago was that?"

"Just a couple of years."

"Do you have time to track down her kids? Get more details from them? I don't want you neglecting your studies."

Quinn perked up. "I'd love to."

Chapter Forty-Four

QUINN DROVE TO FISHERMAN'S Wharf in Maureen's bright yellow BMW with the top down. It was a gorgeous summer day, a rare thing in San Francisco if the prior summer, her first year in The City, was any indication. In a few weeks, fog would roll in and remain until fall.

As she drove through the streets, she traveled through the sounds and smells of San Francisco. Cable car bells clanging. Teenagers laughing on their school lunch break. Seagulls cawing. Hot dogs broiling in corner stands. Salt air. Fish. Lots and lots of fish.

This was her first solo witness interview. She wore jeans, so as not to appear intimidating, and carried the backpack Maureen and Jake had given her. Not that she needed to bring paper or pens – she had a photographic memory and would recall every detail of the interview – but carrying a prop made her feel more authoritative.

Finding Rita Osteen's stepchildren was easier than Quinn thought it would be. Marigold Osteen, the oldest daughter, worked as a host in a high-end restaurant near Fisherman's Wharf.

When Quinn arrived at the restaurant and introduced herself, Marigold asked her to wait a few minutes until she could take a break. It was the end of the lunch hour. Quinn sat in the reception as she watched waiters in black slacks and long-sleeved button-down shirts silently ferry charge cards to the host stand and go back to the tables with receipts. Through the doorway, Quinn could see linen-covered tables topped with glittering glassware and the besuited diners speaking quietly. Behind them were floor-to-ceiling windows overlooking the San Francisco Bay with the Golden Gate Bridge and Marin County in the distance.

This was the view Diego Rivera had painted when he visited San Francisco before the bridge had been built. Elizabeth Shaughnessy, Quinn's great-great-grandmother, had taken him out for the day in her chauffeur-driven open-air Rolls Royce. The story goes that when they reached this spot, he shouted for the driver to stop, climbed out of the car, and set up his easel. While he and Lizzie dined on a picnic of champagne and freshly caught crab, he painted the scene. When the picture was done, he gave it to Lizzie saying, "A small picture *per una bella dama*—for a beautiful lady."

The painting was Lizzie's most prized possession. It hung beside her bed long after Lizzie died. When Maureen inherited the mansion, she sold the painting, the antiques, and the art to fund the foundation she named after Lizzie.

If Maureen hadn't sold the painting, Quinn supposed she would have inherited it someday. She wasn't sure she wanted it. She felt like a pirate, like she didn't belong to this family, no matter what the DNA and the bathroom mirror said. She didn't feel entitled to claim them as her own and she wasn't sure she wanted to.

She hadn't really made a decision to join Maureen's family. When her adopted parents died, she wanted to know more about her birth family – but gaining knowledge about them was a very different thing than being dragged into the fold. Yet that is exactly what happened. She came to San Francisco for a visit, ended up living in Maureen's condo, going to law school, and working in Maureen's office, volunteering for Maureen's nonprofit, without having made the conscious decision that this was what she wanted.

There were times when the glamour and the money and the privilege of the Shaughnessy family dazzled her. She would have loved to have known Lizzie. But there were things she just couldn't accept. Like the exploitation of Chinese laborers. Like the fact she was born from an incestuous rape.

Marigold appeared in front of Quinn. In stark contrast to her name, which suggested a cheerful bright yellow person, Marigold, dressed all in black, was tall, model thin, heavily made-up, with long thick chestnut hair expertly cut to frame her heart-shaped face.

"Things are slowing down," Marigold said. "Let's go for a walk. I need to get out of here."

Out on the streets, they stopped at a coffee stand where Marigold ordered a skinny latte, which she said was her lunch, and Quinn got an herbal tea. They walked beyond Ghirardelli Square and found benches facing the beach. The breeze lifted silvery waves on the bay, and bright white sails flashed as they floated across the water's surface.

"This is my favorite place to go when I need some time to myself," Marigold said. She took a sip of her coffee. "You want to know about my family, is that right? Spoiler alert. We're really screwed up. You have no idea."

"Try me," Quinn said. She still couldn't get her head around the fact that Frank, the father of her biological mother, Maureen, was her father, too. Most days she didn't think about it – it was too big to comprehend.

"Did you have a question, or should I just start talking?"

Maureen always said to let the witness tell their story – don't interrupt. They know best what is important. "Just start talking," Quinn said. "I'll ask questions later, if I need to."

Marigold brushed away a wisp of chestnut hair that had fallen into her mouth. "Okay, try this on. Our mother died years ago. Suicide. She couldn't handle my father's womanizing, and she was afraid that he'd dump her for a younger woman."

"Why didn't she just divorce him?"

"She was a society lady, raised by rich parents for one purpose, and that was to marry well. When they died, they left all their money to their sons because they reasoned that the daughters had made good marriages and didn't need it. So any money we had belonged to my dad. He'd earned it. He was brilliant in finance. She was afraid that she'd lose badly in a divorce because she didn't have money for high-powered lawyers, but he did. And she drank a lot, so she was depressed. They both drank, but she was strung out on diet pills, too. Between the booze and the pills, she was crazy."

Marigold recited these facts clinically as if she had read them from a textbook.

When she fell silent, Quinn said, "That must've been hard. How old were you when she died?"

"Sixteen. Shuttled off to boarding school, preparing for that good marriage, too. Within a year, my father married the witch."

"Rita?"

Marigold laughed. "Yeah, his *personal assistant*. What a cliché! She had wormed her way in a couple years before my mother died when my parents were pretty much living apart. After he married Rita, things changed. He cashed out our trust accounts, gave my sisters and me enough money for each of us to buy a condo, and promised that we'd get the rest when he passed away. He said he had found better investments for the funds. Rita was his financial advisor before she became his personal assistant, so we knew that she had her hands on his money."

"Were you still in contact with him?"

"Less and less. A few days before he died, a nurse called and said he wanted to see me. I had no idea he was so sick that he had a full-time nurse. Rita had left for a few days, checked herself into a spa for a facelift. When I arrived, I was horrified to see how sick he was – with tubes coming out of him everywhere. He said he was sorry. He even cried. Can you believe that? He said that she had got him to change his will, cutting my sisters and me out, and that he was going to fix it. The nurse was there. She heard everything."

"Did he change his will?"

Marigold crushed her emptied paper cup. "He did! The night before he died. The lawyer came to the house, and the nurse saw him sign it. But the will disappeared, and his lawyer lied about it. The nurse thinks Rita killed my dad and got rid of the new will."

"Was that just suspicion, or did she have any evidence?"

"Evidence? You mean like, right after my dad died, when the nurse started collecting the medical equipment, she discovered all his medication was gone. Rita told her she'd flushed the drugs down the toilet because she was worried that if she threw them away, an addict would find them in the garbage. But the nurse figured that if someone counted how many drugs were left, then they'd know Rita had given him an overdose. He was still lying in his bed. The undertakers hadn't come for him, and suddenly Rita's tidying up? Strikes me as a little weird. Like since when did she lift a finger?"

Quinn had found the lawsuit in the court archives. The daughters of Mr. Osteen had sued Rita for their share of the inheritance. There was a trial. Quinn knew they'd lost, but she wanted to hear Marigold's story. "What happened?"

"We couldn't afford an attorney. Rita had Paul Lewis. He convinced the judge that our testimony wasn't good enough to prove there had been a new will, so we got nothing. Not only that, but we also owed her for his attorney fees. So now she's living in the Victorian and I'm hustling tables."

"That totally sucks."

"It sure does." Marigold glanced at her watch. She stood. "I hope the witch gets what she deserves."

Chapter Forty-Five

THE NEXT MORNING, YOLANDA, Quinn, and I were sitting around the table in the conference room, with coffee and muffins before us, as Quinn gave her report about the Marigold Osteen interview. Gerry was back on the couch with his own plate of muffins, mug of coffee, and paperback.

I got up and moved to the whiteboard, uncapped a marker, and wrote "suspects" at the top.

"Rita Osteen is a gold digger," Yolanda said. "She might have killed Tanzini thinking she would get his shares. She's all about the money."

I wrote Rita Osteen's name at the top of the list.

"Bruno Fernandez," Quinn said. "Didn't you guys say he threatened Tanzini at court, pretending to shoot him with a finger gun?"

"We saw it," Yolanda said. "He hates Tanzini. When he came into the office and talked to us, he didn't seem happy we couldn't give him quick satisfaction."

I wrote his name on the board, too.

"What about Henry Watkins?" Quinn asked. "Something fishy was going on between him and Tanzini."

I wagged my head. Unlikely, I thought, but now was not the time to eliminate suspects. Now was the time to broaden the search. I wrote his name on the board, too.

"Yeah, but Henry Watkins was murdered," Yolanda said. "Same M.O. Maybe there was a third guy involved in whatever Henry and Tanzini were up to, someone we don't know about."

I chewed on the marker cap absentmindedly while considering Yolanda's theory.

"Don't do that," she said. "One of these days, you're going to stick the wrong end in your mouth and get ink all over."

I quit chewing and wrote "Mr. X" on the board.

Gerry was now leaning in the conference room doorway. "Aren't you forgetting about someone, Counselor?"

We exchanged looks.

"Just because some guy went to law school doesn't mean he's harmless."

"Paul Lewis," I said. "If what Quinn learned is true, he defrauded the court. He could lose his license, maybe go to jail."

"I don't see that guy getting his hands dirty," Yolanda said.

"Blood washes off," Gerry said.

I wrote Paul Lewis's name on the board. "Let's take a deeper dive into this."

On the right side of the board, I began writing questions, reading them aloud as I went along.

"Number one. Did Paul Lewis write a new will cutting out Osteen's daughters? Number two. The new will, if there was one, disappeared. Who destroyed it? Number three. Paul Lewis testified there was not a new will – for Rita Osteen's benefit."

"How do you figure?" Yolanda asked.

"When Lewis testified there wasn't a new will, the old will, leaving everything to Rita Osteen, remained in effect. She got everything. Number four. A few years later, Paul Lewis drafted the corporation papers for Esme Inc. Rita must have chosen him because she was the only person he knew before Esme Inc was formed. Number five. Paul Lewis represented Alfred Tanzini, Rita Osteen, and Esme. Inc against Esme Castillo. Is Paul Lewis conflicted because he had been involved in drafting the corporate papers, just like he would have been conflicted if he lied about Osteen's will?"

Quinn, having recently taken a legal ethics class posed the next question. "Who does Paul Lewis owe a duty of loyalty to?"

"Rita Osteen," Yolanda said.

I drew an arrow from Lewis's name to Rita's.

"And himself," I said, drawing a star by his name.

Chapter Forty-Six

YOLANDA BUZZED ME ON the intercom. "Vivian Thandi on line one."

"Thanks." I took a deep breath before picking up the handset. "Good morning, Vivian."

"Quick question," she said. "What was your client's relationship with Henry Watkins?"

I guffawed. "That's not how this works, Viv. You know that. I don't aid the prosecution's case. And I don't divulge my client's confidences."

"I take it you haven't spoken to her yet about him."

She was right about that. I had no reason to.

Vivian went on. "Henry Watkins was murdered in his apartment with the same M.O. as Alfred Tanzini."

"So you said in our last meeting."

"Mr. Watkins was an assistant contracts administrator for the San Francisco County Department of Transportation."

I knew all this. "Okay."

"He placed a call to your client on what we believe is the night of his death. They spoke for approximately eight minutes. After that, he spoke to someone else with a private number for approximately twelve minutes. That was the last phone call he made. I'm giving this information to you because it's potentially exculpatory material. If the person he spoke to last killed him, your client may be in the clear for Tanzini's murder because of the similar MO. And if your client has any idea who he spoke to after her, that would greatly assist in our investigation. I'm emailing you the data. Hope to hear back from you soon." Then she disconnected.

This was news.

Generally, the DA's office dumps potentially exculpatory material – that which tended to show the defendant was not guilty – on the defense just before the trial. The late disclosure is usually blamed on getting lost in the paperwork. A jaundiced defense attorney might believe that there was a philosophy of sandbagging the defendant until the last moment, hoping they'd take a plea deal. But as a former DA who was a stooge of police corruption that resulted in hiding exculpatory evidence, I knew that it wasn't always an evil ulterior motive at work – at least not in the DA's office.

Vivian and I had gone the distance in the Tony Paredes trial, and I had won. Which meant that she wasted a big chunk of her time. Maybe this early disclosure was Vivian's attempt to cut her losses. If we went to trial, and I vindicated Esme as I had Tony, Vivian would have wasted another great chunk of her time.

And her win-loss record would be damaged again. Before the Tony Paredes trial, she had won 72 trials and lost one. The one case she'd lost was actually a mistrial because the defendant committed suicide during jury deliberations.

Tony's acquittal was her first real loss.

Maybe she didn't want another one.

I whirled around in my chair to face my computer screen. The inbox dinged and Vivian's email appeared. The attached cell phone analysis showed the call to Esme and then another to a private number.

I hit the intercom button. "Yolanda, how quick can you get Esme in here?"

Twenty-eight minutes later, Esme and Yolanda were sitting on the oxblood leather couch in my office.

I printed the news site stories about the discovery of Henry Watkins' body. The first report did not identify him, but a few days later, after his family had been notified, he was named. The stories said he was found when the police made a welfare check. His coworkers had grown concerned after he failed to come into the office.

I handed Esme and Yolanda each a copy of the news stories. After they read them and looked up at me, I then gave them the cell phone data with the call from Henry Watkins to Esme Castillo highlighted. "It looks like you talked to him the night he died."

Esme slumped into the couch.

My office was so quiet I could hear people talking and laughing on the street below. The sidewalks were full of office workers going to, or coming back from, lunch. I suddenly realized I was hungry.

"Oh," she said, drawing out the word. "That guy."

Yolanda twisted around to look into Esme's face. "What guy?" she asked pointedly.

"This is the guy I saw in Al's apartment once. Then this guy – Henry – called me a few days ago on my cell."

"How did he get your number?" I asked.

"It was on the website, the number to call for deliveries."

"What did he want?"

"He said that he had forgotten some document in Al's apartment, and he needed to get it back. He wondered if I had a key."

Yolanda jumped in. "Why would you have a key?"

"I didn't! It's not like we were living together. This Henry guy just hoped that someone from the bakery would have a second key to Al's place."

Yolanda was my person in charge of common sense whereas I thought like a lawyer, so I often had her sit in on client interviews. But here she was getting a little too proprietary with the facts.

I held up a hand to get their attention. "Did he tell you what the document was?"

"I asked, but he wouldn't say."

"Do you know who he would call next?"

"My guess is Rita Osteen."

Chapter Forty-Seven

DIXON VAUGHN SETTLED BACK into his kitchen table chair and smiled. He had her now.

Scooter had just returned from the city building permits office with a copy of Maureen Gould's application for the remodel of her Pacific Heights palace.

Scooter crossed the kitchen in his high-top sneakers, opened Dixon's fridge, studied the contents, and pulled out a can of beer.

Dixon sneered. "Help yourself, Scooter."

The idiot didn't get the jibe. "Don't call me that. My name is Scott."

"I'll call you what I like. You're drinking my beer. It's eleven in the morning."

"It's happy hour somewhere," Scooter answered, pulling the flip top. He threw back his head and chugged half the can, then threw himself into the chair opposite Dixon.

Dixon ignored him. He turned over a page and went on reading. He had known something was hinky. She inherited the place only last year, and within a matter of months, she had applied for, and received, her permit and the work had been done. Normal people, those who weren't rich and influential, waited years for a permit. But she'd had extensive work done. The heating system, the roof, the electrical system, and the plumbing had to be replaced. Additional restrooms were added. The kitchen was remodeled. And get that! There was an elevator that had to be replaced.

The permit application had been signed off by one of the officials who was under investigation for taking bribes. Two contractors had taken plea deals to testify against him.

Dixon smiled.

"What's that grin about?" Scooter demanded. "The bitch bribed them. Must have. There's no way this permit got approved that quick."

"Maybe it wasn't her. Maybe it was her contractor."

Dixon scowled. "Doesn't matter if it was her or her underlings. She is the privileged elite who broke the rules because she believes they don't apply to her. The Rights Men will love this."

Scooter belched. "Who's the Rights Men?"

"My audience, you idiot."

Chapter Forty-Eight

I WAS BACK AT my desk, researching Rita Osteen when Quinn walked into my office carrying her open laptop. After Esme and Bebe had left, she moved to the conference room to continue studying. Yolanda had gone back to her desk, working on a spreadsheet of the money that had flowed in and out of Esme Inc.

"Mom, did you know about this?"

My shoulders hitched up. What other skeletons were in my ancestors' closet that my daughter could harangue me for?

Best to get it over with.

"What's that?" I asked.

"The Rights of Man podcast."

Not him again. "Show me."

She came around my desk, set the laptop down in front of me, and hit "play."

A John Sousa march blared while an amateurish title graphic swirled to life. A few seconds later, the image cut to Dixon Vaughn sitting in front of a camera with an expensive microphone hanging above him. "Welcome brothers! Thank you for joining me, Dixon Vaughn, your host as we fight the good fight for the rights of man."

Chat room messages scrolled up the page, slowly at first, with men stating their name and saying hello. It sped up as he finished his introduction with "Booya!" "Tell it like it is!" and "Dixon's our man!"

I felt sick.

"Today's episode is about our old friend, Maureen Gould, Queen of the Femicult, and how the rules that you and I live by, brothers, don't apply to her."

I turned to Quinn. "What's he talking about?"

"The mansion." She pointed at the screen. "Watch."

Vaughn held up a file. "This woman bribed a city official to get a permit for remodeling her palace. And here's the proof."

I slammed my palm onto the desk. "What the –! Absolutely not!"

He then proceeded to detail how quickly my permit process had progressed, pointing out that the official who had signed off was now under investigation for bribery.

I picked up my cell phone and hit speed dial on my contractor's number. It went to voicemail. "Victor, we need to talk."

I had just hung up on my call to Victor when Yolanda buzzed the intercom. "Ms. Ullman on line one."

Ms. Ullman was the administrator at the Ullman Family Trust that had approved the only grant I'd received for the foundation.

I put my warmest voice on and answered. "Good afternoon, Ms. Ullman. It's good to hear from you."

"Maybe not so good," she said apologetically. "I'm sorry, Ms. Gould, but we need to pull the award."

I felt like a rubber band had tightened around my skull. I closed my eyes and took a deep breath. "Because?"

"The permit issue. We've been keeping an eye on that podcaster since he began targeting you. This news is devastating. I know, it's terribly unfair. But you understand, we have a limited amount of money, and we need to ensure that the community is best served. If we distribute the funds to you, and you're caught up in some kind of scheme – I know you didn't do anything wrong, let me assure you – but if you're caught up anyway, our donors would be furious with us. Our sources could dry up. It would damage all the very worthwhile projects we help to fund. Again, I am so sorry."

The foundation needed that grant. "Is there any way I can convince you to put the money aside. I hope to get this straightened out quickly – in a matter of a few days."

Her voice was warm when she replied. "And I hope so, too. But how likely is that? Those corruption investigations can linger for years. Look, do your best. And I hope to see your application for the next funding cycle."

I realized too late that promising a result with a few quick calls implied that I had an inside road, which meant influence and was probably the wrong defense in a corruption allegation.

It was far more likely that because of my family's prominence, my pet project was going to be shoved to the bottom of the pile if only so government officials could prove that they weren't playing favorites.

I wanted to cry. But it wasn't scheduled on my calendar.

Chapter Forty-Nine

VICTOR NEVER RETURNED MY message. I called him twice more that afternoon, and he didn't pick up. I didn't leave additional messages. He would have seen my number turn up on his caller ID and, if he checked, he would have heard the one message I'd left. The circumstantial evidence suggested he didn't want to talk to me.

It was Quinn's night to cook. She prepared several vegetarian Indian dishes that filled the condo with exotic spicy aromas while I took a long bath. The atmosphere between Quinn and me was stilted since the evening when she confronted me with the source of the family's wealth. I found myself watching my words, lest I give her an excuse to attack. Not that Quinn made a habit of it, but my mother was hypercritical, which had made me into a closet overeater. As I got fatter, she harangued me about that.

The overeating went away when my mother dumped me in the girls' home, fourteen and pregnant. The nuns were strict about food. There was no chance to sneak into the pantry and steal a bag of cookies or chips. But I still needed the release. When I overate, the act of putting something into my mouth transported me – if only for a moment – from reality and I'd felt like I was wrapped in a gauzy white light.

In place of overeating, I started cutting my arms. The sharp pain sent me to another place, darker than overeating, but away from the reality that I couldn't bear.

Ironically, the few times I saw my mother during a brief home visit, she was pleased with my weight loss, having no idea what I did to myself.

Scars now crossed my arms. I hadn't cut in years, but when I was stressed, the scars would burn, and I would rub them raw.

After my bath, I changed into a soft fleece sweatshirt and yoga pants. I emerged from the bathroom just before I expected Jake to come home.

When he arrived, he walked into the kitchen with Germaine Greer purring on his broad shoulder, and said sincerely, "Something smells good."

Quinn stirred a pot of something colorful and blushed. At least there was someone she liked in the family.

Was that how healthy families worked? Alliances changing as shared experiences affected each member differently? I'd ask Yolanda when I got a chance.

I grabbed a bottle of white wine from the fridge, then took it to the table, snagging a corkscrew on the way. "Business slowing down?"

He shrugged. "I wish. But I got off early tonight. How was your day?"

"Dixon Vaughn did another podcast. He claims I bribed someone to speed up the Foundation's building permit process. I called Victor, but he didn't pick up. What's going on?"

Jake gave me a frown. "I can't talk about it."

A no comment that was as good as a yes.

"What? Is Victor being investigated?"

"If Victor is being investigated, I would have disclosed that I have a conflict of interest so the file would have been assigned to another assistant. You know the drill."

"So Victor is being investigated."

"I didn't say that."

"You didn't have to. What does that mean for my permit? All the work is done. The city signed off on the inspection. I'm in the clear, right? This can't come back on me."

Quinn turned away from the stove. "What do you mean, 'come back on you?' Could you get into trouble?"

It was the first time she looked me in the face in days. My heart fluttered with joy.

We both turned to Jake.

He took a deep breath, eased Germaine off his shoulder, and set her on the floor, something he never did. He usually let her walk on the counter because it bothered me. This night, he was affording me kindness because he knew something that was going to upset me.

I said, "I didn't bribe anyone so there is no evidence to support criminal charges against me. I'm worried about the Foundation. Can they rescind our occupancy certificate?"

Jake looked into my eyes meaningfully.

"Theoretically," I said.

"Theoretically," he said. "If the permit comes under review, they can rescind the occupancy certificate, and there would have to be another inspection before you could start the programs."

I muttered a profanity. We had moved the classes and daycare to other facilities at the Foundation's expense because of the security threat caused by Vaughn's podcasts, but this arrangement was unsustainable. Money was running out quickly.

"Is that a big deal?" Quinn asked.

Jake said, "If there was a review, and another inspection, the mansion would go to the bottom of the pile so that the city offices couldn't be accused of giving your mom preferential treatment. The inspection would be extremely thorough. Victor does good work, so passing the inspection and getting another occupancy permit shouldn't be a problem."

I groaned. I had grant applications pending in which I claimed we were open for business. We had just lost the Ullman grant. If the city revoked the occupancy permit, we'd have to shut down the classes. We couldn't provide daycare. All those mothers and children would be on their own. I had failed them.

"How long will that take?" Quinn asked.

"Months," I said.

"If we're lucky," Jake said.

Sickened, I pulled a chair out from the table and sat down.

Jake came over and stood behind me, rubbing my shoulders. "It'll be okay."

It might be okay. It might be a disaster. But there wasn't anything I could do about it now.

My thoughts immediately turned to Esme's case. As an adult, I replaced overeating and cutting myself with diving into my work. The truth was, I had problems, but in no way did they compare to Esme facing a murder charge. "Vivian called today."

"It's news to me," Jake said. "What did she want to talk about?"

"A murder. Someone killed a man who had business ties to Alfred Tanzini. Apparently, the victim was an official with the County Department of Transportation."

Jake grew very still. "What was his name?"

"Henry Watkins."

Jake gave my shoulders one last squeeze, grabbed his cell phone that he had left on the bar counter, and stalked to our bedroom.

"What was that about?" Quinn asked.

"I don't know," I said. "He'll tell me when he's ready."

I had plenty on my plate besides Jake's secretness. I needed to find out who killed Al Tanzini so I could vindicate Esme. That may, or may not, have something to do with

Henry Watkins' murder. Vivian was on a fishing expedition when she called me – hoping I could solve both crimes in one fell swoop. I didn't have as much faith as she did.

Plus, the Foundation was under attack from Dixon Vaughn. He was trying to intimidate me so I would quit helping women. His podcast, claiming I'd bribed my way through the permit process, had shut down the one grant I'd won. There was no point in applying for more until I had the issue resolved. Meanwhile, I had some donations to limp along with, and the occupancy permit hadn't been pulled yet, so I could continue to provide scaled-down programs until I had the permits and grants sorted.

Quinn brought out a couple of colorful, fragrant dishes, then returned to the kitchen.

"Do you want to help me plan a party?" I asked her.

"Sure," she said as she placed the next two dishes on the table. On her way by, she leaned in and gave me a kiss on the cheek.

Chapter Fifty

WE PLANNED A FUNDRAISER at the Foundation. To promote it, I enlisted Mickey Wong to do a Jackie Kennedy-style tour of the mansion for the television magazine she contributed to.

Mickey arrived on the appointed day, towing a camera person. We began in the foyer. The floor was tiled in a checkerboard of black-and-white marble. The walls and ceiling, as well as the rest of the mansion, had been painted a pale buttermilk color. I chose the color because I didn't want it to feel sterile. A gentle warmth would envelope the women and children who came to the Foundation.

Mickey was my height. Her thick black shoulder-length hair shimmered under the lights as she moved. She wore a black business suit with a black button-down shirt. A tiny microphone was clipped to her blazer, like the one clipped to my blouse. I didn't want to look like a powerful lawyer, but I was no Jackie Kennedy. Instead of a stylish dress or skirt ensemble, I wore a navy-blue silk blouse with matching trousers, and Elizabeth Shaughnessy's pearl necklace. The story wasn't about me. It was about the house.

Mickey looked into the camera lens and nodded. A little red light began to glow on the camera that was shouldered by a sturdy college-aged woman. I marveled at how Mickey looked into the camera like she was talking to another person. I'd burst into laughter if I tried.

"Today we're visiting the Shaughnessy mansion in Pacific Heights. Maureen Gould, the owner of the mansion, is guiding us." She turned to me. "Maureen, tell us about the mansion's history."

I'd memorized a short speech to get over my initial disorientation as we moved from reality into the surreal world of TV. "Thanks for joining me, Micky. The mansion was purchased by my great-grandfather, Black Jack Shaughnessy, after the 1906 earthquake." I pointed to a crack in the plaster work of the domed ceiling. "The mansion made it through, but as you can see it left a few cracks." I patted Mickey's arm reassuringly. "But don't worry, we made it just fine through the '89 shaker."

I rested a hand on the banister Elizabeth Shaughnessy had loved. "This was designed by my great-grandmother, Lizzie. I think it was her favorite part of the house."

I decided against talking about how it symbolized to her the family's achievement of the American dream, how we had gone from poor potato farmers to uber-rich mansion dwellers. Guilt had niggled at me about my own good luck after Quinn's speech about how the Chinese had suffered and been exploited so that others, like the Shaughnessys, could prosper. I had lucked out being born into a rich family.

"When my mother passed away last year, I created a nonprofit corporation named the Elizabeth Shaughnessy Foundation for Abused Women and Children in honor of my great-grandmother. The purpose of the foundation is to help usher displaced women and children into a new life. We offer counseling, resettlement, vocational training, and placement. Next Saturday afternoon, we're holding a fundraiser."

I'd argued with myself about whether to make this a black-tie ticketed affair and invite the upper echelon of San Francisco society or to make it a family-friendly event. The thought of a fancy party made me sick, perhaps because it was during one such party my parents had hosted, that my father visited my bedroom to, in his words, "wish me a good night." Several weeks later, I had morning sickness and was packed off to the girls' home.

I led Mickey down the hall to the sitting room. The ornate Edwardian furniture that had once filled the room was now gone, sold at auction to raise the money to refurbish the building. In their place were comfortable sofas and chairs, upholstered in a royal blue fabric that could withstand any assault or accident. The drapes were a matching color. The gloomy landscape paintings had been sold and were replaced with cheerful images of San Francisco landmarks donated by local artists.

The back windows overlooked what had once been my mother's cherished rose garden. It was beautiful but no place for children to run around. When I was young, I was forbidden to wander into it without supervision – lest I damage one of the bushes. When I took over, the roses were transferred to beds in the side yard and grass was sown.

"This is where folks can hang out and relax. Let's go see the kitchen."

I was feeling more comfortable now, talking to Micky and ignoring the camera person.

The kitchen had been gutted. When I was growing up, it was a mishmash of cabinetry and appliances spanning from when the mansion was built through the decades.

Now it was a gleaming industrial kitchen. Stainless steel cabinets and countertops, two ranges, a large fridge and freezer.

The former pantry room door was closed. It was now where the security office, as we called it, had been placed. After the SWAT incident, I had more security cameras installed. We had three views of every possible port of entry, doors and ground-floor windows. The front and back gardens were covered. Cameras were discreetly tucked into every room of the mansion, except the restrooms.

When the house was occupied, someone was in the old pantry, watching the wall of monitors, each connected to a different surveillance camera discreetly hidden in and outside of the house, flickering twenty-four hours a day. Today, Yolanda's nephew, Jojo, an easy-going, lanky college student and former employee of Esme Inc was on duty behind the door.

I led Mickey into the classroom area, separated from the kitchen by an island. A whiteboard hung on the wall.

"Wow," Mickey said.

"Thanks. This is where we hold nutrition and culinary arts classes."

We left the kitchen and went down a hall to my father's former den. When I was little, it was paneled in dark wood and reeked of cigar smoke. A large partners' desk had been stationed in front of a smoke-stained fireplace and the room was filled with leather furniture.

Even with the stench gone, my stomach turned as we entered. This was the room where my father groomed me. While he worked at his desk, I colored or read books on the couch. Occasionally, he would take a break and pull me onto his lap. When my mother intruded into our private moments, I would feel a strange tension between them. I didn't understand why at the time. Years later, I blamed her for not shielding me and for abandoning me when I became pregnant. But later I realized her surprise visits were intended to protect me, and when she had failed, she sent me as far away as she could to get me away from him. She must have suffered profound guilt.

"This is our admin office," I said. Four desks were arranged, perpendicular to the walls, waiting for social workers and career counselors to fill as they processed paperwork on computers not yet purchased. I opened a side door and beckoned my guests through to what had been the maid's quarters, where there were two chairs and a couch. "This is where our clients will meet with their counselors privately."

The rooms were as changed as I could make them, short of burning the place down, but I was still uncomfortable. "Let's visit the upstairs," I said brightly.

The doors of the six empty bedrooms on the second floor were open so light flooded into the hallway. I relaxed some when we entered the first room, my mother's bedroom. My father never crossed the threshold, which I didn't realize growing up, but I knew I was safe in this room. The ugly plastic folding table that was my desk was stowed in the walk-in closet along with the folding chairs, but the file cabinets remained. "This will be the executive director's office," I said.

The camera person spoke in a surprisingly soft voice. "Do you want footage of this, Mick?"

Mickey shook her head.

I led them down the hall. "These will be classrooms once we're up and running."

Mickey peeked into what had been my bedroom, painted the identical buttermilk color, and gestured for her camera person to enter. "Nice light in here. Let's get some footage."

I was grateful she didn't want me to go into that room. By now, my stomach felt like it was filled with broken glass. How long it would take for my past to stop haunting me?

Mickey wrapped a gentle hand around my wrist. She knew the whole story. I had told it to her when she did a piece on sexual abuse. "Are you holding up okay?" she asked quietly.

I nodded and mustered a smile for her, which must have looked pathetic.

Quietly, she said, "Let me know if you need a break."

"We're almost done."

We took the grand stairway up the next flight. I had pictured this room as my baby's nursery when I entertained fantasies of raising her myself. The worn wooden floor had been replaced with royal blue industrial carpet. The windows were dressed in gauzy yellow curtains, just as I had envisioned in my daydreams when I was pregnant.

"And this is the daycare."

Scattered about were colorful toddler plastic climbing frames, rocking horses, and pint-sized couches and chairs. Yet there was plenty of space left. I didn't know what the older children would need, so I decided to deal with that when the issue arose. Along the walls were toyboxes filled with two or three of every toy I saw in the store.

When Jake met me at the store to pick up the toys, the expression on his face, eyes wide open, as we filled his ancient Blazer to the top to take away my finds, suggested he thought I had overdone it. But he knew how important it was to me, so he didn't comment. I climbed in beside him and said, "I think we can manage it in three trips." He began to choke but recovered after I handed him his go-cup filled with lukewarm coffee.

Mickey broke into my reverie. "Tell me about the fundraiser next Saturday."

"It's going to be a blast. We'll have a cooking demonstration by Esme Castillo of Esme's Casa de Galletas." The court injunction said she couldn't earn money cooking. But it didn't stop her from volunteering. "She's our nutrition instructor. The food will be prepared by her. We'll have a magic show, entertainers, and face painters in the backyard. Lots of food, music, and good times."

Chapter Fifty-One

DIXON VAUGHN SAT IN his recliner, a can of cold beer in one hand, and a remote in the other.

On the screen was the Bitch Queen and some reporter. The Bitch Queen smiled as she pitched her money-grabbing scheme as a little happy shit kiddy party. "Lots of food, music, and good times."

Dixon knew exactly what to do. He flicked off the TV, picked up his cell phone and hit the number two button. "Scooter, get over here."

"Now? Dix, it's late."

"Stop your whining. We got plans to make. Big plans."

Chapter Fifty-Two

DIXON VAUGHN CRUISED THE street, elbow resting on the open window, as he searched for a parking spot for his extended bed pickup truck. The warm air felt good, a sign. Fair weather brought fair friends. The park would soon be packed with his Rights Men followers, and he was going to put on a party for them like they would never forget.

To his left was the Femicult Bitch's mansion. How ironic that her family fortune was made by a card shark saloonkeeper. He was probably a pimp too. Did she get that?

But here she was claiming to be the savior of womankind from male suppression. What a joke.

Dixon turned right, spun his visor to block the sun, and cruised the park across the street from the mansion. He needed a lot of space to park his big truck. When he found Scooter's muscle car, he braked.

He ducked his head to look out the passenger window. Preparations were taking place for the rally. The stage had been set up, and a tent was being erected over the stage to protect it in case of rain. Unlikely since the only clouds slowly sailing across the sky were thin and white, but the band, with all the electrical equipment that could become a deathtrap if exposed to water, insisted on a tent. Some guy snaked electrical cords across the stage, hooking them up to gigantic speakers. Another man fiddled with a high-hat cymbal next to a drum kit.

On the grass, still glistening from dew, Scooter talked to a small clutch of men who Dixon recognized as his most stalwart supporters from the occasional in-person meetings he'd hosted in a sports bar.

This rally would be glorious. Vaughn had sent a press release to all the local news sites promising a thousand-man crowd fed up with being victimized. When the rally story hit the net, it was bound to go viral. His podcast patronage would explode, and their membership dues would flood into his bank account. Dixon Vaughn was on his way to becoming a nationally recognized champion for men's rights.

While Maureen Gould was putting on her little kiddy party at the mansion, Dixon would blast his message to his followers. Anyone who showed up to her fundraiser would be put off because he and his audience would be raising hell. So much for drumming up donations to help women escape from their husbands.

A car pulled up behind Dixon's truck and honked its horn. Dixon rolled down his window and held his hand up high so the other driver could see his raised middle finger. He thought about getting out of his truck to have a discussion with that other driver about courtesy, but the other guy gunned his engine, swerved around the truck, almost clipped it, and raced up the street.

Dixon found a spot near a corner and swooped in. After he jumped out of his truck, he left the door open, blocking anyone's view, as he patted his back pocket to make sure his wallet was still there, and then grabbed his belt and shook out his jeans to make room for his manhood. Feeling free, he slammed the truck door shut.

Showtime!

By now, dozens more men had appeared, walking into the park from every direction. Scooter spotted Dixon and raised his hand excitedly. Dixon jerked his head up in recognition and ambled towards the growing crowd.

A rock band climbed onto the stage. The musicians plugged their guitars into their amplifiers. The lead guitarist swung his hand across the strings, and a high-pitched note screamed through the speakers. Everyone in the park turned towards the stage. Once he had their attention, he let go a riff that led into a rendition of Jimi Hendrix's Star-Spangled Banner solo.

The men raised their fists and shouted "Booya!" Many of them held beers that they then took swigs from. Someone had given Scooter a beer, too. He clinked bottles with the guy next to him and chugged. It was only noon. If he kept this up, he'd be plastered in a couple of hours and useless.

Dixon waded into the group. He slapped backs, exchanged fist bumps and bro handshakes with the men. He welcomed everybody he knew by name because that was the way to build super fans. When he ran across someone whose name he didn't know, he humbly introduced himself and asked for their name and then repeated it as he said it was good to meet them.

Dixon scanned the park. Good, the playground was empty. On the sidewalk, scowling women with strollers or towing small children by the hand walked past quickly. They wanted no part of him.

Likewise, bitches.

At the same time, men were hauling coolers from their double-parked vehicles to the grass. It didn't occur to Dixon to tell Scooter there should be no booze. He should have. When Scooter had first started coming around, he didn't seem to drink that much. Dixon later realized he had been on good behavior. Lately, Scooter seemed to always have a beer in his hand. When it finally occurred to Dixon to look up the guy's criminal records, he discovered a series of alcohol-related assaults Scooter had been arrested on. Most of them were dismissed after he slept off his drunk in jail. The rest were pled out to time served.

Dixon separated himself from the crowd and motioned for Scooter to join him. Scooter loped to him with a beer in each hand. When he came to a halt, he offered a bottle to Dixon.

"No, man," Dixon said. "I need to keep a clear head. And so do you. Lay off that stuff."

"Lighten up, Dix. It's a party. How do you think I got all these guys out here? We even got a taco truck." Scooter pointed to the street where a food truck man was setting up his awning.

"Who's paying for that?" Dixon asked.

Scooter swung his arm in the direction of the crowd as he took a small stumble. He recovered his balance and said, "They are. They brought the booze. And they're buying their own food. But I promised the band you would pay them, just like we talked about. And I already spent the money that you gave me on the stage rental. You like the stage set-up? It's just like you wanted, backed up to the mansion so that everyone who looks at you can see what you're talking about."

Once in a while, Scooter got it right. "It's exactly what I had asked for. Good job!"

Dixon craned his neck in the direction of the mansion. "Are things picking up over there yet?"

Scooter poured the dregs out of a bottle down his neck and wiped his face with the back of his hand. "People have been dribbling in for the last hour or so. That party is supposed to start at one. By then, we will be rocking and rolling."

"Perfect. And how does the schedule look?"

"The band's going to play a set for forty-five minutes, then I'll give you a big introduction, and you come on, do your thing. Man, I can't tell you how excited these guys are to meet you."

Scooter spun around, crashing into Dixon, who had to grab him to keep both of them from falling over. Scooter threw back his head and howled like a mad dog.

"What the hell was that?" Dixon asked.

"The rebel war cry, Dix." Scooter raised his arm and shouted, "Guys! Guys! Here's the man! Come over and meet him."

The crowd swarmed Dixon. He spent the next two hours going from man to man, learning their names, asking about their jobs, and thanking them for their support.

Chapter Fifty-Three

YOLANDA AND I STOOD in front of the mansion's open front doors, greeting guests as they came up from the street. A soft warm breeze carried in the smell of freshly cut grass from the park across the street. The city landscapers had been out early that morning, driving their lawnmowers up and down the lawn. As soon as they left, a semi pulled up and began unloading building materials which were then assembled into a stage. Someone was planning a big do. I hoped the competition for parking wouldn't impact my fundraiser's attendance.

Yolanda, Quinn, Esme, and I spent the morning setting up the party. In the back garden, there were booths for face painters and kids' games. I had originally planned to have a clown come to entertain the children, but Yolanda explained that some little kids are terrified of clowns. If I had raised Quinn, I would have known this. I would have taken her to fairs. I would have been a parent helper in the classrooms. I might have even joined the PTA.

But that's not what happened, so I had no choice but to rely on Yolanda's advice. So instead of clowns, we had a couple of young women dressed up like fairies who would roam through the party and allow their pictures to be taken with the kids.

Esme had been at the mansion since before dawn, baking cookies and assembling finger sandwiches. Originally, I had thought some of the foundation clients would like to help in the kitchen, but Yolanda pointed out that they should be able to enjoy the party with their children just like the ticket holders did. Besides, Quinn would help out.

Yolanda was a wise woman. I was lucky to know her.

That morning when Quinn and I left the condo, Jake gave me a kiss on the cheek. "The weather man says it's going to be a spectacular day. Warm. Blue skies. You're going to do great."

"Aren't you coming?" Quinn asked him.

"Sorry. Got stuff to do. When you come home, you can tell me all about it." He gave Quinn a peck, too.

As I drove to the mansion, Quinn said, "It's weird Jake isn't worried about security."

"We have cameras all over the place, inside and out. Jojo's in the old pantry watching the video feeds. We'll be fine."

"Gerry's not coming either?"

"Mountain man Gerry Waldron at a garden party?"

Quinn laughed. "Yeah, no."

Standing on the portico with Yolanda, I was smiling to myself. I could still feel the soft touch of Jake's lips on my cheek. How lucky was I to find a good man like him?

A troop of Girl Scouts approached from the street, escorted by two women.

"Is there something wrong with that tree?" one girl in a green vest asked the woman closest to her.

I stepped off the porch to join their conversation. "It's a monkey puzzle tree. My great-grandmother planted it."

The woman and girl stood for a moment, pretending to admire it. I had to admit the tree was odd-looking, especially for San Francisco, and not to everyone's taste. My father, Frank, hated it. My mother had been lukewarm towards it, but I think she kept it to goad him. I loved the tree, because I loved everything that reminded me of Lizzie.

"They can live to one thousand years old," I said.

"Wow," the girl said, not impressed. The woman smiled at me politely.

"So glad you could join us," I said. "There's plenty of food and entertainment in the backyard."

As the last girl passed over the threshold, a guitar screamed a high note and began playing the Star-Spangled Banner.

"What's going on over there?" Yolanda asked.

"I don't know. But whoever it is has as much a right to have a party as we do, so we're just going to have to live with it. The music won't be so loud inside the mansion or the back garden."

Senator Foster Heiki came up the walkway, escorting his elegant wife who was turned out in a beige-on-beige sweater ensemble and slacks, beige loafers, discreet gold earrings, and a thin, but expensive gold watch. He wore dress slacks, a white button-down shirt, and his signature retro half-rim eyeglasses. A girl who appeared to be about nine years old, wearing capris and a sparkly top, walked between them holding their hands.

Heiki had been elected this past November to the state Senate representing one of the San Francisco districts. He defeated a man named Rick Stevens, who I had once suspected in a murder for which one of my clients was charged. Heiki was a surprise upset. Stevens had led in the polls, but just before the election, compromising photographs of Stevens had been published.

I couldn't remember where, but I had met Foster Heiki years before. "Good afternoon, Senator," I said, as I held out my hand. "So glad you could join us this afternoon."

"It's a worthy cause," the senator said. "We wouldn't miss it for the world. Have you met my wife, Jennifer? Jennifer, this is Maureen Gould."

"So nice to meet you, Maureen. I'm a great admirer of your work."

Jennifer Heiki was an attorney, but she worked for one of the large charitable organizations that collects donations and redirects the funds to needy causes. It was one of the organizations I hoped to obtain a grant from once I ironed out the permit issue. I had called Ms. Heiki's office, hoping they'd buy tickets for the fundraiser. They bought one hundred tickets, including those that were donated to the Girl Scout troop that had just gone inside.

"We have a carnival in the backyard," I said. "Help yourself to food and drinks. Later, if you like, I'd love to show you around."

"Sounds terrific," Jennifer Heiki said.

As the family strolled into the house, Quinn came down the hall. "We're out of ice already. I need to make a run to the store."

"Want to take Sunny?" I asked as I reached into my pocket for my keys. Quinn loved driving my zippy yellow sports car. And I loved having someone around who enjoyed running errands.

"Well, yeah," Quinn answered. She held her palm out and I dropped the keys into it. As she bounced out the door towards the street where I'd parked my car earlier that day, she pulled off the scrunchy holding her hair up and shook out her red mane.

I watched as she climbed into the sports car. A moment passed and then the convertible's roof retracted and folded into the trunk. She latched her seatbelt, twisted around, and looked over her left shoulder, one hand on the steering wheel, and then peeled out of the parking spot so loudly that the squealing tires could be heard over the rock music in the park.

"Whoa, Nellie!" Yolanda said.

I shrugged. "There's only one way to drive a fast car, and that's fast. She's a safe driver. I'm not concerned."

Chapter Fifty-Four

DIXON WAITED OFF STAGE as Scooter took the microphone and cut loose his rebel war cry. The crowd quieted and looked in his direction.

"Are we having fun?" Scooter yelled into the mic. He wasn't swaying anymore. Good thing, he took Dixon's advice. If the rally turned into a drunken mob, it wouldn't look good when video from the citizen journalists' cell phones went viral.

The crowd shouted "Booya!"

"I can't hear you!"

"Booya!"

Scooter put a hand behind one ear and leaned toward the crowd, as if he was deaf. "What's that?"

"BOOYA!"

Scooter applauded the audience, and they applauded back. When the noise died down, he put his mouth to the microphone. "Thank you to the band! What a great job those guys did!

More shouts and applause. Dixon was impressed by how well Scooter handled the crowd, even drunk.

"Let me tell you my story. Real quick, because I know you want to see Dixon. A few years ago, I was doing sales in an electronics store. One of the other salesclerks was a female. She was hired after I was. I trained her, as a matter of fact. And then one day, our manager was transferred to another store. I figured I was next in line. I interviewed. Felt like I had the job in the bag. They said they had to talk to her, too – just to make it look fair. No worries, I thought. And you know what happened?"

Scooter paused for a response. When none came, he yelled, "Do you know what happened?"

Someone from the crowd yelled, "She got the job!"

"That's right, bro. She got the job. And you know why?"

Another man yelled, "Because she's a woman!"

"That's right, bro! She's a woman and I'm a man. Explain it to me. I had more experience, and more time with the company, but I got passed over because I was a man. So, who's the minority now? I tell you, brothers, it's me and you."

Dixon had never heard this story even though that guy was at his house almost every day. If it was true, Scooter would have told him sooner. But he wasn't bright enough to make it up. Chances are someone told him a similar story and he'd changed the details, so it didn't look like he was stealing.

The crowd was dead quiet.

"And then Dixon Vaughn came along. Dixon Vaughn, retired police officer, and host of the Rights of Man podcast. Let me tell you, Dixon is the real deal. He speaks the truth. Do you want to hear some truth?"

Applause.

Scooter yelled, "Do you want to hear the truth!"

"Booya!" the crowd yelled.

"Booya!" Scooter answered. "Let me introduce, the man himself, Dixon Vaughn!"

Dixon ran up the stairs and strode across the stage. He took Scooter's hand in a bro shake, pulled him in, and slapped him on the back.

When Dixon let him go, he could see a glean of sweat on Scooter's face, even though the day wasn't that warm. The stink of beer was strong. His eyes were glazed over. It looked like he was crying. Dixon felt himself frown briefly.

"You're the man, Dix. Knock them dead."

With that, instead of taking the stairs, Scooter leapt off the front of the stage. He jogged into the crowd where someone handed him a bottle of beer.

Dixon pulled the mic off the stand and paced back and forth across the stage, pointing into the crowd as if he was greeting old friends. He'd read somewhere that Bill Clinton would do that, even if he didn't know a single face. It got him elected. Who knows what the future could hold for Dixon Vaughn?

"Friends, I am sick and tired of women claiming they're victims."

"Tell it, man!" Scooter shouted from the depths of the crowd.

"Anymore, the government – *our* government – bends over backwards for anyone except the lowly male. Can you believe it? This is the country that we fought and died for. Our blood was the price of their freedom. And now, we're getting shoved to the bottom of the pile. And why's that?"

"Why?" The crowd shouted.

Dixon scanned the crowd, building the men's excitement before he answered. Two or three faces were especially familiar. They had that cop look to them, standing apart, observing, ready to pounce. If they were friends, they would be hanging out together. Were they on the job? Was Dixon Vaughn under surveillance?

Let the cops watch him. Maybe they'll see something they like.

"Because we let them. We bend over and take it." With that Dixon waved his rearend, simulated being assaulted from behind and put on a surprised face. The crowd hooted.

He replaced the mic in the stand and struck a spread foot stance behind it. "Men, I have a question for you." He waited for the noise to die down.

"My question for you is this: Are you ready to take back your rights?"

"Hell, yes!" Scooter shouted from the crowd, then he began chanting, "Hell, yes. Hell, yes. Hell, yes." The crowd joined him. Soon Dixon could hear their voices thundering in his chest.

"Shall I name the enemy?"

"Booya!" The crowd shouted. But it wasn't loud enough. The decibels should increase with every response.

"Shall I name the enemy?" Dixon yelled. He pointed the mic at the audience.

"Booya!" The crowd was frantic.

"The Femicult. Satan, thy name is Femicult. That's who we're fighting."

Jeers and hoots from the crowd.

"And the queen of the Femicult is Maureen Gould. Rich, entitled, attorney Maureen Gould. She lives in that palace just behind us." Dixon thrusted his arm in the mansion's direction.

Over the noise of the crowd, Dixon heard the approach of a BMW engine, screaming as it downshifted. There was no mistaking that sound.

A flash of yellow caught Dixon's eye.

Then, Scooter ran past the stage towards the street, whooping a rebel war cry.

QUINN LOVED DRIVING SUNNY II, the powerful sports car Jake had bought Maureen to replace her first BMW, which had been blown up by thugs in front of the mansion. The sidewalk still bore scorch marks where the car had been parked.

Quinn was inside the mansion when Sunny exploded.

Not long after she came to San Francisco, Frank had called to invite her to dinner. Maureen was in the middle of a trial, and Frank was her opponent. Maureen had gone across the bay to find a missing witness, but Frank was at loose ends. Even though they opposed each other in the case, they were still family, Quinn figured. There was no reason not to talk to him – as long as they didn't talk about the case.

When she came to San Francisco to meet Maureen, she didn't know the truth of her paternity. She only knew that Maureen was her mother, her grandmother had passed away, and Frank, Maureen's father, was still living in the mansion. Maureen had refused to talk about Quinn's birth father, which made Quinn even more curious. So when Frank invited her to dinner with a promise to tell her about her father, Quinn jumped at the c hance.

They ended up at the mansion. The excuse was to have cocktails before they went out to eat, but they never went to dinner. Frank plopped himself into a chair in the sitting room and poured himself drink after drink until he was so sloppy drunk, he didn't make sense.

Quinn didn't know what to do. She didn't have a car, and she'd left her phone at Maureen's condo. She'd inched her way halfway out of the room, thinking when she got a chance, she would start walking back to the condo although it was on the opposite side of town. That's when she heard Maureen's BMW roar.

Maureen busted in and began yelling at Frank.

The next thing Quinn knew, there was an explosion on the street. As it turned out, Frank had lured Maureen to the house using Quinn as a hostage on orders from his client. The client's thugs blew up Maureen's car – as a warning to drop the case.

But no one told Maureen Gould what to do. She won the trial. One man went to jail, and another skipped the country.

Quinn loved driving the new BMW Jake had bought to replace Sunny. Most of the time, she only got from one red light to another quickly, but when she had an excuse, she'd open it up on the freeway.

As it happened, today she needed to buy ice for the fundraiser. The gas stations she went to had run out. It was the first nice day in San Francisco in months, and people were loading up on supplies for their picnics and bar-b-ques. Quinn texted Maureen that she had to run down the road to look for ice before she pulled out onto the highway.

Eventually she found a grocery store where she loaded bags and bags into the backseat. She raced back to the mansion, hoping to return before it melted.

She was gone longer than she'd planned. A crowd had filled the park across the street from the mansion, and traffic was backed up for as far as she could see. Once she got to the corner, she could turn down the street and go into the alley behind the mansion. She downshifted and stopped behind another car. Seconds later, a sedan came up behind her and blocked her in.

Movement caught her eye. A man in high-top Converse shoes ran out of the crowd. It was the guy they'd seen on the surveillance video, the one who'd graffitied the house. She was sure of it. He hurdled over the BMW's hood, bracing himself with one hand, causing the car's nose to dip.

Then he was by her side. His hand wrapped around her hair. He jerked her up hard, trying to pull her out, but she was belted in. "You're coming with me, bitch."

He jerked again, really hard. A sharp knife-like pain shot through her neck.

"Like hell I am!" She batted at his hands, but he wound her hair tighter, so tight that his fist was on top of her skull. Her scalp burned.

He was wedged between her and the steering wheel, trying to get at her belt latch, and making the horn blare. His shoulder dug into her chest, pinning her arms. She couldn't move.

ESME LOADED THE LAST of the plastic cups filled with water, and a young woman dressed in black pants and a polo top took the tray and left the kitchen. Another server came in, her tray clamped to her side. "We need more water."

"We're out of cups," Esme said.

"It's hot out there. They're drinking the stuff like they're camels."

A second door led directly from the kitchen to the old pantry that had been converted into a surveillance office. With the conversion, there was less room for storage, so when she was offloading that morning, Esme had left boxes of paper products, including the plastic cups, in the rented van which was parked in the short driveway off the alley behind the mansion.

The pantry door was open. Jojo was lodged in the darkened room, slumped in a chair, long skinny legs stretched out before him, watching the monitors.

"Hey, Jojo, go get me some cups."

"I'm working," he said, without taking his eyes off the screens.

"It's okay. I'll keep an eye on things."

"Might be okay for you, but if anything happens, Yolanda will have my hide."

"I can still kick your butt."

Jojo laughed. He was an easy six inches taller than Esme. "Yeah, well, I'm more scared of Yolanda than I am of you."

"Fine." Esme untied her apron, threw it on the counter, then headed out the back door.

In the alley, she pulled the van keys from her pocket, inserted them in the lock, and opened the heavy door. She climbed inside and began shifting boxes from the front towards the back.

When she had several boxes stacked at the back of the bed, she jumped out. As she turned to grab the first box, she saw through the door's small window someone dressed in a kitchen white uniform approaching from down the alley.

Awesome, some help! After Quinn had left on an errand over an hour ago, Esme was so busy, she felt like she was running a dinner service by herself. Which she was.

But no one had said anything about help.

And if someone was walking from their car, wouldn't they have parked on the street which was just a few hundred feet away?

The person approaching, a woman, walked funny. One of her hands was hidden behind her back, as she kept to one side of the alley, so the van door would hide her approach.

Esme flashed on Gerry's self-defense training class. When he came at Maureen with the plastic knife, he'd hidden it behind his back until the last moment. Just like this woman did.

Esme dropped the box and grabbed the tire iron that was clipped to the van's wall.

Somewhere in the distance, a car horn blared.

Esme needed to move fast, before the woman had her pinned against the van.

She leapt as far away as she could as she slammed the van door, exposing the woman.

The woman lunged.

Esme's vision zoomed in on the flashing blade in the woman's hand. Everything else was a blur. Just as Gerry had shown her, she swung the tire iron down on the extended forearm as hard as she could.

A scream.

Then Esme swung the iron back at the assailant's head.

Silence.

⏣

I WAS ON THE portico, in the process of a just-long-enough farewell to Senator Heiki and his family, when I heard a man's harrowing rebel call coming from the park across the street. A small man, dressed all in black, ran at full speed at the cars stopped in traffic.

On the street, my BMW was locked in by cars. Quinn was at the wheel.

The man hurdled across Sunny's hood and planted himself next to Quinn. His body blocked what he was doing, but I saw his shoulder and arm jerking upwards. She screamed.

I flew.

When I got to the car, he was digging around Quinn, trying to get at her belt latch.

Since I was taller than him, it was easy to drop a figure-four chokehold around his neck. My right arm squeezed his throat while my left hand pulled my right arm even tighter.

People protect their airways. It's instinct.

My face was jammed next to his greasy head, and the reek of sweat and beer filled my nostrils. As he tried to twist out of my hold, I pulled tighter.

He grabbed my right arm with both of his hands, trying to claw it loose, and I pulled even tighter.

He stood and thrust himself back into me. I lost my footing and fell backwards, pulling him down on top of me. A pain shot through my elbow as the full force of both of our weights collided with the sidewalk, followed by a loud crack when my skull hit the concrete.

I must have been knocked out for a few seconds. The next thing I knew, the man's weight was gone and he was facedown, spread eagle on the sidewalk, with Gerry on top of him.

Another man, as big as Gerry, more muscle than fat and clean shaven, said, "I got this." He sounded like Bill, the SWAT guy I met at the mansion.

Gerry moved off the attacker. The other man pulled him to his feet, and said, "I'm putting you under arrest for assault." Then he began reciting the Miranda warning.

That was when Jake appeared.

Chapter Fifty-Five

THE WAITER SHOWED US to a private dining room in the Palace Hotel. Jake had made our Mother's Day brunch reservations for the first slot in the morning so Yolanda and Esme could join us before they went to Yolanda's mother's house.

I wore a dress. What the hell. Most of my adult life, I'd protested what I'd termed Western cultural gender-specific garb. I only wore slacks to court, never skirts. But today I wanted to feel pretty, despite the cast on my arm. Or maybe it was because of the cast on my arm.

Quinn and I had gone dress shopping for the event. I selected a gauzy layered tea-length dress, the fabric of which looked like a watercolor of large flowers in spring colors, sleeveless, of course, to fit over the cast on my right arm. It was the first time I had gone out in public with my arms exposed. Before, I was ashamed of the self-harm scars, now faded to white, on my left arm. But in the past few weeks, I didn't worry that a stranger would see them and know what I had done to myself. They were part of my past.

They were part of me.

As were Lizzie Shaughnessy's pearls, which I touched as we wound our way to the dining room, just to make sure they were still there.

Quinn was elegant in a jade green linen shell and gray linen skirt, despite her Doc Marten boots. The single pearl pendant Jake and I had given her for her birthday hung around her neck and glowed under the soft lighting of the dining room.

Jake wore a court suit and the tie he had worn when we were first married.

Esme was wearing skintight pants, instead of skintight leggings, and a floppy silk top, her Our Lady of Guadalupe medal, and beaded bracelets going halfway up her arms.

I'd thought I'd seen everything in Yolanda's wardrobe, but she surprised me. With four kids, two of them boys with voracious appetites, she was on a budget no matter how much I could afford to pay her. So I knew she shopped at secondhand stores, but she had an eye for labels, good cuts, and color. Today she wore a pale blue knee-length dress with a matching wrap that would have been an appropriate mother of the bride assemble. Gerry, who I suspected didn't own a suit, had put a tie on and appeared to be wearing a new button-down shirt over an also-new pair of slacks.

Jake pulled out a chair for me, then one for Quinn. As we gathered our skirts and slid into place, Yolanda waited patiently for Gerry to get the hint. Jake nodded in her direction, and Gerry finally got it. As he pulled out Yolanda's chair, Esme pulled out her own, giving us all a disapproving frown, and settled herself in.

Quinn quickly thumbed a message, then slipped her phone back into her pocket.

"Texting your boyfriend?" Esme asked.

"He's just a friend."

"Right." Esme elbowed her.

"What am I missing?" I asked.

"Nothing. Nothing at all." Quinn took a sip of water, suppressing a grin.

I'd seen that look before. I'd felt it on my own face frequently when Jake and I started dating.

The waiter stood patiently nearby.

Jake turned to him. "Champagne."

"Two bottles," Gerry said. "Save yourself a trip."

The waiter smiled, and left the room, closing the door quietly.

I patted my cast unconsciously.

"Are you okay?" Jake asked.

I gave a dismissive shake of the head. "Just aching a little."

"What's the doctor say?" Gerry asked.

It had been a month since the mansion fundraiser. I supposed Yolanda filled Gerry in with every detail on a day-to-day basis, but I figured asking a question he already knew the answer to was his way of showing concern.

"Not broken but cracked. Six weeks in the cast. Then physical therapy."

"That's good news."

"I want to thank you for rescuing us, Gerry," I said.

"You already did, and just stop it. I wasn't rescuing you. I was saving that guy from getting killed."

Jake snorted down a laugh and I felt the blood rush to my face. I couldn't argue. If someone hadn't stopped me, I would have kept attacking that man until he quit moving.

Our conversation died down as the waiter appeared, poured champagne for each of us, then left the bottles cradled in ice-filled buckets on the table.

Before the group resumed chatting, Esme spoke. "I need to say something." She waited for our attention.

Yolanda took her hand and nodded for her to continue.

"If it weren't for you, Maureen, and my Tia Yolanda, and Quinn, I would be on my way to jail. I can't thank you enough." She raised her glass. "To the Maureen Gould La w Office."

During the fundraiser, Jojo had been watching the monitors from his small office in the pantry. He had seen Rita Osteen attack Esme. By the time he arrived in the alley, she was on the ground unconscious with Esme standing over her. He called Jake on his cell phone, who had just witnessed Bill arrest the man who'd attacked Quinn. Jake stayed with me while Gerry ran around the corner to the alley to find Rita alive, but unconscious. She was removed from the scene by ambulance, accompanied by a police officer. While she lay in her hospital bed, she had been arrested for the assault of Esme.

The following Monday, I took the evidence I had compiled to the DA's office and sat in the same conference room where they'd questioned Esme. This time, I explained to Vivian and Detectives Dobson and Chong what we had discovered. As a result, Rita Osteen was charged with the murders of Alfred Tanzini and Henry Watkins and the attempted murder of Esme.

The murder charges against Esme were dropped.

"I get she killed those two men," Gerry said. "But why?"

I answered. "Rita Osteen murdered Al Tanzini because she thought she would get his shares if he couldn't make his loan payment. It was in their side deal, the one that she filed with the court to claim she was entitled to her shares. When she killed him, she thought she would automatically become the majority shareholder and had plans for making millions by franchising the business. Then she murdered Henry Watkins because he was making trouble for her about a café contract in the San Francisco Airport, which was part of her plan for the franchise."

Quinn interjected. "But she didn't get Tanzini's shares when he died because the corporation agreement said otherwise. It said the shares were to be distributed pro rata to the living shareholders, which meant Esme was the majority shareholder. And the judge said she needed a full trial to determine which agreement took precedent – a year from now." She sounded just like a lawyer. As my chest swelled with pride, Yolanda chimed in.

"And that's why she decided Esme had to go. Because then Rita Osteen would be the only shareholder, and the company would be hers."

"What about that Bruno Fernandez guy?" Gerry asked. "Is he still asking for a piece of the business?"

The mailman had delivered a letter from Mr. Fernandez earlier that week. "He wrote me, saying that his only reason to come to San Francisco was to track down Al Tanzini and get justice. It wasn't about the money. He couldn't let Tanzini build a new life, leaving behind the destruction he'd caused. Once Tanzini was dead, he wasn't interested in the business anymore. He said he'd be happy to sign whatever papers we needed waiving any interest he might have had."

It would still be a year before we could get the bakery ownership case to trial. Judge Rediger seemed to be worn out on our case and refused to find time on her calendar any sooner. So, I filed a motion for Esme to regain control of the day-to-day business, which the judge granted.

"Esme's free and has her business back. Rita Osteen is in jail on murder charges. What ever happened to Paul Lewis?" Quinn asked.

"He closed his office." That was all I could say.

I wasn't allowed to talk about what I knew because attorney ethical investigations are confidential. A bar investigator called me after Paul Lewis had disappeared. I had no idea if he was out of the country or hiding in his apartment. The police had found a will executed by Rita Osteen's late husband, leaving everything to his children, when they finally processed all the paperwork they'd pulled out of Al Tanzini's apartment. For some reason, Tanzini had a copy of the will. The children were alerted. They reopened the probate case and filed a bar complaint alleging Paul Lewis had committed fraud.

I raised my glass. "To Esme."

Everyone lifted their flutes. "To Esme," they repeated.

"I didn't do anything. It was all you, Maureen, and my aunt."

"And Quinn," Yolanda threw in.

Esme reached over and squeezed Quinn's hand. "And Quinn," she agreed.

"I can't win a case without a client," I said. "It was your life, and your case, and you were the one with the guts to fight."

"It wasn't for me," Esme said. "It was for my grandma. And my family. I'm just the end result of all their work. I couldn't let our heritage get stolen by some thieves."

Yolanda wiped an eye with her freshly polished nail.

"Tia, are you crying?" Esme asked.

"Tears of joy, Esme," Yolanda said. "Tears of joy."

Gerry half-stood and filled everyone's glasses again. "Jake, what's the story with Dixon Vaughn and his little buddy?"

"They were both charged with hate crimes and assault. Vaughn cut a deal quick, putting all the blame off on his henchman, Scott Thomas. Hung the poor bastard out to dry. Thomas didn't help his case much, blabbed all the way back to the police station. He mistook Quinn for Maureen. He'd planned to drag her back to the crowd to, in his words, 'answer for her sins'."

Jake's cell phone buzzed. He pulled it out of his pocket and held it under the table while he read the message. "The cops are responding to a murder scene, a shooting, at an Emeryville address."

"That's where Dixon Vaughn's lives," Yolanda said. She had found it on the business license papers he'd filed for his podcast.

"One fatality, one man in custody."

"Names?" Gerry asked.

"Ages. The fatality is forty-three years old. The person in custody is thirty-five."

We let that soak in. No one needed to explain that Scott Thomas had shot Dixon Vaughn to death.

The waiter arrived for our orders. After I asked for Eggs Benedict, the others did, too.

The atmosphere was leaden with the news of another death.

To change the mood, Jake turned to Quinn with a knowing look on his face. "How did finals go?"

Quinn had been checking her phone for her grades every hour since her last exam. Just as we gathered in the restaurant's foyer, she checked one more time, and a big grin had spread across her face.

"Straight A's."

"How'd your friend that's not your boyfriend do?" Esme asked, her eyes glinting with mischief.

"Same," Quinn said, then hid her face behind her hand.

I looked at Jake in horror. I'd just gotten my daughter back. I didn't know if I was ready for her suitors.

Jake knew when it was time to change the subject. He lifted his glass. "To Quinn!" Jake said.

At this rate, we were all going to get drunk before breakfast arrived. I raised my glass with the others and pretended to take a sip.

Quinn reached into her purse and pulled out a business-sized envelope. She passed it over to me. It had been addressed "To Mom." A big heart was drawn, followed by "Quinn."

"What's this?" I asked.

She shrugged. "Look inside."

Jake settled back into his chair, with yet another knowing look.

"What?" I asked.

"Open it," he said.

The flap was barely tacked down, so when I slid a finger underneath, it easily snapped open. I pulled the documents out and opened them up. It was a court petition stating, "In the matter of the name change of Quinn Marie Brennan."

"You're changing your name?" I asked.

She leaned over my shoulder and pointed to the proposed name change. The name she had chosen was "Quinn Elizabeth Shaughnessy Brennan."

I started crying. When I was carrying her, I had planned to name her Elizabeth Shaughnessy Gould after my great-grandmother.

Jake held up his glass, "To Quinn Elizabeth Shaughnessy Brennan!"

"To Quinn," everyone repeated.

Quinn snuggled into me. "Love you, Mom."

I thew back my head trying to stem the tears. Quinn had forgiven me for the horrid family scandal I'd thrust upon her. She wrapped an arm around me and pulled me in.

Gerry emptied what was left of the champagne into our glasses. "Where's that waiter?" he asked. "We're going to need more booze. This is a celebration!" He stood and raised his glass, "Happy Mother's Day!"

They each stood in turn, glasses raised. "Happy Mother's Day!"

Champagne never tasted so good.

The End

Hope You Enjoyed The Pied Piper!

HELP READERS FIND THEIR next great read! Post a quick review here:
https://www.amazon.com/gp/product/B0D1HC1TDF

Author's Note

When I first began writing *The Pied Piper*, I was inspired by outrage for those brilliant people who had lost control over their creations because they'd been outmaneuvered by others with more business acumen. Like Gary Gygax, who was forced out of TSR, the company he'd co-created to publish Dungeons and Dragons, and Wally Amos, who lost the rights to his Famous Amos cookie recipe.

After my umpteenth revision, it occurred to me that deep down inside, another inspiration for this story was my grandmother, who baked, who taught my mother how to bake, who in turn taught me, and now I'm teaching my granddaughter. One of my clearest memories of my grandmother was when I went to visit while I was driving cross-country, looking for a new place to go after I graduated law school. I walked from the living room into the dining room, looking for her, when she popped out of the kitchen, apron on, spoon in hand, and a dab of boiled frosting upon her nose.

So it was my grandmother to whom I dedicated this book.

At another layer, this is Quinn's story, an adoptee who, in the process of finding an identity, investigates the history of her biological family and struggles with reconciling herself to what she has learned. It's about who we are as individuals, how we fit into the family tree, and to what extent we claim our ancestors' sins as well as their accomplishments.

The ancestry TV shows fascinate me, *Finding Your Roots with Henry Louis Gates, Jr.,* and *Who Do You Think You Are?* How each personality reacts to the news that they were descended from saints or sinners and all those in between is intriguing. In every episode, the featured person is deeply affected by what he or she learns.

For my part, if the research is true, I'm descended on my father's side from the Dudleys, who lost control of the castle (I like to say they lost it in a card game, but I made that up), and King John, who was forced to sign the Magna Carta. But my ancestors aren't just a bunch of losers! Eleanor of Aquitaine is in the family tree as well. Who wouldn't want Katherine Hepburn to be their umpteenth great-grandmother?

I had suffered with the title for several months, before I hit on "The Pied Piper." It happened one day as I was idly thumbing through social media, as one does, when I ran across an article about how Maxfield Parrish's incredible painting of the Pied Piper, which had been originally created for the Palace Hotel in San Francisco after the 1906 earthquake, was rescued from being sold and rehung in the bar that shares its name. The next time I'm in The City, I'll go see it.

The Pied Piper story goes like this: The village of Hamelin was having a rat infestation. It hired the piper to lead away the dreaded rats, which he did. When the villagers reneged on his payment, he led their children away as well.

The heart of my story is about inheritance and legacy – what we receive from our ancestors and what we pass down to our descendants. So, the story of The Pied Piper, someone who stole the village's next generation thus wiping out the ancestor-descendant continuum, felt like an appropriate metaphor.

I hope you enjoyed my story.

Keenan Powell
Anchorage, Alaska
1 November 2024

About the author

Keenan Powell is the Agatha, Lefty, and Silver Falchion nominated author of the Maeve Malloy Mystery series.

Despite being one of original Dungeons and Dragons illustrators, art seemed an impractical pursuit – not an heiress, wouldn't marry well, hated teaching – so she went to law school. The day after graduation, she moved to Alaska.

She is the author of the Maureen Gould Legal Thrillers, Maeve Malloy Legal Thrillers, the Liam Barrett Gilded Age Novels, and numerous short stories.

When not writing or practicing law, Keenan can be found embroidering or studying the Irish language.

Follow her at:

Amazon: https://www.amazon.com/stores/Keenan-Powell/author/B0788TKBJW

Facebook: https://www.facebook.com/keenanwrites

Goodreads: https://www.goodreads.com/author/show/17008872.Keenan_Powell

Bookbub: https://www.bookbub.com/authors/keenan-powell

Acknowledgements

It takes a village, as they say. Bringing forth this book could not have been done without the kind and gentle support of Angie Garza, who gave me the name for Esme's Casa de Galletas (thanks, Angie!), my writer friends, Debbie Burke, Cari Davis, Efrem Seeger, Sandy Manning, Susan Wolfe, and Randal Jackson, Steven Laine, my beta readers, Jenni Legate, Debbie Burke, Rory Bryant, and my editor Jacqueline Green.

And what a cool cover designed for me by Mila Book Covers! I love it!

Also by

The Maureen Gould Legal Thrillers

Implied Consent (Three Hooligans Press, 2023)

The Millionaire (Three Hooligans Press, 2024)

The Pied Piper (Three Hooligans Press, 2025)

The Judge (Three Hooligans Press, 2025)

The Reunion (Three Hooligans Press, 2026)

The Maeve Malloy Legal Thrillers

Deadly Solution (Three Hooligans Press, 2023)

Hell and High Water (Three Hooligans Press, 2024)

Hemlock Needle (Three Hooligans Press, 2024)

The Liam Barrett Gilded Age Novels

The Sorrowful Girl (Three Hooligans Press, 2023)

Short Stories

The Liam Barrett Short Stories: Gilded Age Stories (Three Hooligans Press, 2023)

How I Met Yolanda Martinez (Three Hooligans Press, 2024)

Sneak Preview

Sneak Preview: The Judge

Chapter1

Rachel

Sunday, June 21

Just when, in the hell, did Rachel Newkirk become invisible?

Was it when the first gray hairs sprouted?

She peered into the vanity mirror as her fingers walked through her scalp in their daily search for root growth. At her last touch up, the stylist had suggested she should embrace silver, the new power color. Rachel answered she'd embrace silver when Cher did.

Satisfied with her rich brown hair and tasteful golden highlights, she pursed her mouth. Was it when her lips, never the most plump, had thinned into two slashes? Fillers would fix that problem, at least temporarily, but the promised results, the appearance like bloated leeches, was ridiculous – most definitely not the look she wanted.

She turned her head this way and that, watching the glisten of newly applied moisturizer shift across her features. Her jawline had begun to soften, threatening to slump into jowl, but not quite yet. And her neck was still smooth, but for how much longer?

Her eyes dropped to the bodice of the lacey black negligee she'd bought for the occasion. Was it when her breasts began to sag?

What was that thing that made men stop looking at her?

Tears burned her eyes. She dabbed them away with a tissue, straightened her back.

Chemical peels. Laser chin hair removal. Follicles transplanted to thicken her once luxurious mane. Hot Yoga. Weight training. Pilates. Cycle class in spandex with fifty women bobbing up and down to a deafening disco beat.

The worst of it was her husband, Bill. She considered their gold framed wedding photo angled on the mirrored vanity top. Tall and roguishly handsome with thick sandy hair, murky blue eyes, and a mischievous grin of perfectly aligned teeth, he was one year her junior. It didn't show then, when they were young, both about to enter Stanford law school.

She still remembered the moment that picture was taken. He gazed down upon her with adoration, his arm wrapped tightly around her waist, pulling her in, and whispered the words, "Mrs. William Newkirk." Her beaming face turned up towards his and in that moment, she knew she had achieved her dream. All that she was had metamorphosed into a new glorious, radiant creature inside of whom the souls and minds of she and Bill swirled and caressed and blended until she could no longer distinguish herself from him –not that she would ever want to.

Now the only time he looked at her was when they argued about the house.

On her left hand was the three-carat diamond surrounded by a swirl of smaller diamonds, the symbol of Bill's eternal love for her. If she was no longer Mrs. William Newkirk, who was she? A ghost at forty-eight years old.

Without substance.

Seen through.

Dismissed from the concerns of the living.

Well, tonight, on their twenty-fifth wedding anniversary, Rachel would make certain that William saw her one last time.

Rachel rose from the vanity stool, and crossed the room to her bedside table, enjoying the silky feel of her gown flowing across her hips and thighs. She pulled open the drawer, lifted the revolver she had cleaned earlier that day, and checked the cylinder to satisfy herself that she'd loaded it.

She had.

Happy anniversary, Bill.

Learn more: https://www.amazon.com/dp/B0F31BZTRP